THE WEIRD TALES OF WILLIAM HOPE HODGSON

THE WEIRD TALES OF
WILLIAM HOPE HODGSON

edited by

XAVIER ALDANA REYES

This edition published 2019 by
The British Library
96 Euston Road
London NW1 2DB

Dates attributed to each story relate to first publication

Cataloguing in Publication Data
A catalogue record for this book is available from the British Library

ISBN 978 0 7123 5233 8
e-ISBN 978 0 7123 6482 9

Frontispiece illustration by Enrique Bernardou, 2018

Cover design by Mauricio Villamayor
with illustration by Enrique Bernardou

Text design and typesetting by Tetragon, London
Printed and bound by CPI Group (UK) Ltd, Croydon, CR0 4YY

CONTENTS

INTRODUCTION

In his important essay *Supernatural Horror in Literature* (1927), H. P. Lovecraft wrote of the English author William Hope Hodgson (1877–1918) that his fiction was of 'vast occasional power in its suggestion of lurking worlds and beings behind the ordinary surface of life' and that he was 'second only to Algernon Blackwood in his serious treatment of unreality'. Hodgson has, in time, been recognised as a key player in the development of the weird tale, a subgenre of speculative fiction concerned with the limits of human experience and the unknowability of the natural world that brings together elements of the horror, science fiction and fantasy literary traditions. Hodgson died during the First World War, which means he was not able to publish in the magazine *Weird Tales* (1924–1954), strongly associated with the subgenre, but it is noteworthy that his fiction still found its way into the publication's pages: 'The Hog' appeared in 1947 and four of his other stories were reprinted between 1973 and 1974, during the magazine's first revival. Now regularly included in studies and encyclopaedias of horror literature and the Gothic, the twenty-first century has seen a renewed and sustained interest in Hodgson that has led to books dedicated to his works (Massimo Berruti, S. T. Joshi and Sam Gafford's *William Hope Hodgson: Voices from the Borderland*, from 2014), a specialised journal (*Sargasso: The Journal of William Hope Hodgson Studies*, founded in 2013) and at least one doctoral dissertation (Emily Alder's *William Hope Hodgson's Borderlands*, from 2009). His fiction, once scattered and hard to find, was also published in its entirety by Night Shade Books between 2005 and 2009, and his most celebrated novel, *The*

House on the Borderland (1908), was reprinted by Penguin in their Classics series in 2008.

Hodgson has not always been as well-known or admired, however, and had remained rather forgotten until the late 1980s, when the cultural value of the weird tale began to be reclaimed. It is not difficult to see why. Hodgson's writing is certainly uneven and, even in some of his most powerful works, prone to repetition at the level of vocabulary and content. His style can vary radically, too; it goes all the way from the deliberately archaic prose of his novels *The Boats of the "Glenn Carrig"* (1907) and *The Night Land* (1912) to the fast-paced and dialogue-heavy passages of *The Ghost Pirates* (1909). In virtually all of the tales included in this collection, Hodgson's imaginative invention and ability to conjure up a strong feeling of dread of the unknown shine through and compensate for any of the author's stylistic shortcomings. Regardless, it is true that he was not as sophisticated and accomplished as other master weirdists such as H. P. Lovecraft, Algernon Blackwood and Arthur Machen and that interest and praise has therefore tended to fall upon the latter at Hodgson's expense. Crucially, Hodgson's fictions resist neat generic categorisations and are incredibly heterogeneous. All four of his novels are great achievements in the weird and two of them explore dying Earth scenarios (*The House on the Borderland*, *The Night Land*), but of his some seventy short stories only a handful can be described as horrific or weird. Many of them, like the Captain Jat or Captain Gault stories are sea adventures and cannot be considered fantastic or Gothic. Even some of his most horrific stories, like 'The House among the Laurels' (1910) and 'The Thing Invisible' (1912), which flirt with uncanny events, can conclude with rational explanations that dispel the presence of the supernatural or otherworldly.

Despite the diverse nature of his oeuvre, two main thematic strands do run through Hodgson's work: his passion for the sea (he was a sailor for many years) and his strong interest in spiritualism and the occult. Both of these are evident in his weird tales, upon which Hodgson's reputation currently lies and where, in my view, his imaginative powers are best showcased. In terms of Hodgson's connection to the sea, most of his weird stories take place aboard ships and include very precise nautical terms. His combination of the sea adventure and the weird encounter with barely comprehensible forces is what makes Hodgson's fiction unique. Lovecraft's preoccupation with the unnameability and unknowability of the horrors in supernatural horror ('the assaults of chaos and the daemons of unplumbed space', as he once referred to them) is already evident in Hodgson's work, which often offer only passing glimpses of his nightmare 'things'. Sometimes, as in the 'Sargasso Sea Stories', the source of the weird are marine beasts—monstrous beings, yet apparently of natural origin. In them, the moment of horror is generated by humanity's limited knowledge of the world we inhabit, of our yet virtually unexplored oceans: barely conceivable, destructive creatures do exist about which we know very little and whose shapes are sufficient to conjure up a primeval sense of fear. 'The Thing in the Weeds' (1916) in this collection belongs to this particular strand of his writing, and is an interesting predecessor to Lovecraft's classic 'The Call of Cthulhu' (1928). In other of his sea stories, such as 'A Tropical Horror' (1905), 'The Voice in the Night' (1907), 'The Derelict' (1912) and 'The Riven Night' (posthumously published in 1973), the horrors are a lot more varied, and include everything from a contagious fungus and a man-eating ship to a fantastic sea serpent. One of the aspects that contribute to the effect of Hodgson's nautical horrors is their claustrophobic setting: adrift, marooned and often defenceless, the characters find themselves at the mercy of an unpredictable sea.

Hodgson's interest in psychical research found many outlets in his fiction, and is apparent in works like *The Night Land*, which toys with the idea of projecting one's soul into the future. Similarly, Hodgson's fascination with the occult permeates his collection of short stories *Carnacki, the Ghost-Finder*, which, in its initial publication in 1913, brought together six stories featuring the occult detective of the title. The book was reprinted in 1947 with the inclusion of three other Carnacki stories: 'The Haunted Jarvee' (published posthumously in 1929), the aforementioned 'The Hog' and 'The Find', which had remained unpublished until then. Carnacki naturally has a lot in common with other detectives and psychic doctors of the time, especially with Blackwood's 'John Silence', from which Hodgson drew inspiration, but Hodgson's approach to the supernatural was mixed and often driven by narrative effect. In some stories, 'hauntings' are proven to be false (the aforementioned 'The Thing Invisible' and 'The House among the Laurels'). In others, the existence of the supernatural is the only possible rational explanation to the cases Carnacki investigates, as in 'The Gateway of the Monster' (1910), 'The Whistling Room' (1910) and 'The Hog'—all of them included in this collection. In yet others, as in 'The Horse of the Invisible' (1910), a very intrinsic mixture of rational explanations and weird phenomena are woven together into complex and confounding weird stories that have a lingering effect on readers. Apart from being reflective of Hodgson's sceptical views on the occult, Carnacki's stories are an excellent example of how superstition can be successfully married with scientific reason. For example, Carnacki often uses advanced photographic technology in his investigations, but this does not preclude him from also drawing pentacles on the floor to create protective force barriers.

The various stories in this collection come together to create a fictional mosaic representative of Hodgson's achievements in the weird, and hopes to act as an introduction to this writer for avid Gothic and horror readers. The tales included here are all a testament to the creative abilities of an author who deserves the attention he has been commanding in recent years and who will no doubt continue to be recuperated as a key British figure in the history of weird fiction.

XAVIER ALDANA REYES

Dr. Xavier Aldana Reyes is Senior Lecturer in English Literature and Film at Manchester Metropolitan University and a member of the Manchester Centre for Gothic Studies. He is the editor of Horror: A Literary History *(2016) and* The Gothic Tales of H. P. Lovecraft *(2018), both published by the British Library.*

I would like to dedicate this book to my good friend Sara Martín Alegre.
Gràcies per la teva amistat i per contagiar-me la passió anglosaxona.

ACKNOWLEDGEMENTS

I would like to thank Rob Davies and Jonny Davidson at the British Library for their enthusiasm for this project. It is incredibly exciting to see the British Library supporting weird fiction and rescuing worthy writers from oblivion. I am grateful for their help with the acquisition of the rights to reproduce the stories in this volume, too.

I would also like to thank S. T. Joshi for letting us use his versions of Hodgson's tales. His Centipede Press collection of Hodgson's weird stories, now sadly out of print, was an inspiration for this volume.

Thanks to Night Shade Books for publishing the collected fictions of Hodgson in five exquisite volumes. They made the task of reading the author's complete works a very easy and enjoyable one.

Finally, I am very grateful to Emily Alder for her kind words, free books, encouraging advice and peer-review of the introduction. She is a great Gothic colleague and a true expert on Hodgson.

—1905—

A TROPICAL HORROR

WE ARE A HUNDRED AND THIRTY DAYS OUT FROM MELBOURNE, and for three weeks we have lain in this sweltering calm.

It is midnight, and our watch on deck until four a.m. I go out and sit on the hatch. A minute later, Joky, our youngest 'prentice, joins me for a chatter. Many are the hours we have sat thus and talked in the night watches; though, to be sure, it is Joky who does the talking. I am content to smoke and listen, giving an occasional grunt at seasons to show that I am attentive.

Joky has been silent for some time, his head bent in meditation. Suddenly he looks up, evidently with the intention of making some remark. As he does so, I see his face stiffen with a nameless horror. He crouches back, his eyes staring past me at some unseen fear. Then his mouth opens. He gives forth a strangulated cry and topples backward off the hatch, striking his head against the deck. Fearing I know not what, I turn to look.

Great Heavens! Rising above the bulwarks, seen plainly in the bright moonlight, is a vast slobbering mouth a fathom across. From the huge dripping lips hang great tentacles. As I look the Thing comes further over the rail. It is rising, rising, higher and higher. There are no eyes visible; only that fearful slobbering mouth set on the tremendous trunk-like neck; which, even as I watch, is curling inboard with the stealthy celerity of an enormous eel. Over it comes in vast heaving folds. Will it never end? The ship gives a slow, sullen roll to starboard as she feels the weight. Then the tail, a broad, flat-shaped mass, slips over the teak rail and falls with a loud slump on to the deck.

For a few seconds the hideous creature lies heaped in writhing, slimy coils. Then, with quick, darting movements, the monstrous head travels along the deck. Close by the mainmast stand the harness casks, and alongside of these a freshly opened cask of salt beef with the top loosely replaced. The smell of the meat seems to attract the monster, and I can hear it sniffing with a vast indrawing breath. Then those lips open, displaying four huge fangs; there is a quick forward motion of the head, a sudden crashing, crunching sound, and beef and barrel have disappeared. The noise brings one of the ordinary seamen out of the fo'c'sle. Coming into the night, he can see nothing for a moment. Then, as he gets further aft, he *sees*, and with horrified cries rushes forward. Too late! From the mouth of the Thing there flashes forth a long, broad blade of glistening white, set with fierce teeth. I avert my eyes, but cannot shut out the sickening "Glut! Glut!" that follows.

The man on the "look-out," attracted by the disturbance, has witnessed the tragedy, and flies for refuge into the fo'c'sle, flinging to the heavy iron door after him.

The carpenter and sailmaker come running out from the half-deck in their drawers. Seeing the awful Thing, they rush aft to the cabin with shouts of fear. The Second Mate, after one glance over the break of the poop, runs down the companion-way with the Helmsman after him. I can hear them barring the scuttle, and abruptly I realise that I am on the main-deck alone.

So far I have forgotten my own danger. The past few minutes seem like a portion of an awful dream. Now, however, I comprehend my position and, shaking off the horror that has held me, turn to seek safety. As I do so my eyes fall upon Joky, lying huddled and senseless with fright where he has fallen. I cannot leave him there. Close by stands the empty half-deck—a little steel-built house with iron doors. The lee one is hooked open. Once inside I am safe.

Up to the present the Thing has seemed to be unconscious of my presence. Now, however, the huge barrel-like head sways in my direction; then comes a muffled bellow, and the great tongue flickers in and out as the brute turns and swirls aft to meet me. I know there is not a moment to lose, and, picking up the helpless lad, I make a run for the open door. It is only distant a few yards, but that awful shape is coming down the deck to me in great wreathing coils. I reach the house and tumble in with my burden; then out on deck again to unhook and close the door. Even as I do so something white curls round the end of the house. With a bound I am inside and the door is shut and bolted. Through the thick glass of the ports I see the Thing sweep round the house, in vain search for me.

Joky has not moved yet; so, kneeling down, I loosen his shirt collar and sprinkle some water from the breaker over his face. While I am doing this I hear Morgan shout something; then comes a great shriek of terror, and again that sickening "Glut! Glut!"

Joky stirs uneasily, rubs his eyes, and sits up suddenly.

"Was that Morgan shouting—?" He breaks off with a cry. "Where are we? I have had such awful dreams!"

At this instant there is a sound of running footsteps on the deck, and I hear Morgan's voice at the door.

"Tom, open—!"

He stops abruptly and gives an awful cry of despair. Then I hear him rush forward. Through the porthole, I see him spring into the fore rigging and scramble madly aloft. Something steals up after him. It shows white in the moonlight. It wraps itself around his right ankle. Morgan stops dead, plucks out his sheath-knife, and hacks fiercely at the fiendish thing. It lets go, and in a second he is over the top and running for dear life up the t'gallant rigging.

A time of quietness follows, and presently I see that the day is breaking. Not a sound can be heard save the heavy gasping breathing of the Thing. As the sun rises higher the creature stretches itself out along the deck and seems to enjoy the warmth. Still no sound, either from the men forward or the officers aft. I can only suppose that they are afraid of attracting its attention. Yet, a little later, I hear the report of a pistol away aft, and looking out I see the serpent raise its huge head as though listening. As it does so I get a good view of the fore part, and in the daylight see what the night has hidden.

There, right about the mouth, is a pair of little pig-eyes, that seem to twinkle with a diabolical intelligence. It is swaying its head slowly from side to side; then, without warning, it turns quickly and looks right in through the port. I dodge out of sight; but not soon enough. It has seen me, and brings its great mouth up against the glass.

I hold my breath. My God! If it breaks the glass! I cower, horrified. From the direction of the port there comes a loud, harsh, scraping sound. I shiver. Then I remember that there are little iron doors to shut over the ports in bad weather. Without a moment's waste of time I rise to my feet and slam to the door over the port. Then I go round to the others and do the same. We are now in darkness, and I tell Joky in a whisper to light the lamp, which, after some fumbling, he does.

About an hour before midnight I fall asleep. I am awakened suddenly some hours later by a scream of agony and the rattle of a water-dipper. There is a slight scuffling sound; then that soul-revolting "Glut! Glut!"

I guess what has happened. One of the men forrad has slipped out of the fo'c'sle to try and get a little water. Evidently he has trusted to the darkness to hide his movements. Poor beggar! He has paid for his attempt with his life!

After this I cannot sleep, though the rest of the night passes quietly enough. Towards morning I doze a bit, but wake every few minutes with a start. Joky is sleeping peacefully; indeed, he seems worn out with the terrible strain of the past twenty-four hours. About eight a.m. I call him, and we make a light breakfast off the dry ship's biscuit and water. Of the latter happily we have a good supply. Joky seems more himself, and starts to talk a little—possibly somewhat louder than is safe; for, as he chatters on, wondering how it will end, there comes a tremendous blow against the side of the house, making it ring again. After this Joky is very silent. As we sit there I cannot but wonder what all the rest are doing, and how the poor beggars forrad are faring, cooped up without water, as the tragedy of the night has proved.

Towards noon, I hear a loud bang, followed by a terrific bellowing. Then comes a great smashing of woodwork, and the cries of men in pain. Vainly I ask myself what has happened. I begin to reason. By the sound of the report it was evidently something much heavier than a rifle or pistol, and judging from the mad roaring of the Thing, the shot must have done some execution. On thinking it over further, I become convinced that, by some means, those aft have got hold of the small signal cannon we carry, and though I know that some have been hurt, perhaps killed, yet a feeling of exultation seizes me as I listen to the roars of the Thing, and realise that it is badly wounded, perhaps mortally. After a while, however, the bellowing dies away, and only an occasional roar, denoting more of anger than aught else, is heard.

Presently I become aware, by the ship's canting over to starboard, that the creature has gone over to that side, and a great hope springs up within me that possibly it has had enough of us and is going over the rail into the sea. For a time all is silent and my hope grows stronger. I lean across and nudge Joky, who is sleeping with his head on the table. He starts up sharply with a loud cry.

"Hush!" I whisper hoarsely. "I'm not certain, but I do believe it's gone."

Joky's face brightens wonderfully, and he questions me eagerly. We wait another hour or so, with hope ever rising. Our confidence is returning fast. Not a sound can we hear, not even the breathing of the Beast. I get out some biscuits, and Joky, after rummaging in the locker, produces a small piece of pork and a bottle of ship's vinegar. We fall to with a relish. After our long abstinence from food the meal acts on us like wine, and what must Joky do but insist on opening the door, to make sure the Thing has gone. This I will not allow, telling him that at least it will be safer to open the iron port-covers first and have a look out. Joky argues, but I am immovable. He becomes excited. I believe the youngster is light-headed. Then, as I turn to unscrew one of the after-covers, Joky makes a dash at the door. Before he can undo the bolts I have him, and after a short struggle lead him back to the table. Even as I endeavour to quieten him there comes at the starboard door—the door that Joky has tried to open—a sharp, loud sniff, sniff, followed immediately by a thunderous grunting howl and a foul stench of putrid breath sweeps in under the door. A great trembling takes me, and were it not for the Carpenter's tool-chest I should fall. Joky turns very white and is violently sick, after which he is seized by a hopeless fit of sobbing.

Hour after hour passes, and, weary to death, I lie down on the chest upon which I have been sitting, and try to rest.

It must be about half-past two in the morning, after a somewhat longer doze, that I am suddenly awakened by a most tremendous uproar away forrad—men's voices shrieking, cursing, praying; but in spite of the terror expressed, so weak and feeble; while in the midst, and at times broken off short with that hellishly suggestive "Glut! Glut!" is the unearthly bellowing of the Thing. Fear incarnate seizes me, and I can only fall on my knees and pray. Too well I know what is happening.

Joky has slept through it all, and I am thankful.

Presently, under the door there steals a narrow ribbon of light, and I know that the day has broken on the second morning of our imprisonment. I let Joky sleep on. I will let him have peace while he may. Time passes, but I take little notice. The Thing is quiet, probably sleeping. About midday I eat a little biscuit and drink some of the water. Joky still sleeps. It is best so.

A sound breaks the stillness. The ship gives a slight heave, and I know that once more the Thing is awake. Round the deck it moves, causing the ship to roll perceptibly. Once it goes forrad—I fancy to again explore the fo'c'sle. Evidently it finds nothing, for it returns almost immediately. It pauses a moment at the house, then goes on further aft. Up aloft, somewhere in the fore-rigging, there rings out a peal of wild laughter, though sounding very faint and far away. The Horror stops suddenly. I listen intently, but hear nothing save a sharp creaking beyond the after end of the house, as though a strain had come upon the rigging.

A minute later I hear a cry aloft, followed almost instantly by a loud crash on deck that seems to shake the ship. I wait in anxious fear. What is happening? The minutes pass slowly. Then comes another frightened shout. It ceases suddenly. The suspense has become terrible, and I am no longer able to bear it. Very cautiously I open one of the after port-covers, and peep out to see a fearful sight. There, with its tail upon the deck and its vast body curled round the mainmast, is the monster, its head above the topsail yard, and its great claw-armed tentacle waving in the air. It is the first proper sight that I have had of the

Thing. Good Heavens! It must weigh a hundred tons! Knowing that I shall have time, I open the port itself, then crane my head out and look up. There on the extreme end of the lower topsail yard I see one of the able seamen. Even down here I note the staring horror of his face. At this moment he sees me and gives a weak, hoarse cry for help. I can do nothing for him. As I look the great tongue shoots out and licks him off the yard, much as might a dog a fly off the window-pane.

Higher still, but happily out of reach, are two more of the men. As far as I can judge they are lashed to the mast above the royal yard. The Thing attempts to reach them, but after a futile effort it ceases, and starts to slide down, coil on coil, to the deck. While doing this I notice a great gaping wound on its body some twenty feet above the tail.

I drop my gaze from aloft and look aft. The cabin door is torn from its hinges, and the bulkhead—which, unlike the half-deck, is of teak wood—is partly broken down. With a shudder I realise the cause of those cries after the cannon-shot. Turning I screw my head round and try to see the foremast, but cannot. The sun, I notice, is low, and the night is near. Then I draw in my head and fasten up both port and cover.

How will it end? Oh! how will it end?

After a while Joky wakes up. He is very restless, yet though he has eaten nothing during the day I cannot get him to touch anything.

Night draws on. We are too weary—too dispirited to talk. I lie down, but not to sleep... Time passes.

A ventilator rattles violently somewhere on the main-deck, and there sounds constantly that slurring, gritty noise. Later I hear a cat's agonised howl, and then again all is quiet. Some time after comes a great splash alongside. Then, for some hours all is silent as the grave. Occasionally I sit up on the chest and listen, yet never a whisper of noise comes to me. There is an absolute silence, even the monotonous creak of the gear has died away entirely, and at last a real hope is springing up within me. That splash, this silence—surely I am justified in hoping. I do not wake Joky this time. I will prove first for myself that all is safe. Still I wait. I will run no unnecessary risks. After a time I creep to the after-port and will listen; but there is no sound. I put up my hand and feel at the screw, then again I hesitate, yet not for long. Noiselessly I begin to unscrew the fastening of the heavy shield. It swings loose on its hinge, and I pull it back and peer out. My heart is beating madly. Everything seems strangely dark outside. Perhaps the moon has gone behind a cloud. Suddenly a beam of moonlight enters through the port, and goes as quickly. I stare out. Something moves. Again the light streams in, and now I seem to be looking into a great cavern, at the bottom of which quivers and curls something palely white.

My heart seems to stand still! It is the Horror! I start back and seize the iron port-flap to slam it to. As I do so, something strikes the glass like a steam ram, shatters it to atoms, and flicks past me into the berth. I scream and spring away. The port is quite filled with it. The lamp shows it dimly. It is curling and twisting here and there. It is as thick as a tree, and covered with a smooth slimy skin. At the end is a great claw, like a lobster's, only a thousand times larger. I cower down into the farthest corner... It has broken the tool-chest to pieces with one click of those frightful mandibles. Joky has crawled under a bunk. The Thing sweeps round in my direction. I feel a drop of sweat trickle slowly down my face—it tastes salty. Nearer comes that awful death... Crash! I roll over backwards. It has crushed the water breaker against which I leant, and I am rolling in the water across the floor. The claw drives up, then down, with a quick uncertain movement, striking the deck a dull, heavy blow, a foot from my head. Joky gives a little gasp of horror. Slowly the Thing rises and starts feeling its way round the berth. It plunges into a bunk and pulls out a bolster, nips it in half and drops it, then moves on. It is feeling along the deck. As it does so it comes across a half of the bolster. It seems to toy with it, then picks it up and takes it out through the port…

A wave of putrid air fills the berth. There is a grating sound, and something enters the port again—something white and tapering and set with teeth. Hither and thither it curls, rasping over the bunks, ceiling, and deck, with a noise like that of a great saw at work. Twice it flickers above my head, and I close my eyes. Then off it goes again. It sounds now on the opposite side of the berth and nearer to Joky. Suddenly the harsh, raspy noise becomes muffled, as though the teeth were passing across some soft substance. Joky gives a horrid little scream, that breaks off into a bubbling, whistling sound. I open my eyes. The tip of the vast tongue is curled tightly round something that drips, then is quickly withdrawn, allowing the moonbeams to steal again into the berth. I rise to my feet. Looking round, I note in a mechanical sort of way the wrecked state of the berth—the shattered chests, dismantled bunks, and something else—

"Joky!" I cry, and tingle all over.

There is that awful Thing again at the port. I glance round for a weapon. I will revenge Joky. Ah! there, right under the lamp, where the wreck of the carpenter's chest strews the floor, lies a small hatchet. I spring forward and seize it. It is small, but so keen—so keen! I feel its razor edge lovingly. Then I am back at the port. I stand to one side and raise my weapon. The great tongue is feeling its way to those fearsome remains. It reaches them. As it does so, with a scream of "Joky! Joky!" I strike savagely again and again and again, gasping as I strike; once more, and the monstrous mass falls to the deck, writhing like a hideous eel. A vast, warm flood rushes in through the porthole.

There is a sound of breaking steel and an enormous bellowing. A singing comes in my ears and grows louder—louder. Then the berth grows indistinct and suddenly dark.

Extract from the log of the steamship *Hispaniola*.

> June 24.—Lat.—N. Long.—W. 11 a.m.—Sighted four-masted barque about four points on the port bow, flying signal of distress. Ran down to her and sent a boat aboard. She proved to be the *Glen Doon*, homeward bound from Melbourne to London. Found things in a terrible state. Decks covered with blood and slime. Steel deck-house stove in. Broke open door, and discovered youth of about nineteen in last stage of inanition, also part remains of boy about fourteen years of age. There was a great quantity of blood in the place, and a huge curled-up mass of whitish flesh, weighing about half a ton, one end of which appeared to have been hacked through with a sharp instrument. Found forecastle door open and hanging from one hinge. Doorway bulged, as though something had been forced through. Went inside. Terrible state of affairs, blood everywhere, broken chests, smashed bunks, but no men nor remains. Went aft again and found youth showing signs of recovery. When he came round, gave the name of Thompson. Said they had been attacked by a huge serpent—thought it must have been sea-serpent. He was too weak to say much, but told us there were some men up the mainmast. Sent a hand aloft, who reported them lashed to the royal mast, and quite dead. Went aft to the cabin. Here we found the bulkhead smashed to pieces, and the cabin-door lying on the deck near the after-hatch. Found body of Captain down lazarette, but no officers. Noticed amongst the wreckage part of the carriage of a small cannon. Came aboard again.

Have sent the Second Mate with six men to work her into port. Thompson is with us. He has written out his version of the affair. We certainly consider that the state of the ship, as we found her, bears out in every respect his story.

(Signed) William Norton (Master).

Tom Briggs (1st Mate).

—1907—

THE VOICE IN THE NIGHT

IT WAS A DARK, STARLESS NIGHT. WE WERE BECALMED IN THE Northern Pacific. Our exact position I do not know; for the sun had been hidden during the course of a weary, breathless week, by a thin haze which had seemed to float above us, about the height of our mastheads, at whiles descending and shrouding the surrounding sea.

With there being no wind, we had steadied the tiller, and I was the only man on deck. The crew, consisting of two men and a boy, were sleeping forrard in their den; while Will—my friend, and the master of our little craft—was aft in his bunk on the port side of the little cabin.

Suddenly, from out of the surrounding darkness, there came a hail:

"Schooner, ahoy!"

The cry was so unexpected that I gave no immediate answer, because of my surprise.

It came again—a voice curiously throaty and inhuman, calling from somewhere upon the dark sea away on our port broadside:

"Schooner, ahoy!"

"Hullo!" I sung out, having gathered my wits somewhat. "What are you? What do you want?"

"You need not be afraid," answered the queer voice, having probably noticed some trace of confusion in my tone. "I am only an old—man."

The pause sounded oddly; but it was only afterwards that it came back to me with any significance.

"Why don't you come alongside, then?" I queried somewhat snappishly; for I liked not his hinting at my having been a trifle shaken.

"I—I—can't. It wouldn't be safe. I—" The voice broke off, and there was silence.

"What do you mean?" I asked, growing more and more astonished. "Why not safe? Where are you?"

I listened for a moment; but there came no answer. And then, a sudden indefinite suspicion, of I knew not what, coming to me, I stepped swiftly to the binnacle, and took out the lighted lamp. At the same time, I knocked on the deck with my heel to waken Will. Then I was back at the side, throwing the yellow funnel of light out into the silent immensity beyond our rail. As I did so, I heard a slight, muffled cry, and then the sound of a splash, as though someone had dipped oars abruptly. Yet I cannot say that I saw anything with certainty; save, it seemed to me, that with the first flash of the light, there had been something upon the waters, where now there was nothing.

"Hullo, there!" I called. "What foolery is this!"

But there came only the indistinct sounds of a boat being pulled away into the night.

Then I heard Will's voice, from the direction of the after scuttle:

"What's up, George?"

"Come here, Will!" I said.

"What is it?" he asked, coming across the deck.

I told him the queer thing which had happened. He put several questions; then, after a moment's silence, he raised his hands to his lips, and hailed:

"Boat, ahoy!"

From a long distance away, there came back to us a faint reply, and my companion repeated his call. Presently, after a short period of silence, there grew on our hearing the muffled sound of oars; at which Will hailed again.

This time there was a reply:

"Put away the light."

"I'm damned if I will," I muttered; but Will told me to do as the voice bade, and I shoved it down under the bulwarks.

"Come nearer," he said, and the oar-strokes continued. Then, when apparently some half-dozen fathoms distant, they again ceased.

"Come alongside," exclaimed Will. "There's nothing to be frightened of aboard here!"

"Promise that you will not show the light?"

"What's to do with you," I burst out, "that you're so infernally afraid of the light?"

"Because—" began the voice, and stopped short.

"Because what?" I asked, quickly.

Will put his hand on my shoulder.

"Shut up a minute, old man," he said, in a low voice. "Let me tackle him."

He leant more over the rail.

"See here, Mister," he said, "this is a pretty queer business, you coming upon us like this, right out in the middle of the blessed Pacific. How are we to know what sort of a hanky-panky trick you're up to? You say there's only one of you. How are we to know, unless we get a squint at you—eh? What's your objection to the light, anyway?"

As he finished, I heard the noise of the oars again, and then the voice came; but now from a greater distance, and sounding extremely hopeless and pathetic.

"I am sorry—sorry! I would not have troubled you, only I am hungry, and—so is she."

The voice died away, and the sound of the oars, dipping irregularly, was borne to us.

"Stop!" sung out Will. "I don't want to drive you away. Come back! We'll keep the light hidden, if you don't like it."

He turned to me:

"It's a damned queer rig, this; but I think there's nothing to be afraid of?"

There was a question in his tone, and I replied.

"No, I think the poor devil's been wrecked around here, and gone crazy."

The sound of the oars drew nearer.

"Shove that lamp back in the binnacle," said Will; then he leaned over the rail, and listened. I replaced the lamp, and came back to his side. The dipping of the oars ceased some dozen yards distant.

"Won't you come alongside now?" asked Will in an even voice. "I have had the lamp put back in the binnacle."

"I—I cannot," replied the voice. "I dare not come nearer. I dare not even pay you for the—the provisions."

"That's all right," said Will, and hesitated. "You're welcome to as much grub as you can take—" Again he hesitated.

"You are very good," exclaimed the voice. "May God, Who understands everything, reward you—" It broke off huskily.

"The—the lady?" said Will, abruptly. "Is she—"

"I have left her behind upon the island," came the voice.

"What island?" I cut in.

"I know not its name," returned the voice. "I would to God—!" it began, and checked itself as suddenly.

"Could we not send a boat for her?" asked Will at this point.

"No!" said the voice, with extraordinary emphasis. "My God! No!"

There was a moment's pause; then it added, in a tone which seemed a merited reproach:

"It was because of our want I ventured— Because her agony tortured me."

"I am a forgetful brute," exclaimed Will. "Just wait a minute, whoever you are, and I will bring you up something at once."

In a couple of minutes he was back again, and his arms were full of various edibles. He paused at the rail.

"Can't you come alongside for them?" he asked.

"No—I *dare not,*" replied the voice, and it seemed to me that in its tones I detected a note of stifled craving—as though the owner hushed a mortal desire. It came to me then in a flash, that the poor old creature out there in the darkness, was *suffering* for actual need of that which Will held in his arms; and yet, because of some unintelligible dread, refraining from dashing to the side of our little schooner, and receiving it. And with the lightning-like conviction, there came the knowledge that the Invisible was not mad; but sanely facing some intolerable horror.

"Damn it, Will!" I said, full of many feelings, over which predominated a vast sympathy. "Get a box. We must float off the stuff to him in it."

This we did—propelling it away from the vessel, out into the darkness, by means of a boathook. In a minute, a slight cry from the Invisible came to us, and we knew that he had secured the box.

A little later, he called out a farewell to us, and so heartful a blessing, that I am sure we were the better for it. Then, without more ado, we heard the ply of oars across the darkness.

"Pretty soon off," remarked Will, with perhaps just a little sense of injury.

"Wait," I replied. "I think somehow he'll come back. He must have been badly needing that food."

"And the lady," said Will. For a moment he was silent; then he continued:

"It's the queerest thing ever I've tumbled across, since I've been fishing."

"Yes," I said, and fell to pondering.

And so the time slipped away—an hour, another, and still Will stayed with me; for the queer adventure had knocked all desire for sleep out of him.

The third hour was three parts through, when we heard again the sound of oars across the silent ocean.

"Listen!" said Will, a low note of excitement in his voice.

"He's coming, just as I thought," I muttered.

The dipping of the oars grew nearer, and I noted that the strokes were firmer and longer. The food had been needed.

They came to a stop a little distance off the broadside, and the queer voice came again to us through the darkness:

"Schooner, ahoy!"

"That you?" asked Will.

"Yes," replied the voice. "I left you suddenly; but—but there was great need."

"The lady?" questioned Will.

"The—lady is grateful now on earth. She will be more grateful soon in—in heaven."

Will began to make some reply, in a puzzled voice; but became confused, and broke off short. I said nothing. I was wondering at the curious pauses, and, apart from my wonder, I was full of a great sympathy.

The voice continued:

"We—she and I, have talked, as we shared the result of God's tenderness and yours—"

Will interposed; but without coherence.

"I beg of you not to—to belittle your deed of Christian charity this night," said the voice. "Be sure that it has not escaped His notice."

It stopped, and there was a full minute's silence. Then it came again:

"We have spoken together upon that which—which has befallen us. We had thought to go out, without telling any, of the terror which has come into our—lives. She is with me in believing that tonight's happenings are under a special ruling, and that it is God's wish that we should tell to you all that we have suffered since—since—"

"Yes?" said Will, softly.

"Since the sinking of the *Albatross*."

"Ah!" I exclaimed, involuntarily. "She left Newcastle for 'Frisco some six months ago, and hasn't been heard of since."

"Yes," answered the voice. "But some few degrees to the North of the line she was caught in a terrible storm, and dismasted. When the day came, it was found that she was leaking badly, and, presently, it falling to a calm, the sailors took to the boats, leaving—leaving a young lady—my fiancée—and myself upon the wreck.

"We were below, gathering together a few of our belongings, when they left. They were entirely callous, through fear, and when we came up upon the decks, we saw them only as small shapes afar off upon the horizon. Yet we did not despair, but set to work and constructed a small raft. Upon this we put such few matters as it would hold, including a quantity of water and some ship's biscuit. Then, the vessel being very deep in the water, we got ourselves onto the raft, and pushed off.

"It was later, when I observed that we seemed to be in the way of some tide or current, which bore us from the ship at an angle; so that in the course of three hours, by my watch, her hull became invisible to our sight, her broken masts remaining in view for a somewhat longer period. Then, towards evening, it grew misty, and so through the night. The next day we were still encompassed by the mist, the weather remaining quiet.

"For four days, we drifted through this strange haze, until, on the evening of the fourth day, there grew upon our ears the murmur of breakers at a distance. Gradually it became plainer, and, somewhat after midnight, it appeared to sound upon either hand at no very great space. The raft was raised upon a swell several times, and then we were in smooth water, and the noise of the breakers was behind.

"When the morning came, we found that we were in a sort of great lagoon; but of this we noticed little at the time; for close before us, through the enshrouding mist, loomed the hull of a large sailing-vessel. With one accord, we fell upon our knees and thanked God; for we thought that here was an end to our perils. We had much to learn.

"The raft drew near to the ship, and we shouted on them, to take us aboard; but none answered. Presently, the raft touched against the side of the vessel, and, seeing a rope hanging downwards, I seized it and began to climb. Yet I had much ado to make my way up, because of a kind of grey, lichenous fungus, which had seized upon the rope, and which blotched the side of the ship, lividly.

"I reached the rail, and clambered over it, on to the deck. Here, I saw that the decks were covered, in great patches, with the grey masses, some of them rising into nodules several feet in height; but at the time, I thought less of this matter than of the possibility of there being people aboard the ship. I shouted; but none answered. Then I went to the door below the poop-deck. I opened it, and peered in. There was a great smell of staleness, so that I knew in a moment that nothing living was within, and with the knowledge, I shut the door quickly; for I felt suddenly lonely.

"I went back to the side, where I had scrambled up. My—my sweetheart was still sitting quietly upon the raft. Seeing me look down, she called up to know whether there were any aboard of the ship. I replied that the vessel had the appearance of having been long deserted; but that if she would wait a little, I would see whether there was anything in the shape of a ladder, by which she could ascend to the deck. Then we would make a search through the vessel together. A little later, on the opposite side of the decks, I found a rope side-ladder. This I carried across, and a minute afterwards, she was beside me.

"Together, we explored the cabins and apartments in the after-part of the ship; but nowhere was there any sign of life. Here and there, within the cabins themselves, we came across odd patches of that queer fungus; but this, as my sweetheart said, could be cleansed away.

"In the end, having assured ourselves that the after portion of the vessel was empty, we picked our ways to the bows, between the ugly grey nodules of that strange growth; and here we made a further search, which told us that there was indeed none aboard but ourselves.

"This being now beyond any doubt, we returned to the stern of the ship, and proceeded to make ourselves as comfortable as possible. Together, we cleared out and cleaned two of the cabins; and, after that, I made examination whether there was anything eatable in the ship. This I soon found was so, and thanked God in my heart for His goodness. In addition to this, I discovered the whereabouts of the freshwater pump, and having fixed it, I found the water drinkable, though somewhat unpleasant to the taste.

"For several days, we stayed aboard the ship, without attempting to get to the shore. We were busily engaged in making the place habitable. Yet even thus early, we became aware that our lot was even less to be desired than might have been imagined; for though, as a first step, we scraped away the odd patches of growth that studded the floors and walls of the cabins and saloon, yet they returned almost to their original size within the space of twenty-four hours, which not only discouraged us, but gave us a feeling of vague unease.

"Still, we would not admit ourselves beaten, so set to work afresh, and not only scraped away the fungus, but soaked the places where it had been, with carbolic, a can-full of which I had found in the pantry. Yet, by the end of the week, the growth had returned in full strength, and, in addition, it had spread to other places, as though our touching it had allowed germs from it to travel elsewhere.

"On the seventh morning, my sweetheart woke to find a small patch of it growing on her pillow, close to her face. At that, she came to me, so soon as she could get her garments upon her. I was in the galley at the time, lighting the fire for breakfast.

"'Come here, John,' she said, and led me aft. When I saw the thing upon her pillow, I shuddered, and then and there we agreed to go right out of the ship, and see whether we could not fare to make ourselves more comfortable ashore.

"Hurriedly, we gathered together our few belongings, and even among these, I found that the fungus had been at work; for one of her shawls had a little lump of it growing near one edge. I threw the whole thing over the side, without saying anything to her.

"The raft was still alongside; but it was too clumsy to guide, and I lowered down a small boat that hung across the stern, and in this we made our way to the shore. Yet, as we drew near to it, I became gradually aware that here the vile fungus, which had driven us from the ship, was growing riot. In places it rose into horrible, fantastic mounds, which seemed almost to quiver, as with a quiet life, when the wind blew across them. Here and there, it took on the forms of vast fingers, and in others it just spread out flat and smooth and treacherous. Odd places, it appeared as grotesque stunted trees, seeming extraordinarily kinked and gnarled— The whole quaking vilely at times.

"At first, it seemed to us that there was no single portion of the surrounding shore which was not hidden beneath the masses of the hideous lichen; yet, in this, I found we were mistaken; for somewhat later, coasting along the shore at a little distance, we descried a smooth white patch of what appeared to be fine sand, and there we landed. It was not sand. What it was, I do not know. All that I have observed, is that upon it, the fungus will not grow; while everywhere else, save where the sand-like earth wanders oddly, path-wise, amid the grey desolation of the lichen, there is nothing but that loathsome greyness.

"It is difficult to make you understand how cheered we were to find one place that was absolutely free from the growth, and here we deposited our belongings. Then we went back to the ship for such things as it seemed to us we should need. Among other matters, I managed to bring ashore with me one of the ship's sails, with which I constructed two small tents, which, though exceedingly rough-shaped, served the purposes for which they were intended. In these, we lived and stored our various necessities, and thus for a matter of some four weeks, all went smoothly and without particular unhappiness. Indeed, I may say with much of happiness—for—for we were together.

"It was on the thumb of her right hand, that the growth first showed. It was only a small circular spot, much like a little grey mole. My God! how the fear leapt to my heart when she showed me the place. We cleansed it, between us, washing it with carbolic and water. In the morning of the following day, she showed her hand to me again. The grey warty thing had returned. For a little while, we looked at one another in silence. Then, still wordless, we started again to remove it. In the midst of the operation, she spoke suddenly.

"'What's that on the side of your face, Dear!' Her voice was sharp with anxiety. I put my hand up to feel.

"'There! Under the hair by your ear.—A little to the front a bit.' My finger rested upon the place, and then I knew.

"'Let us get your thumb done first,' I said. And she submitted, only because she was afraid to touch me until it was cleansed. I finished washing and disinfecting her thumb, and then she turned to my face. After it was finished, we sat together and talked awhile of many things; for there had come into our lives sudden, very terrible thoughts. We were, all at once, afraid of something worse than death. We spoke of loading the boat with provisions and water, and making our way out on to the sea; yet we were helpless, for many causes, and—and the growth had attacked us already. We decided to stay. God would do with us what was His will. We would wait.

"A month, two months, three months passed, and the places grew somewhat, and there had come others. Yet we fought so strenuously with the fear, that its headway was but slow, comparatively speaking.

"Occasionally, we ventured off to the ship for such stores as we needed. There, we found that the fungus grew persistently. One of the nodules on the maindeck became soon as high as my head.

"We had now given up all thought or hope of leaving the island. We had realised that it would be unallowable to go among healthy humans, with the thing from which we were suffering.

"With this determination and knowledge in our minds, we knew that we should have to husband our food and water; for we did not know, at that time, but that we should possibly live for many years.

"This reminds me that I have told you that I am an old man. Judged by years this is not so. But—but—"

He broke off; then continued somewhat abruptly:

"As I was saying, we knew that we should have to use care in the matter of food. But we had no idea then how little food there was left, of which to take care. It was a week later, that I made the discovery that all the other bread tanks—which I had supposed full—were empty, and that (beyond odd tins of vegetables and meat, and some other matters) we had nothing on which to depend, but the bread in the tank which I had already opened.

"After learning this, I bestirred myself to do what I could, and set to work at fishing in the lagoon; but with no success. At this, I was somewhat inclined to feel desperate, until the thought came to me to try outside the lagoon, in the open sea.

"Here, at times, I caught odd fish; but, so infrequently, that they proved of but little help in keeping us from the hunger which threatened. It seemed to me that our deaths were likely to come by hunger, and not by the growth of the thing which had seized upon our bodies.

"We were in this state of mind when the fourth month wore out. Then I made a very horrible discovery. One morning, a little before midday, I came off from the ship, with a portion of the biscuits which were left. In the mouth of her tent, I saw my sweetheart sitting, eating something.

"'What is it, my Dear?' I called out as I leapt ashore. Yet, on hearing my voice, she seemed confused, and, turning, slyly threw something towards the edge of the little clearing. It fell short, and, a vague suspicion having arisen within me, I walked across and picked it up. It was a piece of the grey fungus.

"As I went to her, with it in my hand, she turned deadly pale; then a rose red.

"I felt strangely dazed and frightened.

"'My Dear! My Dear!' I said, and could say no more. Yet, at my words, she broke down and cried bitterly. Gradually, as she calmed, I got from her the news that she had tried it the preceding day, and—and liked it. I got her to promise on her knees not to touch it again, however great our hunger. After she had promised, she told me that the desire for it had come suddenly, and that, until the moment of desire, she had experienced nothing towards it, but the most extreme repulsion.

"Later in the day, feeling strangely restless, and much shaken with the thing which I had discovered, I made my way along one of the twisted paths—formed by the white, sand-like substance—which led among the fungoid growth. I had, once before, ventured along there; but not to any great distance. This time, being involved in perplexing thought, I went much further than hitherto.

"Suddenly, I was called to myself, by a queer hoarse sound on my left. Turning quickly, I saw that there was movement among an extraordinarily shaped mass of fungus, close to my elbow. It was swaying uneasily, as though it possessed life of its own. Abruptly, as I stared, the thought came to me that the thing had a grotesque resemblance to the figure of a distorted human creature. Even as the fancy flashed into my brain, there was a slight, sickening noise of tearing, and I saw that one of the branch-like arms was detaching itself from the surrounding grey masses, and coming towards me. The head of the thing—a shapeless grey ball, inclined in my direction. I stood stupidly, and the vile arm brushed across my face. I gave out a frightened cry, and ran back a few paces. There was a sweetish taste upon my lips, where the thing had touched me. I licked them, and was immediately filled with an inhuman desire. I turned and seized a mass of the fungus. Then more, and—more. I was insatiable. In the midst of devouring, the remembrance of the morning's discovery swept into my mazed brain. It was sent by God. I dashed the fragment I held, to the ground. Then, utterly wretched and feeling a dreadful guiltiness, I made my way back to the little encampment.

"I think she knew, by some marvellous intuition which love must have given, so soon as she set eyes on me. Her quiet sympathy made it easier for me, and I told her of my sudden weakness; yet omitted to mention the extraordinary thing which had gone before. I desired to spare her all unnecessary terror.

"But, for myself, I had added an intolerable knowledge, to breed an incessant terror in my brain; for I doubted not but that I had seen the end of one of those men who had come to the island in the ship in the lagoon; and in that monstrous ending, I had seen our own.

"Thereafter, we kept from the abominable food, though the desire for it had entered into our blood. Yet, our drear punishment was upon us; for, day by day, with monstrous rapidity, the fungoid growth took hold of our poor bodies. Nothing we could do would check it materially, and so—and so—we who had been human, became— Well, it matters less each day. Only—only we had been man and maid!

"And day by day, the fight is more dreadful, to withstand the hunger-lust for the terrible lichen.

"A week ago we ate the last of the biscuit, and since that time I have caught three fish. I was out here fishing tonight, when your schooner drifted upon me out of the mist. I hailed you. You know the rest, and may God, out of His great heart, bless you for your goodness to a—a couple of poor outcast souls."

There was the dip of an oar—another. Then the voice came again, and for the last time, sounding through the slight surrounding mist, ghostly and mournful.

"God bless you! Good-bye!"

"Good-bye," we shouted together, hoarsely, our hearts full of many emotions.

I glanced about me. I became aware that the dawn was upon us.

The sun flung a stray beam across the hidden sea; pierced the mist dully, and lit up the receding boat with a gloomy fire. Indistinctly, I saw something nodding between the oars. I thought of a sponge—a great, grey nodding sponge— The oars continued to ply. They were grey—as was the boat—and my eyes searched a moment vainly for the conjunction of hand and oar. My gaze flashed back to the—head. It nodded forward as the oars went backward for the stroke. Then the oars were dipped, the boat shot out of the patch of light, and the—the thing went nodding into the mist.

—1909—

OUT OF THE STORM

"HUSH!" SAID MY FRIEND THE SCIENTIST, AS I WALKED INTO his laboratory. I had opened my lips to speak; but stood silent for a few minutes at his request.

He was sitting at his instrument, and the thing was tapping out a message in a curiously irregular fashion—stopping a few seconds, then going on at a furious pace.

It was during a somewhat longer than usual pause that, growing slightly impatient, I ventured to address him.

"Anything important?" I asked.

"For God's sake, shut up!" he answered back in a high, strained voice.

I stared. I am used to pretty abrupt treatment from him at times when he is much engrossed in some particular experiment; but this was going a little too far, and I said so.

He was writing, and, for reply, he pushed several loosely written sheets over to me with the one curt word, "Read!"

With a sense half of anger, half of curiosity, I picked up the first and glanced at it. After a few lines, I was gripped and held securely by a morbid interest. I was reading a message from one in the last extremity. I will give it word for word:

"John, we are sinking! I wonder if you really understand what I feel at the present time—you sitting comfortably in your laboratory, I out here upon the waters, already one among the dead. Yes, we are doomed. There is no such thing as help in our case. We are sinking—steadily, remorselessly. God! I must keep up and be a man! I need not tell you that I am in the operator's room. All the rest are on deck—or dead in the hungry thing which is smashing the ship to pieces.

"I do not know where we are, and there is no one of whom I can ask. The last of the officers was drowned nearly an hour ago, and the vessel is now little more than a sort of breakwater for the giant seas.

"Once, about half an hour ago, I went out onto the deck. My God! the sight was terrible. It is a little after midday; but the sky is the colour of mud—do you understand?—grey mud! Down from it there hang vast lappets of clouds. Not such clouds as I have ever before seen; but monstrous, mildewed-looking hulls. They show solid, save where the frightful wind tears their lower edges into great feelers that swirl savagely above us, like the tentacles of some enormous Horror.

"Such a sight is difficult to describe to the living; though the Dead of the Sea know of it without words of mine. It is such a sight that none is allowed to see and live. It is a picture for the doomed and the dead; one of the sea's hell-orgies—one of the *Thing's* monstrous gloatings over the living—say the alive-in-death, those upon the brink. I have no right to tell of it to you; to speak of it to one of the living is to initiate innocence into one of the infernal mysteries—to talk of foul things to a child. Yet I care not! I will expose, in all its hideous nakedness, the death-side of the sea. The undoomed living shall know some of the things that death has hitherto so well guarded. Death knows not of this little instrument beneath my hands that connects me still with the quick, else would he haste to quiet me.

"Hark you, John! I have learnt undreamt of things in this little time of waiting. I know now why we are afraid of the dark. I had never imagined such secrets of the sea and the grave (which are one and the same).

"Listen! Ah, but I was forgetting you cannot hear! I can! The Sea is— Hush! the Sea is laughing, as though Hell cackled from the mouth of an ass. It is jeering. I can hear its voice echo like Satanic thunder amid the mud overhead— It is calling to me! call— I must go— The sea calls!

"Oh! God, art Thou indeed God? Canst Thou sit above and watch calmly that which I have just seen? Nay! Thou art no God! Thou art weak and puny beside this foul *Thing* which Thou didst create in Thy lusty youth. *It* is *now* God—and I am one of its children.

"Are you there, John? Why don't you answer! Listen! I ignore God; for there is a stronger than He. My God is here, beside me, around me, and will be soon above me. You know what that means. It is merciless. *The sea is now all the God there is!* That is one of the things I have learnt.

"Listen! *it* is laughing again. God is *it*, not He.

"It called, and I went out onto the decks. All was terrible. *It* is in the waist—everywhere. *It* has swamped the ship. Only the forecastle, bridge and poop stick up out from the bestial, reeking *Thing*, like three islands in the midst of shrieking foam. At times gigantic billows assail the ship from both sides. They form momentary arches above the vessel—arches of dull, curved water half a hundred feet towards the hideous sky. Then they descend—roaring. Think of it! You cannot.

"There is an infection of sin in the air: it is the exhalations from the *Thing*. Those left upon the drenched islets of shattered wood and iron are doing the most horrible things. The *Thing* is teaching them. Later, I felt the vile informing of its breath; but I have fled back here—to pray for death.

"On the forecastle, I saw a mother and her little son clinging to an iron rail. A great billow heaved up above them—descended in a falling mountain of brine. It passed, and they were still there. The *Thing* was only toying with them; yet, all the same, it had torn the hands of the child from the rail, and the child was clinging frantically to its Mother's arm. I saw another vast hill hurl up to port and hover above them. Then the Mother stooped and bit like a foul beast at the hands of her wee son. She was afraid that his little additional weight would be more than she could hold. I heard his scream even where I stood—it drove to me upon that wild laughter. It told me again that God is not He, but *It*. Then the hill thundered down upon those two. It seemed to me that the *Thing* gave a bellow as it leapt. It roared about them churning and growling; then surged away, and there was only one—the Mother. There appeared to me to be blood as well as water upon her face, especially about her mouth; but the distance was too great, and I cannot be sure. I looked away. Close to me, I saw something further—a beautiful young girl (her soul hideous with the breath of the *Thing*) struggling with her sweetheart for the shelter of the chart-house side. He threw her off; but she came back at him. I saw her hand come from her head, where still clung the wreckage of some form of headgear. She struck at him. He shouted and fell away to leeward, and she—smiled, showing her teeth. So much for that. I turned elsewhere.

"Out upon the *Thing*, I saw gleams, horrid and suggestive, below the crests of the waves. I have never seen them until this time. I saw a rough sailorman washed away from the vessel. One of the huge breakers snapped at him!—Those things were teeth. *It* has teeth. I heard them clash. I heard his yell. It was no more than a mosquito's shrilling amid all that laughter; but it was very terrible. There is worse than death.

"The ship is lurching very queerly with a sort of sickening heave—

*

"I fancy I have been asleep. No—I remember now. I hit my head when she rolled so strangely. My leg is doubled under me. I think it is broken; but it does not matter—

"I have been praying. I—I— What was it? I feel calmer, more resigned, now. I think I have been mad. What was it that I was saying? I cannot remember. It was something about—about—God. I—I believe I blasphemed. May He forgive me! Thou knowest, God, that I was not in my right mind. Thou knowest that I am very weak. Be with me in the coming time! I have sinned; but Thou art all merciful.

"Are you there, John? It is very near the end now. I had so much to say; but it all slips from me. What was it that I said? I take it all back. I was mad, and—and God knows. He is merciful, and I have very little pain now. I feel a bit drowsy.

"I wonder whether you are there, John. Perhaps, after all, no one has heard the things I have said. It is better so. The Living are not meant—and yet, I do not know. If you are there, John, you will—you will tell *her* how it was; but not—not— Hark! there was such a thunder of water overhead just then. I fancy two vast seas have met in mid-air across the top of the bridge and burst all over the vessel. It must be soon now—and there was such a number of things I had to say! I can hear voices in the wind. They are singing. It is like an enormous dirge—

"I think I have been dozing again. I pray God humbly that it be soon! You will not—not tell *her* anything about, about what I may have said, will you, John? I mean those things which I ought not to have said. What was it I did say? My head is growing strangely confused. I wonder whether you really do hear me. I may be talking only to that vast roar outside. Still, it is some comfort to go on, and I will not believe that you do not hear all I say. Hark again! A mountain of brine must have swept clean over the vessel. She has gone right over on to her side... She is back again. It will be very soon now—

"Are you there, John? Are you there? It is coming! The Sea has come for me! It is rushing down through the companionway! It—it is like a vast jet! My God! I am dr-own-ing! I—am—dr—"

—1910—

THE GATEWAY OF THE MONSTER

IN RESPONSE TO CARNACKI'S USUAL CARD OF INVITATION TO HAVE dinner and listen to a story, I arrived promptly at 427, Cheyne Walk, to find the three others who were always invited to these happy little times, there before me. Five minutes later, Carnacki, Arkright, Jessop, Taylor and I were all engaged in the "pleasant occupation" of dining.

"You've not been long away, this time," I remarked, as I finished my soup; forgetting momentarily, Carnacki's dislike of being asked even to skirt the borders of his story until such time as he was ready. Then he would not stint words.

"No," he replied, with brevity; and I changed the subject, remarking that I had been buying a new gun, to which piece of news he gave an intelligent nod, and a smile, which I think showed a genuinely good-humoured appreciation of my intentional changing of the conversation.

Later, when dinner was finished, Carnacki snugged himself comfortably down in his big chair, along with his pipe, and began his story, with very little circumlocution:

"As Dodgson was remarking just now, I've only been away a short time, and for a very good reason too—I've only been away a short distance. The exact locality I am afraid I must not tell you; but it is less than twenty miles from here; though, except for changing a name, that won't spoil the story. And it *is* a story too! One of the most extraordinary things I have ever run against.

"I received a letter a fortnight ago from a man I will call Anderson, asking for an appointment. I arranged a time, and when he turned up, I found that he wished me to look into, and see whether I could not clear up, a long-standing and well-authenticated case of what he termed 'haunting.' He gave me very full particulars, and, finally, as the thing seemed to present something unique, I decided to take it up.

"Two days later, I drove up to the house, late in the afternoon, and discovered it a very old place, standing quite alone in its own grounds.

"Anderson had left a letter with the butler, I found, pleading excuses for his absence, and leaving the whole house at my disposal for my investigations.

"The butler evidently knew the object of my visit, and I questioned him pretty thoroughly during dinner, which I had in rather lonely state. He is an elderly and privileged servant, and had the history of the Grey Room exact in detail. From him I learned more particulars regarding two things that Anderson had mentioned in but a casual manner. The first was that the door of the Grey Room would be heard in the dead of night to open, and slam heavily, and this even though the butler knew it was locked, and the key on the bunch in his pantry. The second was that the bedclothes would always be found torn off the bed, and hurled in a heap in a corner.

"But it was the door slamming that chiefly bothered the old butler. Many and many a time, he told me, had he lain awake and just shivered with fright, listening; for, at times the door would be slammed time after time, thud! thud! thud! so that sleep was impossible.

"From Anderson, I knew already that the room had a history extending back over a hundred and fifty years. Three people had been strangled in it—an ancestor of his and his wife and child. This is authentic, as I had taken very great pains to make sure; so that you can imagine it was with a feeling that I had a striking case to investigate, that I went upstairs after dinner to have a look at the Grey Room.

"Peters, the butler, was in rather a state about my going, and assured me with much solemnity that in all the twenty years of his service, no one had ever entered that room after night-fall. He begged me, in quite a fatherly way, to wait till the morning, when there would be no danger, and then he could accompany me himself.

"Of course, I told him not to bother. I explained that I should do no more than look round a bit, and, perhaps, fix a few seals. He need not fear; I was used to that sort of thing. But he shook his head, when I said that.

"'There isn't many ghosts like ours, sir,' he assured me, with mournful pride. And, by Jove! he was right, as you will see.

"I took a couple of candles, and Peters followed, with his bunch of keys. He unlocked the door; but would not come inside with me. He was evidently in quite a fright, and renewed his request, that I would put off my examination, until daylight. Of course, I laughed at him, and told him he could stand sentry at the door, and catch anything that came out.

"'It never comes outside, sir,' he said, in his funny, old, solemn manner. Somehow, he managed to make me feel as if I were going to have the creeps right away. Anyway, it was one to him, you know.

"I left him there, and examined the room. It is a big apartment, and well-furnished in the grand style, with a huge four-poster, which stands with its head to the end wall. There were two candles on the mantelpiece, and two on each of the three tables that were in the room. I lit the lot, and after that, the room felt a little less inhumanly dreary; though, mind you, it was quite fresh, and well kept, in every way.

"After I had taken a good look round, I sealed lengths of *bébé* ribbon across the windows, along the walls, over the pictures, and over the fireplace and the wall-closets.

"All the time, as I worked, the butler stood just without the door, and I could not persuade him to enter; though I jested with him a little, as I stretched the ribbons, and went here and there about my work. Every now and again, he would say: 'You'll excuse me, I'm sure, sir; but I do wish you would come out, sir. I'm fair in a quake for you.'

"I told him he need not wait; but he was loyal enough in his way to what he considered his duty. He said he could not go away and leave me all alone there. He apologised; but made it very clear that I did not realise the danger of the room; and I could see, generally, that he was getting into a really frightened state. All the same, I had to make the room so that I should know if anything material entered it; so I asked him not to bother me, unless he really heard or saw something. He was beginning to fret my nerves, and the 'feel' of the room was bad enough already, without making things any nastier.

"For a time further, I worked, stretching ribbons across, a little above the floor, and sealing them so that the merest touch would break the seals, were anyone to venture into the room in the dark, with the intention of playing the fool.

"All this had taken me far longer than I had anticipated; and, suddenly, I heard a clock strike eleven. I had taken off my coat soon after commencing work; now, however, as I had practically made an end of all that I intended to do, I walked across to the settee, and picked it up. I was in the act of getting into it, when the old butler's voice (he had not said a word for the last hour) came sharp and frightened: 'Come out, sir, quick! There's something going to happen!' Jove! but I jumped, and then, in the same moment, one of the candles on the table to the left of the bed went out. Now, whether it was the wind, or what, I do not know; but, just for a moment, I was enough startled to make a run for the door; though I am glad to say that I pulled up, before I reached it. I simply could not bunk out, with the butler standing there, after having, as it were, read him a sort of lesson on 'bein' brave, y'know.' So I just turned right round, picked up the two candles off the mantelpiece, and walked across to the table near the bed. Well, I saw nothing. I blew out the candle that was still alight; then I went to those on the two other tables, and blew them out. Then, outside of the door, the old man called again: 'Oh! sir, do be told! Do be told!'

"'All right, Peters,' I said, and, by Jove, my voice was not as steady as I should have liked! I made for the door, and had a bit of work not to start running. I took some thundering long strides, though, as you can imagine. Near the entrance, I had a sudden feeling that there was a cold wind in the room. It was almost as if the window had been suddenly opened a little. I got to the door, and the old butler gave back a step, in a sort of instinctive way.

"'Collar the candles, Peters!' I said, pretty sharply, and shoved them into his hands. I turned, and caught the handle, and slammed the door shut, with a crash. Somehow, do you know, as I did so, I thought I felt something pull back on it; but it must have been only fancy. I turned the key in the lock, and then again, double-locking the door.

"I felt easier then, and set-to and sealed the door. In addition, I put my card over the keyhole, and sealed it there; after which I pocketed the key, and went downstairs—with Peters, who was nervous and silent, leading the way. Poor old beggar! It had not struck me until that moment that he had been enduring a considerable strain during the last two or three hours.

"About midnight, I went to bed. My room lay at the end of the corridor upon which opens the door of the Grey Room. I counted the doors between it and mine, and found that five rooms lay between. And I am sure you can understand that I was not sorry.

"Just as I was beginning to undress, an idea came to me, and I took my candle and sealing-wax, and sealed the doors of all the five rooms. If any door slammed in the night, I should know just which one.

"I returned to my room, locked myself in, and went to bed. I was waked suddenly from a deep sleep by a loud crash somewhere out in the passage. I sat up in bed, and listened; but heard nothing. Then I lit my candle. I was in the very act of lighting it, when there came the bang of a door being violently slammed, along the corridor.

"I jumped out of bed, and got my revolver. I unlocked the door, and went out into the passage, holding my candle high, and keeping the pistol ready. Then a queer thing happened. I could not go a step towards the Grey Room. You all know I am not really a cowardly chap. I've gone into too many cases connected with ghostly things, to be accused of that; but I tell you I funked it; simply funked it, just like any blessed kid. There was something precious unholy in the air that night. I backed into my bedroom, and shut and locked the door. Then I sat on the bed all night, and listened to the dismal thudding of a door up the corridor. The sound seemed to echo through all the house.

"Daylight came at last, and I washed and dressed. The door had not slammed for about an hour, and I was getting back my nerve again. I felt ashamed of myself; though, in some ways it was silly; for when you're meddling with that sort of thing, your nerve is bound to go, sometimes. And you just have to sit quiet and call yourself a coward until the safety of the day comes. Sometimes it is more than just cowardice, I fancy. I believe at times it is Something warning you, and fighting *for* you. But, all the same, I always feel mean and miserable, after a time like that.

"When the day came properly, I opened my door, and, keeping my revolver handy, went quietly along the passage. I had to pass the head of the stairs, on the way; and who should I see coming up, but the old butler, carrying a cup of coffee. He had merely tucked his nightshirt into his trousers, and he'd an old pair of carpet slippers on.

"'Hullo, Peters!' I said, feeling suddenly cheerful; for I was as glad as any lost child to have a live human being close to me. 'Where are you off to with the refreshments?'

"The old man gave a start, and slopped some of the coffee. He stared up at me, and I could see that he looked white and done-up. He came on up the stairs, and held out the little tray to me.

"'I'm very thankful indeed, sir, to see you safe and well,' he said. 'I feared, one time, you might risk going into the Grey Room, sir. I've lain awake all night, with the sound of the Door. And when it came light, I thought I'd make you a cup of coffee. I knew you would want to look at the seals, and somehow it seems safer if there's two, sir.'

"'Peters,' I said, 'you're a brick. This is very thoughtful of you.' And I drank the coffee. 'Come along,' I told him, and handed him back the tray. 'I'm going to have a look at what the Brutes have been up to. I simply hadn't the pluck to in the night.'

"'I'm very thankful, sir,' he replied. 'Flesh and blood can do nothing, sir, against devils; and that's what's in the Grey Room after dark.'

"I examined the seals on all the doors, as I went along, and found them right; but when I got to the Grey Room, the seal was broken; though the visiting-card, over the keyhole, was untouched. I ripped it off, and unlocked the door, and went in, rather cautiously, as you can imagine; but the whole room was empty of anything to frighten one; and there was heaps of light. I examined all my seals, and not a single one was disturbed. The old butler had followed me in, and, suddenly, he said, 'The bedclothes, sir!'

"I ran up to the bed, and looked over; and, surely, they were lying in the corner to the left of the bed. Jove! you can imagine how queer I felt. Something *had* been in the room. I stared for a while, from the bed to the clothes on the floor. I had a feeling that I did not want to touch either. Old Peters, though, did not seem to be affected that way. He went over to the bed-coverings, and was going to pick them up, as, doubtless, he had done every day these twenty years back; but I stopped him. I wanted nothing touched, until I had finished my examination. This, I must have spent a full hour over, and then I let Peters straighten up the bed; after which we went out, and I locked the door; for the room was getting on my nerves.

"I had a short walk, and then breakfast; which made me feel more my own man. Then to the Grey Room again; and, with Peters' help, and one of the maids, I had everything taken out except the bed, even the very pictures.

"I examined the walls, floor and ceiling then, with probe, hammer and magnifying-glass; but found nothing unusual. I can assure you, I began to realise, in very truth, that some incredible thing had been loose in the room during the past night.

"I sealed up everything again, and went out, locking and sealing the door as before.

"After dinner that night, Peters and I unpacked some of my stuff, and I fixed up my camera and flashlight opposite to the door of the Grey Room, with a string from the trigger of the flashlight to the door. You see, if the door were really opened, the flashlight would blare out, and there would be, possibly, a very queer picture to examine in the morning.

"The last thing I did, before leaving, was to uncap the lens; and after that I went off to my bedroom, and to bed; for I intended to be up at midnight; and to insure this, I set my little alarm to call me; also I left my candle burning.

"The clock woke me at twelve, and I got up and into my dressing-gown and slippers. I shoved my revolver into my right side-pocket, and opened my door. Then, I lit my dark-room lamp, and withdrew the slide, so that it would give a clear light. I carried it up the corridor, about thirty feet, and put it down on the floor, with the open side away from me; so that it would show me anything that might approach along the dark passage. Then I went back, and sat in the doorway of my room, with my revolver handy, staring up the passage towards the place where I knew my camera stood outside of the door of the Grey Room.

"I should think I had watched for about an hour and a half, when, suddenly, I heard a faint noise, away up the corridor. I was immediately conscious of a queer prickling sensation about the back of my head, and my hands began to sweat a little. The following instant the whole end of the passage flicked into sight in the abrupt glare of the flashlight. Then came the succeeding darkness, and I peered nervously up the corridor, listening tensely, and trying to find what lay beyond the faint, red glow of my dark-lamp, which now seemed ridiculously dim, by contrast with the tremendous blaze of the flash-powder... And then, as I stooped forward, staring and listening, there came the crashing thud of the door of the Grey Room. The sound seemed to fill the whole of the large corridor, and go echoing hollowly through the house. I tell you, I felt horrible—as if my bones were water. Simply beastly. Jove! how I did stare, and how I listened. And then it came again, thud, thud, thud, and then a silence that was almost worse than the noise of the door; for I kept fancying that some brutal thing was stealing upon me along the corridor.

"Suddenly, my lamp was put out, and I could not see a yard before me. I realised all at once that I was doing a very silly thing, sitting there, and I jumped up. Even as I did so, I *thought* I heard a sound in the passage, quite *near* to me. I made one backward spring into my room, and slammed and locked the door.

"I sat on my bed, and stared at the door. I had my revolver in my hand; but it seemed an abominably useless thing. Can you understand? I felt that there was something the other side of my door. For some unknown reason, I *knew* it was pressed up against the door, and it was soft. That was just what I thought. Most extraordinary thing to imagine, when you come to think of it!

"Presently, I got hold of myself a bit, and marked out a pentacle hurriedly with chalk on the polished floor; and there I sat in it until it was almost dawn. And all the time, away up the corridor, the door of the Grey Room thudded at solemn and horrid intervals. It was a miserable, brutal night.

"When the day began to break, the thudding of the door came gradually to an end, and at last, I grabbed together my courage, and went along the corridor, in the half light, to cap the lens of my camera. I can tell you, it took some doing; but if I had not gone, my photograph would have been spoilt, and I was tremendously keen to save it. I got back to my room, and then set-to and rubbed out the five-pointed star in which I had been sitting.

"Half an hour later there was a tap at my door. It was Peters, with my coffee. When I had drunk it, we both walked along to the Grey Room. As we went, I had a look at the seals on the other doors; but they were untouched. The seal on the door of the Grey Room was broken, as also was the string from the trigger of the flashlight; but the visiting-card over the keyhole was still there. I ripped it off, and opened the door.

"Nothing unusual was to be seen, until we came to the bed; then I saw that, as on the previous day, the bedclothes had been torn off, and hurled into the left-hand corner, exactly where I had seen them before. I felt very queer; but I did not forget to look at all the seals, only to find that not one had been broken.

"Then I turned and looked at old Peters, and he looked at me, nodding his head.

"'Let's get out of here!' I said. 'It's no place for any living human to enter, without proper protection.'

"We went out then, and I locked and sealed the door, again.

"After breakfast, I developed the negative; but it showed only the door of the Grey Room, half opened. Then I left the house, as I wanted to get certain matters and implements that might be necessary to life; perhaps to the spirit; for I intended to spend the coming night in the Grey Room.

"I got back in a cab, about half past five, with my apparatus, and this, Peters and I carried up to the Grey Room, where I piled it carefully in the centre of the floor. When everything was in the room, including a cat which I had brought, I locked and sealed the door, and went towards my bedroom, telling Peters I should not be down to dinner. He said 'Yes, sir,' and went downstairs, thinking that I was going to turn-in; which was what I wanted him to believe, as I knew he would have worried both himself and me, if he had known what I intended.

"But I merely got my camera and flashlight from my bedroom, and hurried back to the Grey Room. I entered, and locked and sealed myself in, and set to work; for I had a lot to do before it got dark.

"First, I cleared away all the ribbons across the floor; then I carried the cat—still fastened in its basket—over towards the far wall, and left it. I returned then to the centre of the room, and measured out a space twenty-one feet in diameter, which I swept with a 'broom of hyssop.' About this, I drew a circle of chalk, taking care never to step over the circle.

"Beyond this, I smudged, with a bunch of garlic, a broad belt right around the chalked circle, and when this was complete, I took from among my stores in the centre a small jar of a certain water. I broke away the parchment, and withdrew the stopper. Then, dipping my left forefinger in the little jar, I went round the circle again, making upon the floor, just within the line of chalk, the Second Sign of the Saaamaaa Ritual, and joining each Sign most carefully with the left-handed crescent. I can tell you, I felt easier when this was done, and the 'water-circle' complete.

"Then, I unpacked some more of the stuff that I had brought, and placed a lighted candle in the 'valley' of each Crescent. After that, I drew a Pentacle, so that each of the five points of the defensive star touched the chalk circle. In the five points of the star, I placed five portions of a certain bread, each wrapped in linen; and in the five 'vales,' five opened jars of the water I had used to make the 'water-circle.' And now I had my first protective barrier complete.

"Now, anyone, except you who know something of my methods of investigation, might consider all this a piece of useless and foolish superstition; but you all remember the Black Veil case, in which I believe my life was saved by a very similar form of protection; whilst Aster, who sneered at it, and would not come inside, died.

"I got the idea from the Sigsand MS., written, so far as I can make out, in the fourteenth century. At first, naturally, I imagined it was just an expression of the superstition of his time; and it was not until long after my first reading that it occurred to me to test his 'Defence,' which I did, as I've just said, in that horrible Black Veil business. You know how *that* turned out. Later, I used it several times, and always

I came through safe, until that Moving Fur case. It was only a partial 'Defence' there, and I nearly died in the pentacle. After that, I came across Professor Garder's 'Experiments with a Medium.' When they surrounded the Medium with a current of a certain number of vibrations, in vacuum, he lost his power—almost as if it cut him off from the Immaterial.

"That made me think; and led eventually to the Electric Pentacle, which is a most marvellous 'Defence' against certain manifestations. I used the shape of the defensive star for this protection, because I have, personally, no doubt at all but that there is some extraordinary virtue in the old magic figure. Curious thing for a Twentieth Century man to admit, is it not? But then, as you all know, I never did, and never will, allow myself to be blinded by a little cheap laughter. I ask questions, and keep my eyes open!

"In this last case, I had little doubt that I had run up against an ab-natural monster, and I meant to take every possible care; for the danger is abominable.

"I turned-to now to fit the Electric Pentacle, setting it so that each of its 'points' and 'vales' coincided exactly with the 'points' and 'vales' of the drawn pentagram upon the floor. Then I connected up the battery, and the next instant the pale blue glare from the intertwining vacuum tubes shone out.

"I glanced about me then, with something of a sigh of relief, and realised suddenly that the dusk was upon me; for the window was grey and unfriendly. Then I stared round at the big, empty room, over the double-barrier of electric and candle light; and had an abrupt, extraordinary sense of weirdness thrust upon me—in the air, you know, it seemed; as it were a sense of something inhuman impending. The room was full of the stench of bruised garlic, a smell I hate.

"I turned now to my camera, and saw that it and the flashlight were in order. Then I tested the action of my revolver, carefully; though I had little thought that it would be needed. Yet, to what extent materialisation of an ab-natural creature is possible, given favourable conditions, no one can say; and I had no idea what horrible thing I was going to see, or feel the presence of. I might, in the end, have to fight with a material thing. I did not know, and could only be prepared. You see, I never forgot that three people had been strangled in the bed close to me; and the fierce slamming of the door, I had heard myself. I had no doubt that I was investigating a dangerous and ugly case.

"By this time, the night had come (though the room was very light with the burning candles), and I found myself glancing behind me, constantly, and then all round the room. It was nervy work waiting for that thing to come into the room.

"Suddenly, I was aware of a little, cold wind sweeping over me, coming from behind. I gave one great nerve-thrill, and a prickly feeling went all over the back of my head. Then I hove myself round with a sort of stiff jerk, and stared straight against that queer wind. It seemed to come from the corner of the room to the left of the bed—the place where both times I had found the heap of tossed bedclothes. Yet I could see nothing unusual; no opening— Nothing!...

"Abruptly, I was aware that the candles were all a-flicker in that unnatural wind... I believe I just squatted there and stared in a horribly frightened, wooden way for some minutes. I shall never be able to let you know how disgustingly horrible it was sitting in that vile, cold wind! And then, flick! flick! flick! all the candles round the outer barrier went out; and there was I, locked and sealed in that room, and with no light beyond the weakish blue glare of the Electric Pentacle.

"A time of abominable tenseness passed, and still that wind blew upon me; and then, suddenly, I knew that something stirred in the corner to the left of the bed. I was made conscious of it, rather by some inward, unused sense, than by either sight or sound; for the pale, short-radius glare of the Pentacle gave but a very poor light for seeing by. Yet, as I stared, something began slowly to grow upon my sight—a moving shadow, a little darker than the surrounding shadows. I lost the thing amid the vagueness, and for a moment or two I glanced swiftly from side to side, with a fresh, new-sense of impending danger. Then my attention was directed to the bed. All the coverings were being drawn steadily off, with a hateful, stealthy sort of motion. I heard the slow, dragging slither of the clothes, but I could see nothing of the thing that pulled. I was aware in a funny, subconscious, introspective fashion that the 'creep' had come upon me, prickling all over my head, yet that I was cooler mentally than I had been for some minutes; sufficiently so to feel that my hands were sweating coldly, and to shift my revolver, half-consciously, whilst I rubbed my right hand dry upon my knee; though never, for an instant, taking my gaze or my attention from those moving clothes.

"The faint noises from the bed ceased once, and there was a most intense silence, with only the dull thudding of the blood beating in my head. Yet, immediately afterwards, I heard again the slurring sound of the bedclothes being dragged off the bed. In the midst of my nervous tension I remembered the camera, and reached round for it; but without looking away from the bed. And then, you know, all in a moment, the whole of the bed-coverings were torn off with extraordinary violence, and I heard the flump they made as they were hurled into the corner.

"There was a time of absolute quietness then, for perhaps a couple of minutes; and you can imagine how horrible I felt. The bedclothes had been thrown with such savageness! And, then again, the abominable unnaturalness of the thing that had just been done before me!

"Suddenly, over by the door, I heard a faint noise—a sort of crickling sound, and then a pitter or two upon the floor. A great, nervous thrill swept over me, seeming to run up my spine and over the back of my head; for the seal that secured the door had just been broken. Something was there. I could not see the door; at least, I mean to say that it was impossible to say how much I actually saw, and how much my imagination supplied. I made it out only as a continuation of the grey walls... And then it seemed to me that something dark and indistinct moved and wavered there among the shadows.

"Abruptly, I was aware that the door was opening, and with an effort I reached again for my camera; but before I could aim it, the door was slammed with a terrific crash that filled the whole room with a sort of hollow thunder. I jumped, like a frightened child. There seemed such a power behind the noise; as if a vast, wanton Force were 'out.' Can you understand?

"The door was not touched again; but, directly afterwards, I heard the basket, in which the cat lay, creak. I tell you, I fairly pringled all along my back. I knew that I was going to learn definitely whether whatever was abroad was dangerous to Life. From the cat there rose suddenly a hideous caterwaul, that ceased abruptly; and then—too late—I snapped off the flashlight. In the great glare, I saw that the basket had been overturned, and the lid was wrenched open, with the cat lying half in, and half out upon the floor. I saw nothing else; but I was full of the knowledge that I was in the presence of some Being or Thing that had power to destroy.

"During the next two or three minutes, there was an odd, noticeable quietness in the room, and you must remember I was half-blinded, for the time, because of the flashlight; so that the whole place seemed to be pitchy dark just beyond the shine of the pentacle. I tell you it was most horrible. I just knelt there in the star, and whirled round on my knees, trying to see whether anything was coming at me.

"My power of sight came gradually, and I got a little hold of myself; and abruptly I saw the thing I was looking for, close to the 'water-circle.' It was big and indistinct, and wavered curiously, as though the shadow of a vast spider hung suspended in the air, just beyond the barrier. It passed swiftly round the circle, and seemed to probe ever towards me; but only to draw back with extraordinary jerky movements, as might a living person who touched the hot bar of a grate.

"Round and round it moved, and round and round I turned. Then, just opposite to one of the 'vales' in the pentacles, it seemed to pause, as though preliminary to a tremendous effort. It retired almost beyond the glow of the vacuum light, and then came straight towards me, appearing to gather form and solidity as it came. There seemed a vast, malign determination behind the movement, that must succeed. I was on my knees, and I jerked back, falling onto my left hand and hip, in a wild endeavour to get back from the advancing thing. With my right hand I was grabbing madly for my revolver, which I had let slip. The brutal thing came with one great sweep straight over the garlic and the 'water-circle,' almost to the vale of the pentacle. I believe I yelled. Then, just as suddenly as it had swept over, it seemed to be hurled back by some mighty, invisible force.

"It must have been some moments before I realised that I was safe; and then I got myself together in the middle of the pentacles, feeling horribly gone and shaken, and glancing round and round the barrier; but the thing had vanished. Yet I had learnt something; for I knew now that the Grey Room was haunted by a monstrous hand.

"Suddenly, as I crouched there, I saw what had so nearly given the monster an opening through the barrier. In my movements within the pentacle, I must have touched one of the jars of water; for just where the thing had made its attack, the jar that guarded the 'deep' of the 'vale' had been moved to one side, and this had left one of the 'five doorways' unguarded. I put it back, quickly, and felt almost safe again; for I had found the cause, and the 'Defence' was still good. I began to hope again that I should see the morning come in. When I saw that thing so nearly succeed, I'd had an awful, weak, overwhelming feeling that the 'barriers' could never bring me safe through the night, against such a Force. You can understand?

"For a long time I could not see the hand; but, presently, I thought I saw, once or twice, an odd wavering, over among the shadows near the door. A little later, as though in a sudden fit of malignant rage, the dead body of the cat was picked up, and beaten with dull, sickening blows against the solid floor. That made me feel rather queer.

"A minute afterwards, the door was opened and slammed twice with tremendous force. The next instant, the thing made one swift, vicious dart at me, from out of the shadows. Instinctively, I started sideways from it, and so plucked my hand from upon the Electric Pentacle, where—for a wickedly careless moment—I had placed it. The monster was hurled off from the neighbourhood of the pentacles; though—owing to my inconceivable foolishness—it had been enabled for a second time to pass the outer barriers. I can tell you, I shook for a time, with sheer funk. I moved right to the centre of the pentacles again, and knelt there, making myself as small and compact as possible.

"As I knelt, I began to have presently, a vague wonder at the two 'accidents' which had so nearly allowed the brute to get at me. Was I being *influenced* to unconscious voluntary actions that endangered me? The thought took hold of me; and I watched my every movement. Abruptly, I stretched a tired leg, and knocked over one of the jars of water. Some was spilled; but because of my suspicious watchfulness, I had it upright and back within the vale, while yet some of the water remained. Even as I did so, the vast, black, half-materialised hand beat up at me out of the shadows, and seemed to leap almost into my face; so nearly did it approach; but for the third time it was thrown back by some altogether enormous, overmastering force. Yet, apart from the dazed fright in which it left me, I had for a moment that feeling of spiritual sickness, as if some delicate, beautiful, inward grace had suffered, which is felt only upon the too near approach of the ab-human, and is more dreadful in a strange way, than any physical pain that can be suffered. I knew by this, more of the extent and closeness of the danger; and for a long time I was simply cowed by the butt-headed brutality of that Force upon my spirit. I can put it no other way.

"I knelt again in the centre of the pentacles, watching myself with as much fear, almost, as the monster; for I knew now that, unless I guarded myself from every sudden impulse that came to me, I might simply work my own destruction. Do you see how horrible it all was?

"I spent the rest of the night in a haze of sick fright, and so tense that I could not make a single movement naturally. I was in such fear that any desire for action that came to me might be prompted by the Influence that I knew was at work on me. And outside of the barrier, that ghastly thing went round and round, grabbing and grabbing in the air at me. Twice more was the body of the dead cat molested. The second time, I heard every bone in its body scrunch and crack. And all the time the horrible wind was blowing upon me from the corner of the room to the left of the bed.

"Then, just as the first touch of dawn came into the sky, the unnatural wind ceased, in a single moment; and I could see no sign of the hand. The dawn came slowly, and presently the wan light filled all the room, and made the pale glare of the Electric Pentacle look more unearthly. Yet, it was not until the day had fully come, that I made any attempt to leave the barrier; for I did not know but that there was some method abroad, in the sudden stopping of that wind, to entice me from the pentacles.

"At last, when the dawn was strong and bright, I took one last look round, and ran for the door. I got it unlocked, in a nervous, clumsy fashion; then locked it hurriedly, and went to my bedroom, where I lay on the bed, and tried to steady my nerves. Peters came, presently, with the coffee, and when I had drunk it, I told him I meant to have a sleep, as I had been up all night. He took the tray, and went out quietly; and after I had locked my door, I turned in properly, and at last got to sleep.

"I woke about midday, and after some lunch, went up to the Grey Room. I switched off the current from the Pentacle, which I had left on, in my hurry; also, I removed the body of the cat. You can understand, I did not want anyone to see the poor brute.

"After that, I made a very careful search of the corner where the bedclothes had been thrown. I made several holes through the woodwork, and probed; but found nothing. Then it occurred to me to try with my instrument under the skirting. I did so, and heard my wire ring on metal. I turned the hook-end of the probe that way, and fished for the thing. At the second go, I got it. It was a small object, and I took it to the window. I found it to be a curious ring, made of some greyish metal. The curious thing about it was that it was made in the form of a pentagon; that is, the same shape as the inside of the magic pentacle; but without the 'mounts' which form the points of the defensive star. It was free from all chasing or engraving.

"You will understand that I was excited, when I tell you that I felt sure I held in my hand the famous Luck Ring of the Anderson family;

which, indeed, was of all things the one most intimately connected with the history of the haunting. This ring had been handed on from father to son, through generations; and always—in obedience to some ancient family traditions—each son had to promise never to wear the ring. The ring, I may say, was brought home by one of the Crusaders, under very peculiar circumstances; but the story is too long to go into here.

"It appears that young Sir Hulbert, an ancestor of Anderson's, made a bet one evening, in drink, you know, that he would wear the ring that night. He did so, and in the morning his wife and child were found strangled in the bed, in the very room in which I stood. Many people, it would seem, thought young Sir Hulbert was guilty of having done the thing in drunken anger; and he, in an attempt to prove his innocence, slept a second night in the room. He also was strangled.

"Since then, no one has spent a night in the Grey Room, until I did so. The ring had been lost so long, that its very existence had become almost a myth; and it was most extraordinary to stand there, with the actual thing in my hand, as you can understand.

"It was whilst I stood there, looking at the ring, that I got an idea. Supposing that it were, in a way, a doorway— You see what I mean? A sort of gap in the world-hedge, if I may so phrase my idea. It was a queer thought, I know, and possibly was not my own; but one of those mental nudgings from the Outside.

"You see, the wind had come from that part of the room where the ring lay. I pondered the thought a lot. Then the shape—the inside of a pentacle. It had no 'mounts,' and without mounts, as the Sigsand MS. has it: 'Thee mownts wych are thee Five Hills of safetie. To lack is to gyve pow'r to thee daemon; and surelie to fayvor thee Evill Thynge.' You see, the very shape of the ring was significant. I determined to test it.

"I unmade my pentacle; for it must be 'made' afresh *and around* the one to be protected. Then I went out and locked the door; after which I left the house, to get certain matters, for neither 'yarbs nor fyre nor water' must be used a second time. I returned about seven-thirty; and as soon as the things I had brought had been carried up to the Grey Room, I dismissed Peters for the night, just as I had done the evening before. When he had gone downstairs, I let myself into the room, and locked and sealed the door. I went to the place in the centre of the room where all the stuff had been packed, and set to work with all my speed to construct a barrier about me and the ring.

"I do not remember whether I explained to you. But I had reasoned that, if the ring were in any way a 'medium of admission,' and it were enclosed with me in the Electric Pentacle, it would be, to express it loosely, insulated. Do you see? The Force which had visible expression as a Hand, would have to stay beyond the Barrier which separates the Ab from the Normal; for the 'gateway' would be removed from accessibility.

"As I was saying, I worked with all my speed to get the barrier completed about me and the ring; for it was already later than I cared to be in that room 'unprotected.' Also, I had a feeling that there would be a vast effort made that night to regain the use of the ring. For I had the strongest conviction that the ring was a necessity to materialisation. You will see whether I was right.

"I completed the barriers in about an hour, and you can imagine something of the relief I felt when I saw the pale glare of the Electric Pentacle once more all about me. From then, onwards, for about two hours, I sat quietly, facing the corner from which the wind came.

"About eleven o'clock I had a queer knowledge that something was near to me; yet nothing happened for a whole hour after that. Then, suddenly, I felt the cold, queer wind begin to blow upon me. To my astonishment, it seemed now to come from behind me, and I whipped round, with a hideous quake of fear. The wind met me in the face. It was blowing up from the floor close to me. I stared down, in a sickening maze of new frights. What on earth had I done now! The ring was there, close beside me, where I had put it. Suddenly, as I stared, bewildered, I was aware that there was something queer about the ring—funny shadowy movements and convolutions. I look at them, stupidly. And then, abruptly, I knew that the wind was blowing up at me from the ring. A queer indistinct smoke became visible to me, seeming to pour upwards through the ring, and mix with the moving shadows. Suddenly, I realised that I was in more than any mortal danger; for the convoluting shadows about the ring were taking shape, and the death-hand was forming *within* the Pentacle. My Goodness! do you realise it! I had brought the 'gateway' into the pentacles, and the brute was coming through—pouring into the material world, as gas might pour out from the mouth of a pipe.

"I should think that I knelt for a couple of moments in a sort of stunned fright. Then, with a mad, awkward movement, I snatched at the ring, intending to hurl it out of the Pentacle. Yet, it eluded me, as though some invisible, living thing jerked it hither and thither. At last, I gripped it; but, in the same instant, it was torn from my grasp with incredible and brutal force. A great, black shadow covered it, and rose into the air, and came at me. I saw that it was the Hand, vast and nearly perfect in form. I gave one crazy yell, and jumped over the Pentacle and the ring of burning candles, and ran despairingly for the door. I fumbled idiotically and ineffectually with the key, and all the time I stared, with a fear that was like insanity, towards the Barriers. The hand was plunging towards me; yet, even as it had been unable to pass into the pentacle when the ring was without;

so, now that the ring was within, it had no power to pass out. The monster was chained, as surely as any beast would be, were chains rivetted upon it.

"Even then, in that moment, I got a flash of this knowledge; but I was too utterly shaken with fright, to reason; and the instant I managed to get the key turned, I sprang into the passage, and slammed the door, with a crash. I locked it, and got to my room, somehow; for I was trembling so that I could hardly stand, as you can imagine. I locked myself in, and managed to get the candle lit; then I lay down on the bed, and kept quiet for an hour or two, and so I grew steadier.

"I got a little sleep, later; but woke when Peters brought my coffee. When I had drunk it, I felt altogether better, and took the old man along with me whilst I had a look into the Grey Room. I opened the door and peeped in. The candles were still burning, wan against the daylight; and behind them was the pale, glowing star of the Electric Pentacle. And there, in the middle, was the ring—the gateway of the monster, lying demure and ordinary.

"Nothing in the room was touched, and I knew that the brute had never managed to cross the Pentacles. Then I went out, and locked the door.

"After a further sleep of some hours, I left the house. I returned in the afternoon, in a cab. I had with me an oxy-hydrogen jet, and two cylinders, containing the gases. I carried the things to the Grey Room; and there, in the centre of the Electric Pentacle, I erected the little furnace. Five minutes later, the Luck Ring, once the 'luck' but now the 'bane' of the Anderson family, was no more than a little splash of hot metal."

Carnacki felt in his pocket, and pulled out something wrapped in tissue paper. He passed it to me. I opened it, and found a small circle of greyish metal, something like lead, only harder and rather brighter.

"Well?" I asked, at length, after examining it and handing it round to the others. "Did that stop the haunting?"

Carnacki nodded. "Yes," he said. "I slept three nights in the Grey Room, before I left. Old Peters nearly fainted when he knew that I meant to; but by the third night he seemed to realise that the house was just safe and ordinary. And, you know, I believe, in his heart, he hardly approved."

Carnacki stood up, and began to shake hands. "Out you go!" he said, genially.

And, presently, we went pondering to our various homes.

—*1910*—

THE HORSE OF THE INVISIBLE

I HAD THAT AFTERNOON RECEIVED AN INVITATION FROM CARNACKI. When I reached his place I found him sitting alone. As I came into the room he rose with a perceptibly stiff movement and extended his left hand. His face seemed to be badly scarred and bruised, and his right hand was bandaged. He shook hands, and offered me his paper, which I refused. Then he passed me a handful of photographs, and returned to his reading.

Now, that is just Carnacki. Not a word had come from him, and not a question from me. He would tell us all about it later. I spent about half an hour, looking at the photographs, which were chiefly 'snaps' (some by flashlight) of an extraordinarily pretty girl; though, in some of the photographs it was wonderful that her prettiness was so evident; for so frightened and startled was her expression, that it was difficult not to believe that she had been photographed in the presence of some imminent and overwhelming danger.

The bulk of the photographs were of interiors of different rooms and passages, and in every one the girl might be seen, either full length in the distance, or closer, with perhaps little more than a hand or arm, or portion of the head or dress included in the photograph. All of these had evidently been taken with some definite aim, that did not have for its first purpose the picturing of the girl, but obviously of her surroundings; and they made me very curious, as you can imagine.

Near the bottom of the pile, however, I came upon something *definitely* extraordinary. It was a photograph of the girl, standing abrupt and clear in the great blaze of a flashlight, as was plain to be seen. Her face was turned a little upward, as if she had been frightened suddenly by some noise. Directly above her, as though half-formed and coming down out of the shadows, was the shape of a single, enormous hoof.

I examined this photograph for a long time, without understanding it more than that it had probably to do with some queer Case in which Carnacki was interested.

When Jessop, Arkright, and Taylor came in, Carnacki quietly held out his hand for the photographs, which I returned in the same spirit, and afterwards we all went in to dinner. When we had spent a quiet hour at the table, we pulled our chairs round, and made ourselves snug; and Carnacki began:

"I've been North," he said, speaking slowly and painfully, between puffs at his pipe. "Up to Hisgins of East Lancashire. It has been a pretty strange business all round, as I fancy you chaps will think, when I have finished. I knew, before I went, something about the 'horse story,' as I have heard it called; but I had never thought of it as coming my way, somehow. Also, I know *now* that I had never considered it seriously—in spite of my rule always to keep an open mind. Funny creatures, we humans!

"Well, I got a wire, asking for an appointment, which of course told me that there was some trouble. On the date I fixed, old Captain Hisgins himself came up to see me. He told me a great many new details about the horse story; though, naturally, I had always known the main points, and understood that if the first child were a girl, that girl would be haunted by the Horse, during her courtship.

"It is, as you can see already, an extraordinary story; and though I have always known about it, I have never thought it to be anything more than an old-time legend, as I have already hinted. You see, for seven generations the Hisgin Family have had men-children for their first-born, and even the Hisgins themselves have long considered the tale to be little more than a myth.

"To come to the present, the eldest child of the reigning family is a girl, and she has been often teased and warned in jest by her friends and relations that she is the first girl to be the eldest for seven generations, and that she would have to keep her men friends at arm's length, or go into a nunnery, if she hoped to escape the haunting. And this, I think, shows us how thoroughly the tale had grown to be considered as nothing worthy of the least serious thought. Don't you think so?

"Two months ago, Miss Hisgins became engaged to Beaumont, a young Naval Officer, and on the evening of the very day of the engagement, before it was even formally announced, a most extraordinary thing happened, which resulted in Captain Hisgins making the appointment, and my ultimately going down to their place to look into the thing.

"From the old family records and papers that were entrusted to me, I found that there could be no possible doubt but that prior to something like a hundred and fifty years ago there were some very extraordinary and disagreeable coincidences, to put the thing in the least emotional way. In the whole of the two centuries prior to that date, there were five first-born girls, out of a total of seven generations of the family. Each of these girls grew up to Maidenhood, and each became engaged, and each one died during the period of the engagement, two by suicide, one by falling from a window, one from a 'broken-heart' (presumably heart-failure, owing to sudden shock through fright). The fifth girl was killed one evening in the park round the house; but just how, there seemed to be no *exact* knowledge; only that there was an impression that she had been kicked by a horse. She was dead, when found.

"Now, you see, all of these deaths might be attributed, in a way—even the suicides—to natural causes, I mean, as distinct from supernatural. You see? Yet, in every case, the Maidens had undoubtedly suffered some extraordinary and terrifying experiences during their various courtships; for in all of the records there was mention either of the neighing of an unseen horse, or of the sounds of an invisible horse galloping, as well as many other peculiar and quite inexplicable manifestations. You begin to understand now, I think, just how extraordinary a business it was that I was asked to look into.

"I gathered from one account that the haunting of the girls was so constant and horrible that two of the girls' lovers fairly ran away from their lady-loves. And I think it was this, more than anything else, that made me feel that there had been something more in it, than a mere succession of uncomfortable coincidences.

"I got hold of these facts, before I had been many hours in the house; and after this, I went pretty carefully into the details of the thing that happened on the night of Miss Hisgin's engagement to Beaumont. It seems that as the two of them were going through the big lower corridor, just after dusk and before the lamps had been lighted, there had been a sudden, horrible neighing in the corridor, close to them. Immediately afterward, Beaumont received a tremendous blow or kick, which broke his right forearm. Then the rest of the family and the servants came running, to know what was wrong. Lights were brought, and the corridor and, afterwards, the whole house searched; but nothing unusual was found.

"You can imagine the excitement in the house, and the half incredulous, half believing talk about the old legend. Then, later, in the middle of the night, the old Captain was waked by the sound of a great horse galloping round and round the house.

"Several times after this, both Beaumont and the girl said that they had heard the sounds of hoofs near to them, after dusk, in several of the rooms and corridors.

"Three nights later, Beaumont was waked by a strange neighing in the night-time, seeming to come from the direction of his sweetheart's bedroom. He ran hurriedly for her father, and the two of them raced to her room. They found her awake, and ill with sheer terror, having been awakened by the neighing, seemingly close to her bed.

"The night before I arrived, there had been a fresh happening, and they were all in a frightfully nervy state, as you can imagine.

"I spent most of the first day, as I have hinted, in getting hold of details; but after dinner, I slacked off, and played billiards all the evening with Beaumont and Miss Hisgins. We stopped about ten o'clock, and had coffee, and I got Beaumont to give me full particulars about the thing that had happened the evening before.

"He and Miss Hisgins had been sitting quietly in her aunt's boudoir, whilst the old lady chaperoned them, behind a book. It was growing dusk, and the lamp was at her end of the table. The rest of the house was not yet lit, as the evening had come earlier than usual.

"Well, it seems that the door into the hall was open, and suddenly, the girl said: 'S'ush! what's that?'

"They both listened, and then Beaumont heard it—the sound of a horse, outside of the front door.

"'Your father?' he suggested; but she reminded him that her father was not riding.

"Of course, they were both ready to feel queer, as you can suppose; but Beaumont made an effort to shake this off, and went into the hall to see whether anyone was at the entrance. It was pretty dark in the hall, and he could see the glass panels of the inner draught-door, clear-cut in the darkness of the hall. He walked over to the glass, and looked through into the drive beyond; but there was nothing in sight.

"He felt nervous and puzzled, and opened the inner door and went out on to the carriage-circle. Almost directly afterward, the great hall door swung-to with a crash behind him. He told me that he had a sudden awful feeling of having been trapped in some way—that is how *he* put it. He whirled round, and gripped the door-handle; but something seemed to be holding it with a vast grip on the other side. Then, before he could be fixed in his mind that this was so, he was able to turn the handle, and open the door.

"He paused a moment in the doorway, and peered into the hall; for he had hardly steadied his mind sufficiently to know whether he was really frightened or not. Then he heard his sweetheart blow him a kiss out of the greyness of the big, unlit hall, and he knew that she had followed him, from the boudoir. He blew her a kiss back, and stepped inside the doorway, meaning to go to her. And then, suddenly, in a flash of sickening knowledge, he knew that it was not his sweetheart who had blown him that kiss. He knew that something was trying to tempt him alone into the darkness, and that the girl had never left the boudoir. He jumped back, and in the same instant of time, he heard the kiss again, nearer to him. He called out at the top of his voice: 'Mary, stay in the boudoir. Don't move out of the boudoir until I come to you.' He heard her call something in reply, from the boudoir, and then he had struck a clump of a dozen, or so, matches, and was holding them above his head, and looking round the hall. There was no one in it; but even as the matches burned out, there came the sounds of a great horse galloping down the empty drive.

"Now, you see, both he and the girl had heard the sounds of the horse galloping; but when I questioned more closely, I found that the aunt had heard nothing; though, it is true, she is a bit deaf, and she was further back in the room. Of course, both he and Miss Hisgins had been in an extremely nervous state, and ready to hear anything. The door might have been slammed by a sudden puff of wind, owing to some inner door being opened; and as for the grip on the handle, that may have been nothing more than the sneck catching.

"With regard to the kisses and the sounds of the horse galloping, I pointed out that these might have seemed ordinary enough sounds, if they had been only cool enough to reason. As I told him, and as he knew, the sounds of a horse galloping, carry a long way on the wind; so that what he had heard might have been nothing more than a horse being ridden, some distance away. And as for the kiss, plenty of quiet noises—the rustle of a paper or a leaf—have a somewhat similar sound, especially if one is in an over-strung condition, and imagining things.

"I finished preaching this little sermon on common-sense, versus hysteria, as we put out the lights and left the billiard room. But neither Beaumont nor Miss Hisgins would agree that there had been any fancy on their parts.

"We had come out of the billiard room, by this, and were going along the passage; and I was still doing my best to make both of them see the ordinary, commonplace possibilities of the happening, when what killed my pig, as the saying goes, was the sound of a hoof in the dark billiard room, we had just left.

"I felt the 'creep' come on me in a flash, up my spine and over the back of my head. Miss Hisgins whooped like a child with the whooping-cough, and ran up the passage, giving little gasping screams. Beaumont, however, ripped round on his heels, and jumped back a couple of yards. I gave back too, a bit, as you can understand.

"'There it is,' he said, in a low, breathless voice. 'Perhaps you'll believe now.'

"'There's certainly something,' I whispered, never taking my gaze off the closed door of the billiard room.

"'H'sh!' he muttered. 'There it is again.'

"There was a sound like a great horse pacing round and round the billiard room, with slow, deliberate steps. A horrible cold fright took me, so that it seemed impossible to take a full breath, you know the feeling; and then I saw we must have been walking backwards, for we found ourselves suddenly at the opening of the long passage.

"We stopped there, and listened. The sounds went on steadily, with a horrible sort of deliberateness; as if the brute were taking a sort of malicious gusto in walking about all over the room which we had just occupied. Do you understand just what I mean?

"Then there was a pause, and a long time of absolute quiet, except for an excited whispering from some of the people down in the big hall. The sound came plainly up the wide stair-way. I fancy they were gathered round Miss Hisgins, with some notion of protecting her.

"I should think Beaumont and I stood there, at the end of the passage, for about five minutes, listening for any noise in the billiard room. Then I realised what a horrible funk I was in, and I said to him: 'I'm going to see what's there.'

"'So'm I,' he answered. He was pretty white; but he had heaps of pluck. I told him to wait one instant, and I made a dash into my bedroom, and got my camera and flashlight. I slipped my revolver into my right-hand pocket, and a knuckle-duster over my left fist, where it was ready, and yet would not stop me from being able to work my flashlight.

"Then I ran back to Beaumont. He held out his hand, to show me that he had his pistol, and I nodded; but whispered to him not to be too quick to shoot, as there might be some silly practical-joking at work, after all. He had got a lamp from a bracket in the upper hall, which he was holding in the crook of his damaged arm, so that we had a good light. Then we went down the passage, towards the billiard room; and you can imagine that we were a pretty nervous couple.

"All this time, there had not been a sound; but, abruptly when we were within perhaps a couple of yards of the door, we heard the sudden clumping of a hoof on the solid *parquet*-floor of the billiard room. In the instant afterward, it seemed to me that the whole place shook beneath the ponderous hoof-falls of some huge thing, *coming towards the door*. Both Beaumont and I gave back a pace or two, and then realised, and hung on to our courage, as you might say, and waited. The great tread came right up to the door, and then stopped, and there was an instant of absolute silence, except that, so far as I was concerned, the pulsing in my throat and temples almost deafened me.

"I daresay we waited quite half a minute, and then came the further restless clumping of a great hoof. Immediately afterward, the sounds came right on, as if some invisible thing passed through the closed door, and the ponderous tread was upon us. We jumped, each of us, to our side of the passage, and I know that I spread myself stiff against the wall. The clungk clunck, clungk clunck, of the great hoof-falls passed right between us, and slowly and with deadly deliberateness, down the passage. I heard them through a haze of blood-beats in my ears and temples, and my body extraordinarily rigid and pringling, and I was horribly breathless. I stood for a little time like this, my head turned, so that I could see up the passage. I was conscious only that there was a hideous danger abroad. Do you understand?

"And then, suddenly, my pluck came back to me. I was aware that the noise of the hoof-beats sounded near the other end of the passage. I twisted quickly, and got my camera to bear, and snapped off the flashlight. Immediately afterward, Beaumont let fly a storm of shots down the passage, and began to run, shouting: 'It's after Mary. Run! Run!'

"He rushed down the passage, and I after him. We came out on to the main landing and heard the sound of a hoof on the stairs, and after that, nothing. And from thence, onward, nothing.

"Down, below us in the big hall, I could see a number of the household round Miss Hisgins, who seemed to have fainted; and there were several of the servants clumped together a little way off, staring up at the main landing, and no one saying a single word. And about some twenty steps up the stairs was old Captain Hisgins with a drawn sword in his hand, where he had halted just below the last hoof-sound. I think I never saw anything finer than the old man standing there between his daughter and that infernal thing.

"I daresay you can understand the queer feeling of horror I had at passing that place on the stairs where the sounds had ceased. It was as if the monster were still standing there, invisible. And the peculiar thing was that we never heard another sound of the hoof, either up or down the stairs.

"After they had taken Miss Hisgins to her room, I sent word that I should follow, so soon as they were ready for me. And, presently, when a message came to tell me that I could come any time, I asked her father to give me a hand with my instrument-box, and between us we carried it into the girl's bedroom. I had the bed pulled well out into the middle of the room; after which, I erected the Electric Pentacle round the bed.

"Then I directed that lamps should be placed round the room, but that on no account must any light be made within the pentacle, neither must anyone pass in or out. The girl's mother, I had placed within the pentacle, and directed that her maid should sit without, ready to carry any message, so as to make sure that Mrs. Hisgins did not have to leave the pentacle. I suggested also, that the girl's father should stay the night in the room, and that he had better be armed.

"When I left the bedroom, I found Beaumont waiting outside the door, in a miserable state of anxiety. I told him what I had done, and explained to him that Miss Hisgins was probably perfectly safe within the 'protection'; but that, in addition to her father remaining the night in the room, I intended to stand guard at the door. I told him that I should like him to keep me company, for I knew that he could never sleep, feeling as he did, and I should not be sorry to have a companion. Also, I wanted to have him under my own observation; for there was no doubt but that he was actually in greater danger in some ways than the girl. At least, that was my opinion; and is still, as I think you will agree later.

"I asked him whether he would object to my drawing a pentacle round him for the night, and got him to agree; but I saw that he did not know whether to be superstitious about it, or to regard it more as a piece of foolish mumming; but he took it seriously enough, when I gave him some particulars about the Black Veil case, when young Aster died. You remember, he said it was a piece of silly superstition, and stayed outside. Poor devil!

"The night passed quietly enough, until a little while before dawn, when we both heard the sounds of a great horse galloping round and round the house, just as old Captain Hisgins had described it. You can imagine how queer it made me feel, and directly afterward, I heard someone stir within the bedroom. I knocked at the door; for I was uneasy, and the Captain came. I asked whether everything was right; to which he replied, yes; and immediately asked me whether I had heard the sounds of the galloping; so that I knew he had heard them also. I suggested that it might be as well to leave the bedroom door open a little, until the dawn came in, as there was certainly something abroad. This was done, and he went back into the room, to be near his wife and daughter.

"I had better say here, that I was doubtful whether there was any value in the 'Defence' about Miss Hisgins; for what I term the 'personal-sounds' of the manifestation were so extraordinarily material, that I was inclined to parallel the case with that one of Harford's, where the hand of the child kept materialising within the pentacle, and patting the floor. As you will remember, that was a hideous business.

"Yet, as it chanced, nothing further happened; and so soon as daylight had fully come, we all went off to bed.

"Beaumont knocked me up about midday, and I went down and made breakfast into lunch. Miss Hisgins was there, and seemed in very fair spirits, considering. She told me that I had made her feel almost safe, for the first time for days. She told me also that her cousin, Harry Parsket, was coming down from London, and she knew that he would do anything to help fight the ghost. And after that, she and Beaumont went out into the grounds, to have a little time together.

"I had a walk in the grounds myself, and went round the house; but saw no traces of hoof-marks; and after that, I spent the rest of the day, making an examination of the house; but found nothing.

"I made an end of my search, before dark, and went to my room to dress for dinner. When I got down, the cousin had just arrived; and I found him one of the nicest men I have met for a long time. A chap with a tremendous amount of pluck, and the particular kind of man I like to have with me, in a bad case like the one I was on.

"I could see that what puzzled him most was our belief in the genuineness of the haunting; and I found myself almost wanting something to happen, just to show him how true it was. As it chanced, something did happen, with a vengeance.

"Beaumont and Miss Hisgins had gone out for a stroll just before the dusk, and Captain Hisgins asked me to come into his study for a short chat whilst Parsket went upstairs with his traps, for he had no man with him.

"I had a long conversation with the old Captain, in which I pointed out that the 'haunting' had evidently no particular connection with the house, but only with the girl herself, and that the sooner she was married, the better, as it would give Beaumont a right to be with her at all times; and further than this, it might be that the manifestations would cease, if the marriage were actually performed.

"The old man nodded agreement to this, especially to the first part, and reminded me that three of the girls who were said to have been 'haunted,' had been sent away from home, and met their deaths whilst away. And then in the midst of our talk there came a pretty frightening interruption; for all at once the old butler rushed into the room, most extraordinarily pale—

"'Miss Mary, Sir! Miss Mary, Sir!' he gasped. 'She's screaming… out in the Park, Sir! And they say they can hear the Horse—'

"The Captain made one dive for a rack of arms, and snatched down his old sword, and ran out, drawing it as he ran. I dashed out and up the stairs, snatched my camera-flashlight and a heavy revolver, gave one yell at Parsket's door: 'The Horse!' and was down and into the grounds.

"Away in the darkness there was a confused shouting, and I caught the sounds of shooting, out among the scattered trees. And then, from a patch of blackness to my left, there burst suddenly an infernal gobbling sort of neighing. Instantly I whipped round and snapped off the flashlight. The great light blazed out momentarily, showing me the leaves of a big tree close at hand, quivering in the night breeze; but I saw nothing else; and then the ten-fold blackness came down upon me, and I heard Parsket shouting a little way back to know whether I had seen anything.

"The next instant he was beside me, and I felt safer for his company; for there was some incredible thing near to us, and I was momentarily blind, because of the brightness of the flashlight. 'What was it? What was it?' he kept repeating in an excited voice. And all the time I was staring into the darkness and answering, mechanically, 'I don't know. I don't know.'

"There was a burst of shouting somewhere ahead, and then a shot. We ran towards the sounds, yelling to the people not to shoot; for in the darkness and panic there was this danger also. Then there came two of the game-keepers, racing hard up the drive, with lanterns and their guns; and immediately afterward a row of lights dancing towards us from the house, carried by some of the men-servants.

"As the lights came up, I saw that we had come close to Beaumont. He was standing over Miss Hisgins, and he had his revolver in his hand. Then I saw his face, and there was a great wound across his forehead. By him, was the Captain, turning his naked sword this way and that, and peering into the darkness; a little behind him stood the old butler, a battle-axe, from one of the arm-stands in the hall, in his hands. Yet there was nothing strange to be seen anywhere.

"We got the girl into the house, and left her with her mother and Beaumont, whilst a groom rode for a doctor. And then the rest of us, with four other keepers, all armed with guns and carrying lanterns, searched round the home-park. But we found nothing.

"When we got back, we found that the Doctor had been. He had bound up Beaumont's wound, which, luckily was not deep, and ordered Miss Hisgins straight to bed. I went upstairs with the Captain, and found Beaumont on guard outside of the girl's door. I asked him how he felt; and then, so soon as the girl and her mother were ready for us, Captain Hisgins and I went into the bedroom, and fixed the pentacle again round the bed. They had already got lamps about the room; and after I had set the same order of watching, as on the previous night, I joined Beaumont, outside of the door.

"Parsket had come up, while I had been in the bedroom, and between us, we got some idea from Beaumont as to what had happened out in the Park. It seems that they were coming home after their stroll, from the direction of the West Lodge. It had got quite dark; and, suddenly, Miss Hisgins said 'Hush!' and came to a standstill. He stopped, and listened; but heard nothing for a little. Then he caught it—the sound of a horse, seemingly a long way off, galloping towards them over the grass. He told the girl that it was nothing, and started to hurry her towards the house; but she was not deceived, of course. In less than a minute, they heard it quite close to them in the darkness, and they started running. Then Miss Hisgins caught her foot, and fell. She began to scream, and that is what the butler heard. As Beaumont lifted the girl, he heard the hoofs come thudding right at him. He stood over her, and fired all five chambers of his revolver right at the sounds. He told us that he was sure he saw something that looked like an enormous horse's head, right upon him, in the light of the last flash of his pistol. Immediately afterwards, he was struck a tremendous blow, which knocked him down; and then the Captain and the butler came running up, shouting. The rest, of course, we knew.

"About ten o'clock, the butler brought us up a tray; for which I was very glad; as the night before I had got rather hungry. I warned Beaumont, however, to be very particular not to drink any spirits, and I also made him give me his pipe and matches. At midnight I drew a pentacle round him; and Parsket and I sat one on each side of him; but outside of the pentacle; for I had no fear that there would be any manifestation made against anyone, except Beaumont or Miss Hisgins.

"After that, we kept pretty quiet. The passage was lit by a big lamp at each end; so that we had plenty of light; and we were all armed, Beaumont and I with revolvers, and Parsket with a shot-gun. In addition to my weapon, I had my camera and flashlight.

"Now and again we talked in whispers; and twice the Captain came out of the bedroom to have a word with us. About half past one, we had all grown very silent; and suddenly, about twenty minutes later, I held up my hand, silently; for there seemed to me to be a sound of galloping, out in the night. I knocked on the bedroom door, for the Captain to open it, and when he came, I whispered to him that we thought we heard the Horse. For some time, we stayed, listening, and both Parsket and the Captain thought they heard it; but now I was not so sure, neither was Beaumont. Yet afterwards, I thought I heard it again.

"I told Captain Hisgins I thought he had better go back into the bedroom, and leave the door a little open, and this he did. But from that time onward, we heard nothing; and presently the dawn came in, and we all went very thankfully to bed.

"When I was called at lunch-time, I had a little surprise; for Captain Hisgins told me that they had held a family council, and had decided to take my advice, and have the marriage without a day's more delay than possible. Beaumont was already on his way to London to get a special licence, and they hoped to have the wedding next day.

"This pleased me; for it seemed the sanest thing to be done, in the extraordinary circumstances; and meanwhile I should continue my investigations; but until the marriage was accomplished, my chief thought was to keep Miss Hisgins near to me.

"After lunch, I thought I would take a few experimental photographs of Miss Hisgins and her *surroundings*. Sometimes the camera sees things that would seem very strange to normal human eyesight.

"With this intention, and partly to make an excuse to keep her in my company as much as possible, I asked Miss Hisgins to join me in my experiments. She seemed glad to do this, and I spent several hours with her, wandering all over the house, from room to room; and whenever the impulse came, I took a flashlight of her and the room or corridor in which we chanced to be at the moment.

"After we had gone right through the house in this fashion, I asked her whether she felt sufficiently brave to repeat the experiments in the cellars. She said, yes; and so I rooted out Captain Hisgins and Parsket; for I was not going to take her even into what you might call artificial darkness, without help and companionship at hand.

"When we were ready, we went down into the wine-cellar, Captain Hisgins carrying a shot-gun, and Parsket a specially prepared background and a lantern. I got the girl to stand in the middle of the cellar, whilst Parsket and the Captain held out the background behind her. Then I fired off the flashlight, and we went into the next cellar, where we repeated the experiment.

"Then, in the third cellar, a tremendous, pitch-dark place, something extraordinary and horrible manifested itself. I had stationed Miss Hisgins in the centre of the place, with her father and Parsket holding the background, as before. When all was ready, and just as I pressed the trigger of the 'flash,' there came in the cellar that dreadful, gobbling neighing, that I had heard out in the Park. It seemed to come from somewhere above the girl; and in the glare of the sudden light, I saw that she was staring tensely upward, but at no visible thing. And then in the succeeding comparative darkness, I was shouting to the Captain and Parsket to run Miss Hisgins out into the daylight.

"This was done, instantly; and I shut and locked the door afterwards making the First and Eighth signs of the Saaamaaa Ritual opposite to each post, and connecting them across the threshold with a triple line.

"In the meanwhile, Parsket and Captain Hisgins carried the girl to her Mother, and left her there, in a half-fainting condition; whilst I stayed on guard outside of the cellar door, feeling pretty horrible, for I knew that there was some disgusting thing inside; and along with this feeling there was a sense of half-ashamedness, rather miserable, you know, because I had exposed Miss Hisgins to the danger.

"I had got the Captain's shot-gun, and when he and Parsket came down again, they were each carrying guns and lanterns. I could not possibly tell you the utter relief of spirit and body that came to me, when I heard them coming; but just try to imagine what it was like, standing outside of that cellar. Can you?

"I remember noticing, just before I went to unlock the door, how white and ghastly Parsket looked, and the old Captain was grey-looking; and I wondered whether my face was like theirs. And this, you know, had its own distinct effect upon my nerves; for it seemed to bring the beastliness of the thing bash down on to me in a fresh way. I know it was only sheer will-power that carried me up to the door and made me turn the key.

"I paused one little moment, and then with a nervy jerk, sent the door wide open, and held my lantern over my head. Parsket and the Captain came one on each side of me, and held up their lanterns; but the place was absolutely empty. Of course, I did not trust to a casual look of this kind; but spent several hours with the help of the two others in sounding every square foot of the floor, ceiling and walls.

"Yet, in the end, I had to admit that the place itself was absolutely normal; and so we came away. But I sealed the door, and outside, opposite each door-post, I made the First and Last signs of the

Saaamaaa Ritual, joining them as before, with a triple line. Can you imagine what it was like, searching that cellar?

"When we got upstairs, I inquired very anxiously how Miss Hisgins was, and the girl came out herself to tell me that she was all right and that I was not to trouble about her, or blame myself, as I told her I had been doing.

"I felt happier then, and went off to dress for dinner; and after that was done, Parsket and I took one of the bathrooms, to develop the negatives that I had been taking. Yet none of the plates had anything to tell us, until we came to the one that was taken in the cellar. Parsket was developing, and I had taken a batch of the fixed plates out into the lamplight, to examine them.

"I had just gone carefully through the lot, when I heard a shout from Parsket, and when I ran to him, he was looking at a partly-developed negative, which he was holding up to the red-lamp. It showed the girl plainly, looking upward, as I had seen her; but the thing that astonished me, was the shadow of an enormous hoof, right above her, as if it were coming down upon her out of the shadows. And, you know, I had run her bang into that danger. That was the thought that was chief in my mind.

"As soon as the developing was complete, I fixed the plate, and examined it carefully in a good light. There was no doubt about it at all; the thing above Miss Hisgins was an enormous, shadowy hoof. Yet I was no nearer to coming to any definite knowledge; and the only thing I could do was to warn Parsket to say nothing about it to the girl; for it would only increase her fright; but I showed the thing to her father, for I considered it right that he should know.

"That night, we took the same precautions for Miss Hisgins' safety, as on the two previous nights; and Parsket kept me company;

yet the dawn came in, without anything unusual having happened, and I went off to bed.

"When I got down to lunch, I learnt that Beaumont had wired to say that he would be in soon after four; also that a message had been sent to the Rector. And it was generally plain that the ladies of the house were in a tremendous fluster.

"Beaumont's train was late, and he did not get home until five; but even then the Rector had not put in an appearance; and the butler came in to say that the coachman had returned without him, as he had been called away unexpectedly. Twice more during the evening the carriage was sent down; but the clergyman had not returned; and we had to delay the marriage until the next day.

"That night, I arranged the 'Defence' round the girl's bed, and the Captain and his wife sat up with her, as before. Beaumont, as I expected, insisted on keeping watch with me, and he seemed in a curiously frightened mood; not for himself, you know; but for Miss Hisgins. He had a horrible feeling, he told me, that there would be a final, dreadful attempt on his sweetheart that night.

"This, of course, I told him was nothing but nerves; yet, really, it made me feel very anxious; for I have seen too much, not to know that, under such circumstances, a premonitory *conviction* of impending danger, is not necessarily to be put down entirely to nerves. In fact, Beaumont was so simply and earnestly convinced that the night would bring some extraordinary manifestation, that I got Parsket to rig up a long cord from the wire of the butler's bell, to come along the passage handy.

"To the butler himself, I gave directions not to undress, and to give the same order to two of the footmen. If I rang, he was to come instantly, with the footmen, carrying lanterns; and the lanterns were to be kept ready lit all night. If, for any reason, the bell did not ring, and I blew my whistle, he was to take that as a signal in place of the bell.

"After I had arranged all these minor details, I drew a pentacle about Beaumont, and warned him very particularly to stay within it, whatever happened. And when this was done, there was nothing to do but wait, and pray that the night would go as quietly as the night before.

"We scarcely talked at all, and by about one a.m., we were all very tense and nervous; so that, at last, Parsket got up and began to walk up and down the corridor, to steady himself a bit. Presently, I slipped off my pumps, and joined him; and we walked up and down, whispering occasionally, for something over an hour, until in turning I caught my foot in the bell-cord, and went down on my face; but without hurting myself, or making a noise.

"When I got up, Parsket nudged me.

"'Did you notice that the bell never rang,' he whispered.

"'Jove!' I said, 'you're right.'

"'Wait a minute,' he answered. 'I'll bet it's only a kink somewhere in the cord.' He left his gun, and slipped along the passage, and taking the top lamp, tiptoed away into the house, carrying Beaumont's revolver ready in his right-hand. He was a plucky chap, as I remember thinking then, and again, later.

"Just then, Beaumont motioned to me for absolute quiet. Directly afterwards, I heard the thing for which he listened—the sound of a horse galloping, out in the night. I think that I may say, I fairly shivered. The sound died away, and left a horrible, desolate, eerie feeling in the air, you know. I put my hand out to the bell-cord, hoping that Parsket had got it clear. Then I waited, glancing before and behind.

"Perhaps two minutes passed, full of what seemed like an almost unearthly quiet. And then, suddenly, down the corridor, at the lighted end, there sounded the clumping of a great hoof; and instantly the lamp was thrown down with a tremendous crash, and we were in the dark. I tugged hard on the cord, and blew the whistle; then I raised my snapshot, and fired the flashlight. The corridor blazed into brilliant light; but there was nothing; and then the darkness fell like thunder. I heard the Captain at the bedroom-door, and shouted to him to bring out a lamp, *quick*; but instead, something started to kick the door, and I heard the Captain shouting within the bedroom, and then the screaming of the women. I had a sudden horrible fear that the monster had got into the bedroom; but in the same instant, from up the corridor, there came abruptly the vile, gobbling neighing that we had heard in the park and the cellar. I blew the whistle again, and groped blindly for the bell-cord, shouting to Beaumont to stay in the Pentacle, whatever happened. I yelled again to the Captain to bring out a lamp, and there came a smashing sound against the bedroom door. Then I had my matches in my hand, to get some light, before that incredible, unseen Monster was upon us.

"The match scraped on the box, and flared up, dully; and in the same instant, I heard a faint sound behind me. I whipped round, in a kind of mad terror, and saw something, in the light of the match—a monstrous horse-head, close to Beaumont.

"'Look out, Beaumont!' I shouted in a sort of scream. 'It's behind you!'

"The match went out, abruptly, and instantly there came the huge bang of Parsket's double-barrel (both barrels at once), fired evidently single-handed by Beaumont close to my ear, as it seemed. I caught a momentary glimpse of the great head, in the flash, and of an enormous hoof amid the belch of fire and smoke, seeming to be descending upon Beaumont. In the same instant, I fired three chambers of my revolver. There was the sound of a dull blow, and then that horrible, gobbling neigh, broke out close to me. I fired twice at the sound. Immediately afterward, Something struck me, and I was knocked backwards. I got on to my knees, and shouted for help, at the top of my voice. I heard the women screaming behind the closed door of the bedroom, and was dully aware that the door was being smashed from the inside; and directly afterwards I knew that Beaumont was struggling with some hideous thing, near to me. For an instant, I held back, stupidly, paralysed with funk; and then, blindly and in a sort of rigid chill of goose-flesh, I went to help him, shouting his name. I can tell you, I was nearly sick, with the naked fear I had on me. There came a little, choking scream, out of the darkness; and, at that, I jumped forward into the dark. I gripped a vast, furry ear. Then something struck me another great blow, knocking me sick. I hit back, weak and blind, and gripped with my other hand at the incredible thing. Abruptly, I was dimly aware of a tremendous crash behind me, and a great burst of light. There were other lights in the passage, and a noise of feet and shouting. My hand-grips were torn from the thing they held; I shut my eyes stupidly, and heard a loud yell above me; and then a heavy blow, like a butcher chopping meat; and then something fell upon me.

"I was helped to my knees by the Captain and the butler. On the floor lay an enormous horse-head, out of which protruded a man's trunk and legs. On the wrists were fixed great hoofs. It was the monster. The Captain cut something with the sword that he held in his hand, and stooped, and lifted off the mask; for that is what it was. I saw the face then of the man who had worn it. It was Parsket. He had a bad wound across the forehead, where the Captain's sword had bit through the mask. I looked bewilderedly from him to Beaumont, who was sitting up, leaning against the wall of the corridor. Then I stared at Parsket, again.

"'By Jove!' I said, at last; and then I was quiet; for I was so ashamed for the man. You can understand, can't you? And he was opening his eyes. And, you know, I had grown so to like him.

"And then, you know, just as Parsket was getting back his wits, and looking from one to the other of us, and beginning to remember, there happened a strange and incredible thing. For from the end of the corridor, there sounded, suddenly, the clumping of a great hoof. I looked that way, and then instantly at Parsket, and saw a horrible fear in his face and eyes. He wrenched himself round, weakly, and stared in mad terror up the corridor to where the sound had been; and the rest of us stared, in a frozen group. I remember hearing vaguely, half sobs and whispers from Miss Hisgins' bedroom, all the while that I stared frightenedly, up the corridor.

"The silence lasted several seconds; and then, abruptly, there came again the clumping of the great hoof, away at the end of the corridor. And immediately afterward, the clungk, clunk—clungk, clunk, of mighty hoofs coming down the passage, towards us.

"Even then, you know, most of us thought it was some mechanism of Parsket's still at work; and we were in the queerest mixture of fright and doubt. I think everyone looked at Parsket. And suddenly the Captain shouted out:

"'Stop this damned fooling at once. Haven't you done enough!'

"For my part, I was now frightened; for I had a *sense* that there was something horrible and wrong. And then Parsket managed to gasp out:

"'It's not me! My God! It's not me! My God! It's not me!'

"And then, you know, it seemed to come home to everyone in an instant that there was really some dreadful thing coming down the passage. There was a mad rush to get away, and even old Captain Hisgins gave back with the butler and the footmen.

Beaumont fainted outright, as I found afterwards; for he had been badly mauled. I just flattened back against the wall, kneeling, as I was, too stupid and dazed even to run. And almost in the same instant the ponderous hoof-falls sounded close to me, and seeming to shake the solid floor, as they passed. Abruptly the great sounds ceased, and I knew in a sort of sick fashion that the thing had halted opposite to the open door of the girl's bedroom. And then I was aware that Parsket was standing rocking in the doorway, with his arms spread across, so as to fill the doorway with his body. I saw with less bewilderment. Parsket was extraordinarily pale, and the blood was running down his face from the wound in his forehead; and then I noticed that he seemed to be looking at something in the passage, with a peculiar, desperate, fixed, incredibly masterful gaze. But, there was really nothing to be seen. And suddenly, the clungk, clunk—clungk, clunk, recommenced, and passed onward down the passage. In the same moment, Parsket pitched forward out of the doorway on to his face.

"There were shouts from the huddle of men down the passage, and the two footmen and the butler simply ran, carrying their lanterns; but the Captain went against the side-wall with his back, and put the lamp he was carrying over his head. The dull tread of the Horse went past him, and left him unharmed; and I heard the monstrous hoof-falls going away and away through the quiet house; and after that a dead silence.

"Then the Captain moved, and came towards us, very slow and shaky, and with an extraordinarily grey face.

"I crept towards Parsket, and the Captain came to help me. We turned him over; and, you know, I knew in a moment that he was dead; but you can imagine what a feeling it sent through me.

"I looked up at the Captain; and suddenly he said:

"'That— That— That—' and I know that he was trying to tell me that Parsket had stood between his daughter and whatever it was that had gone down the passage. I stood up, and steadied him; though I was not very steady myself. And suddenly, his face began to work, and he went down on to his knees by Parsket, and cried like some shaken child. Then the women came out of the doorway of the bedroom; and I turned away and left him to them, whilst I went over to Beaumont.

"That is practically the whole story; and the only thing that is left to me is to try to explain some of the puzzling parts, here and there.

"Perhaps you have seen that Parsket was in love with Miss Hisgins; and this fact is the key to a good deal that was extraordinary. He was doubtless responsible for some portions of the 'haunting'; in fact, I think for nearly everything; but, you know, I can prove nothing, and what I have to tell you is chiefly the result of deduction.

"In the first place, it is obvious that Parsket's intention was to frighten Beaumont away; and when he found that he could not do this, I think he grew so desperate that he really intended to kill him. I hate to say this; but the facts force me to think so.

"I am quite certain that it was Parsket who broke Beaumont's arm. He knew all the details of the so-called 'Horse Legend,' and got the idea to work upon the old story, for his own end. He evidently had some method of slipping in and out of the house, probably through one of the many French windows, or possibly he had a key to one or two of the garden doors; and when he was supposed to be away, he was really coming down, on the quiet, and hiding somewhere in the neighbourhood.

"The incident of the kiss in the dark hall, I put down to sheer nervous imaginings on the part of Beaumont and Miss Hisgins; yet, I must say that the sound of the horse outside of the front door, is a little difficult to explain away. But I am still inclined to keep to my first idea on this point, that there was nothing really unnatural about it.

"The hoof-sounds in the billiard room and down the passage, were done by Parsket, from the floor below, by pomping up against the panelled ceiling, with a block of wood tied to one of the window-hooks. I proved this, by an examination, which showed the dints in the woodwork.

"The sounds of the horse galloping round the house, were possibly made also by Parsket, who must have had a horse tied up in the plantation, near by, unless, indeed, he made the sounds himself; but I do not see how he could have gone fast enough to produce the illusion. In any case, I don't feel perfect certainty on this point. I failed to find any hoof-marks, as you remember.

"The gobbling neighing in the park was a ventriloquial achievement on the part of Parsket; and the attack out there on Beaumont was also by him, so that when I thought he was in his bedroom, he must have been outside all the time, and joined me after I ran out of the front-door. This is almost probable; I mean that Parsket was the cause; for if it had been something more serious, he would certainly have given up his foolishness, knowing that there was no longer any need for it. I cannot imagine how he escaped being shot, both then, and in the last mad action, of which I have just told you. He was enormously without fear of any kind for himself, as you can see.

"The time when Parsket was with us, when we thought we heard the Horse galloping round the house, we must have been deceived. No one was *very* sure, except, of course, Parsket, who would naturally encourage the belief.

"The neighing in the cellar, is where I consider there came the first suspicion into Parsket's mind that there was something more at work than his sham-haunting. The neighing was done by him, in the same way that he did it in the park; but when I remember how ghastly he looked, I feel sure that the sounds must have had some infernal quality added to them, which frightened the man himself. Yet, later, he would persuade himself that he had been getting fanciful. Of course, I must not forget that the effect upon Miss Hisgins must have made him feel pretty miserable.

"Then, about the clergyman being called away, we found afterwards that it was a bogus errand, or rather, call; and it is apparent that Parsket was at the bottom of this, so as to get a few more hours in which to achieve his end; and what that was, a very little imagination will show you; for he had found that Beaumont would not be frightened away. I hate to think this; but I'm bound to. Anyway, it is obvious that the man was temporarily a bit off his normal balance. Love's a queer disease!

"Then, there is no doubt at all but that Parsket left the cord to the butler's bell hitched somewhere, so as to give him an excuse to slip away naturally to clear it. This also gave him the opportunity to remove one of the passage lamps. Then he had only to smash the other, and the passage was in utter darkness, for him to make the attempt on Beaumont.

"In the same way, it was he who locked the door of the bedroom, and took the key (it was in his pocket). This prevented the Captain from bringing a light, and coming to the rescue. But Captain Hisgins broke down the door, with the heavy fender-curb; and it was his smashing the door that sounded so confusing and frightening in the darkness of the passage.

"The photograph of the monstrous hoof above Miss Hisgins in the cellar, is one of the things that I am less sure about. It might have been faked by Parsket, whilst I was out of the room, and this would have been easy enough, to anyone who knew how. But, you know, it does not look like a fake. Yet, there is as much evidence of probability that it was faked, as against; and the thing is too vague for an examination to help to a definite decision; so that I will express no opinion, one way or the other. It is certainly a horrible photograph.

"And now I come to that last, dreadful thing. There has been no further manifestation of anything abnormal; so that there is an extraordinary uncertainty in my conclusions. IF we had not heard those last sounds, and if Parsket had not shown that enormous sense of fear, the whole of this case could be explained in the way in which I have shown. And, in fact, as you have seen, I am of the opinion that almost all of it can be cleared up; but I see no way of going past the thing we heard at the last, and the fear that Parsket showed.

"His death— No, that proves nothing. At the inquest it was described somewhat untechnically as due to heart-spasm. That is normal enough, and leaves us quite in the dark as to whether he died because he stood between the girl and some incredible thing of monstrosity.

"The look on Parsket's face, and the thing he called out, when he heard the great hoof-sounds coming down the passage, seem to show that he had the sudden realisation of what before then may have been nothing more than a horrible suspicion. And his fear and appreciation of some tremendous danger approaching was probably more keenly real even than mine. And then he did the one fine, great thing!"

"And the cause?" I said. "What caused it?"

Carnacki shook his head.

"God knows," he answered, with a peculiar, sincere reverence. "IF that thing was what it seemed to be, one might suggest an explanation, which would not offend one's reason, but which may be utterly wrong. Yet I have thought, though it would take a long lecture on Thought Induction to get you to appreciate my reasons, that Parsket had produced what I might term a kind of 'induced haunting,' a kind of induced simulation of his mental conceptions, due to his desperate thoughts and broodings. It *is* impossible to make it clearer, in a few words."

"But the old story!" I said. "Why may not there have been something in *that*?"

"There may have been something in it," said Carnacki. "But I do not think it had anything to do with *this*. I have not clearly thought out my reasons, yet; but later I may be able to tell you why I think so."

"And the marriage. And the cellar—was there anything found there?" asked Taylor.

"Yes, the marriage was performed that day, in spite of the tragedy," Carnacki told us. "It was the wisest thing to do—considering the things that I cannot explain. Yes, I had the floor of that big cellar up; for I had a feeling I might find something there to give me some light. But there was nothing.

"You know, the whole thing is tremendous and extraordinary. I shall never forget the look on Parsket's face. And afterwards the disgusting sounds of those great hoofs going away through the quiet house."

Carnacki stood up:

"Out you go!" he said, in friendly fashion, using the recognised formula.

And we went presently out into the quiet of the Embankment, and so to our homes.

—1910—

THE WHISTLING ROOM

CARNACKI SHOOK A FRIENDLY FIST AT ME, AS I ENTERED, LATE. Then, he opened the door into the dining room, and ushered the four of us—Jessop, Arkright, Taylor and myself—in to dinner.

We dined well, as usual, and, equally as usual, Carnacki was pretty silent during the meal. At the end, we took our wine and cigars to our accustomed positions, and Carnacki—having got himself comfortable in his big chair—began without any preliminary:

"I have just got back from Ireland, again," he said. "And I thought you chaps would be interested to hear my news. Besides, I fancy I shall see the thing clearer, after I have told it all out straight. I must tell you this, though, at the beginning—up to the present moment, I have been utterly and completely 'stumped.' I have tumbled upon one of the most peculiar cases of 'haunting'—or devilment of some sort—that I have come against. Now listen.

"I have been spending the last few weeks at Iastrae Castle, about twenty miles North-East of Galway. I got a letter about a month ago from a Mr. Sid K. Tassoc, who it seemed had bought the place lately, and moved in, only to find that he had got a very peculiar piece of property.

"When I reached there, he met me at the station, driving a jaunting-car, and drove me up to the castle, which, by the way, he called a 'house-shanty.' I found that he was 'pigging it' there with his boy brother and another American, who seemed to be half-servant and half-companion. It appears that all the servants had left the place, in a body, as you might say; and now they were managing among themselves, assisted by some day-help.

"The three of them got together a scratch feed, and Tassoc told me all about the trouble, whilst we were at table. It is most extraordinary, and different from anything that I have had to do with; though that Buzzing Case was very queer, too.

"Tassoc began right in the middle of his story. 'We've got a room in this shanty,' he said, 'which has got a most infernal whistling in it; sort of haunting it. The thing starts any time; you never know when, and it goes on until it frightens you. All the servants have gone, as I've told you. It's not ordinary whistling, and it isn't the wind. Wait till you hear it.'

"'We're all carrying guns,' said the boy; and slapped his coat pocket.

"'As bad as that?' I said; and the older brother nodded. 'I may be soft,' he replied; 'but wait till you've heard it. Sometimes I think it's some infernal thing, and the next moment, I'm just as sure that someone's playing a trick on us.'

"'Why?' I asked. 'What is to be gained?'

"'You mean,' he said, 'that people usually have some good reason for playing tricks as elaborate as this. Well, I'll tell you. There's a lady in this province, by the name of Miss Donnehue, who's going to be my wife, this day two months. She's more beautiful than they make them, and so far as I can see, I've just stuck my head into an Irish hornet's nest. There's about a score of hot young Irishmen been courting her these two years gone, and now that I've come along and cut them out, they feel raw against me. Do you begin to understand the possibilities?'

"'Yes,' I said. 'Perhaps I do in a vague sort of way; but I don't see how all this affects the room?'

"'Like this,' he said. 'When I'd fixed it up with Miss Donnehue, I looked out for a place, and bought this little house-shanty. Afterwards, I told her—one evening during dinner, that I'd decided to tie up here. And then she asked me whether I wasn't afraid of the whistling room. I told her it must have been thrown in gratis, as I'd heard nothing about it. There were some of her men friends present, and I saw a smile go round. I found out, after a bit of questioning, that several people have bought this place during the last twenty odd years. And it was always on the market again, after a trial.

"'Well, the chaps started to bait me a bit, and offered to take bets after dinner that I'd not stay six months in this shanty. I looked once or twice to Miss Donnehue, so as to be sure I was "getting the note" of the talkee-talkee; but I could see that she didn't take it as a joke, at all. Partly, I think, because there was a bit of a sneer in the way the men were tackling me, and partly because she really believes there is something in this yarn of the whistling room.

"'However, after dinner, I did what I could to even things up with the others. I nailed all their bets, and screwed them down good and safe. I guess some of them are going to be hard hit, unless I lose; which I don't mean to. Well, there you have practically the whole yarn.'

"'Not quite,' I told him. 'All that I know, is that you have bought a castle, with a room in it that is in some way "queer," and that you've been doing some betting. Also, I know that your servants have got frightened, and run away. Tell me something about the whistling?'

"'O, that!' said Tassoc; 'that started the second night we were in. I'd had a good look round the room in the daytime, as you can understand; for the talk up at Arlestrae—Miss Donnehue's place—had made me wonder a bit. But it seems just as usual as some of the other rooms in the old wing, only perhaps a bit more lonesome feeling. But that may be only because of the talk about it, you know.

"'The whistling started about ten o'clock, on the second night, as I said. Tom and I were in the library, when we heard an awfully queer whistling, coming along the East Corridor— The room is in the East Wing, you know.

"'"That's that blessed ghost!" I said to Tom, and we collared the lamps off the table, and went up to have a look. I tell you, even as we dug along the corridor, it took me a bit in the throat, it was so beastly queer. It was a sort of tune, in a way; but more as if a devil or some rotten thing were laughing at you, and going to get round at your back. That's how it makes you feel.

"'When we got to the door, we didn't wait; but rushed it open; and then I tell you the sound of the thing fairly hit me in the face. Tom said he got it the same way— Sort of felt stunned and bewildered. We looked all round, and soon got so nervous, we just cleared out, and I locked the door.

"'We came down here, and had a stiff peg each. Then we landed fit again, and began to feel we'd been nicely had. So we took sticks, and went out into the grounds, thinking after all it must be some of these confounded Irishmen working the ghost-trick on us. But there was not a leg stirring.

"'We went back into the house, and walked over it, and then paid another visit to the room. But we simply couldn't stand it. We fairly ran out, and locked the door again. I don't know how to put it into words; but I had a feeling of being up against something that was rottenly dangerous. You know! We've carried our guns ever since.

"'Of course, we had a real turn-out of the room next day, and the whole house-place; and we even hunted round the grounds; but there was nothing queer. And now I don't know what to think; except that the sensible part of me tells me that it's some plan of these Wild Irishmen to try to take a rise out of me.'

"'Done anything since?' I asked him.

"'Yes,' he said—'Watched outside of the door of the room at nights, and chased round the grounds, and sounded the walls and floor of the room. We've done everything we could think of; and it's beginning to get on our nerves; so we sent for you.'

"By this, we had finished eating. As we rose from the table, Tassoc suddenly called out: 'Ssh! Hark!'

"We were instantly silent, listening. Then I heard it, an extraordinary hooning whistle, monstrous and inhuman, coming from far away through corridors to my right.

"'By God!' said Tassoc; 'and it's scarcely dark yet! Collar those candles, both of you, and come along.'

"In a few moments, we were all out of the door and racing up the stairs. Tassoc turned into a long corridor, and we followed, shielding our candles as we ran. The sound seemed to fill all the passage as we drew near, until I had the feeling that the whole air throbbed under the power of some wanton Immense Force—a sense of an actual taint, as you might say, of monstrosity all about us.

"Tassoc unlocked the door; then, giving it a push with his foot, jumped back, and drew his revolver. As the door flew open, the sound beat out at us, with an effect impossible to explain to one who has not heard it—with a certain, horrible personal note in it; as if in there in the darkness you could picture the room rocking and creaking in a mad, vile glee to its own filthy piping and whistling and hooning; and yet all the time aware of you in particular. To stand there and listen, was to be stunned by Realisation. It was as if someone showed you the mouth of a vast pit suddenly, and said: That's Hell. And you *knew* that they had spoken the truth. Do you get it, even a little bit?

"I stepped a pace into the room, and held the candle over my head, and looked quickly round. Tassoc and his brother joined me, and the man came up at the back, and we all held our candles high. I was deafened with the shrill, piping hoon of the whistling; and then, clear in my ear, something seemed to be saying to me: 'Get out of here—quick! Quick! Quick!'

"As you chaps know, I never neglect that sort of thing. Sometimes it may be nothing but nerves; but as you will remember, it was just such a warning that saved me in the 'Grey Dog' Case, and in the 'Yellow Finger' Experiments; as well as other times. Well, I turned sharp round to the others: 'Out!' I said. 'For God's sake, *out* quick!' And in an instant I had them into the passage.

"There came an extraordinary yelling scream into the hideous whistling, and then, like a clap of thunder, an utter silence. I slammed the door, and locked it. Then, taking the key, I looked round at the others.

"They were pretty white, and I imagine I must have looked that way too. And there we stood a moment, silent.

"'Come down out of this, and have some whisky,' said Tassoc, at last, in a voice he tried to make ordinary; and he led the way. I was the back man, and I knew we all kept looking over our shoulders. When we got downstairs, Tassoc passed the bottle round. He took a drink, himself, and slapped his glass on to the table. Then sat down with a thud.

"'That's a lovely thing to have in the house with you, isn't it!' he said. And directly afterwards: 'What on earth made you hustle us all out like that, Carnacki?'

"'Something seemed to be telling me to get out, *quick*,' I said. 'Sounds a bit silly-superstitious, I know; but when you are meddling with this sort of thing, you've got to take notice of queer fancies, and risk being laughed at.'

"I told him then about the 'Grey Dog' business, and he nodded a lot to that. 'Of course,' I said, 'this may be nothing more than those would-be rivals of yours playing some funny game; but, personally, though I'm going to keep an open mind, I feel that there is something beastly and dangerous about this thing.'

"We talked for a while longer, and then Tassoc suggested billiards, which we played in a pretty half-hearted fashion, and all the time cocking an ear to the door, as you might say, for sounds; but none came, and later, after coffee, he suggested early bed, and a thorough overhaul of the room on the morrow.

"My bedroom was in the newer part of the castle, and the door opened into the picture gallery. At the East end of the gallery was the entrance to the corridor of the East Wing; this was shut off from the gallery by two old and heavy oak doors, which looked rather odd and quaint beside the more modern doors of the various rooms.

"When I reached my room, I did not go to bed; but began to unpack my instrument-trunk, of which I had retained the key. I intended to take one or two preliminary steps at once, in my investigation of the extraordinary whistling.

"Presently, when the castle had settled into quietness, I slipped out of my room, and across to the entrance of the great corridor. I opened one of the low, squat doors, and threw the beam of my pocket searchlight down the passage. It was empty, and I went through the doorway, and pushed-to the oak behind me. Then along the great passageway, throwing my light before and behind, and keeping my revolver handy.

"I had hung a 'protection belt' of garlic round my neck, and the smell of it seemed to fill the corridor and give me assurance; for, as you all know, it is a wonderful 'protection' against the more usual Aeiirii forms of semi-materialisation, by which I supposed the whistling might be produced; though, at that period of my investigation, I was still quite prepared to find it due to some perfectly natural cause;

for it is astonishing the enormous number of cases that prove to have nothing abnormal in them.

"In addition to wearing the necklet, I had plugged my ears loosely with garlic, and as I did not intend to stay more than a few minutes in the room, I hoped to be safe.

"When I reached the door, and put my hand into my pocket for the key, I had a sudden feeling of sickening funk. But I was not going to back out, if I could help it. I unlocked the door and turned the handle. Then I gave the door a sharp push with my foot, as Tassoc had done, and drew my revolver, though I did not expect to have any use for it, really.

"I shone the searchlight all round the room, and then stepped inside, with a disgustingly horrible feeling of walking slap into a waiting Danger. I stood a few seconds, expectant, and nothing happened, and the empty room showed bare from corner to corner. And then, you know, I realised that the room was full of an abominable silence; can you understand that? A sort of purposeful silence, just as sickening as any of the filthy noises the Things have power to make. Do you remember what I told you about that 'Silent Garden' business? Well, this room had just that same *malevolent* silence—the beastly quietness of a thing that is looking at you and not seeable itself, and thinks that it has got you. O, I recognised it instantly, and I whipped the top off my lantern, so as to have light over the *whole* room.

"Then I set-to, working like fury, and keeping my glance all about me. I sealed the two windows with lengths of human hair, right across, and sealed them at every frame. As I worked, a queer, scarcely perceptible tenseness stole into the air of the place, and the silence seemed, if you can understand me, to grow more solid. I knew then that I had no business there without 'full protection'; for I was practically certain that this was no mere Aeiirii development;

but one of the worse forms, as the Saiitii; like that 'Grunting Man' case—you know.

"I finished the window, and hurried over to the great fireplace. This is a huge affair, and has a queer gallows-iron, I think they are called, projecting from the back of the arch. I sealed the opening with seven human hairs—the seventh crossing the six others.

"Then, just as I was making an end, a low, mocking whistle grew in the room. A cold, nervous prickling went up my spine, and round my forehead from the back. The hideous sound filled all the room with an extraordinary, grotesque parody of human whistling, too gigantic to be human—as if something gargantuan and monstrous made the sounds softly. As I stood there a last moment, pressing down the final seal, I had little doubt but that I had come across one of those rare and horrible cases of the *Inanimate* reproducing the functions of the *Animate*. I made a grab for my lamp, and went quickly to the door, looking over my shoulder, and listening for the thing that I expected. It came, just as I got my hand upon the handle—a squeal of incredible, malevolent anger, piercing through the low hooning of the whistling. I dashed out, slamming the door and locking it.

"I leant a little against the opposite wall of the corridor, feeling rather funny; for it had been a hideously narrow squeak... 'Theyr be noe sayfetie to be gained bye gayrds of holieness when the monyster hath pow'r to speak throe woode and stoene.' So runs the passage in the Sigsand MS., and I proved it in that 'Nodding Door' business. There is no protection against this particular form of monster, except, possibly, for a fractional period of time; for it can reproduce itself in, or take to its purposes, the very protective material which you may use, and has power to '*forme* wythine the pentycle'; though not immediately. There is, of course, the possibility of the Unknown Last Line of the Saaamaaa Ritual being uttered; but it is too uncertain to count upon, and the danger is too hideous; and even then it has no power to protect for more than 'maybee fyve beats of the harte,' as the Sigsand has it.

"Inside of the room, there was now a constant, meditative, hooning whistling; but presently this ceased, and the silence seemed worse; for there is such a sense of hidden mischief in a silence.

"After a little, I sealed the door with crossed hairs, and then cleared off down the great passage, and so to bed.

"For a long time I lay awake; but managed eventually to get some sleep. Yet, about two o'clock I was waked by the hooning whistling of the room coming to me, even through the closed doors. The sound was tremendous, and seemed to beat through the whole house with a presiding sense of terror. As if (I remember thinking) some monstrous giant had been holding mad carnival with itself at the end of that great passage.

"I got up and sat on the edge of the bed, wondering whether to go along and have a look at the seal; and suddenly there came a thump on my door, and Tassoc walked in, with his dressing-gown over his pyjamas.

"'I thought it would have waked you, so I came along to have a talk,' he said. 'I can't sleep. Beautiful! Isn't it!'

"'Extraordinary!' I said, and tossed him my case.

"He lit a cigarette, and we sat and talked for about an hour; and all the time that noise went on, down at the end of the big corridor.

"Suddenly, Tassoc stood up:

"'Let's take our guns, and go and examine the brute,' he said, and turned towards the door.

"'No!' I said. 'By Jove—NO! I can't say anything definite, yet; but I believe that room is about as dangerous as it well can be.'

"'Haunted—*really* haunted?' he asked, keenly and without any of his frequent banter.

"I told him, of course, that I could not say a definite *yes* or *no* to such a question; but that I hoped to be able to make a statement, soon. Then I gave him a little lecture on the False Re-Materialisation of the Animate-Force through the Inanimate-Inert. He began then to understand the particular way in which the room might be dangerous, if it were really the subject of a manifestation.

"About an hour later, the whistling ceased quite suddenly, and Tassoc went off again to bed. I went back to mine, also, and eventually got another spell of sleep.

"In the morning, I walked along to the room. I found the seals on the door intact. Then I went in. The window seals and the hair were all right; but the seventh hair across the great fireplace was broken. This set me thinking. I knew that it might, very possibly, have snapped, through my having tensioned it too highly; but then, again, it might have been broken by something else. Yet, it was scarcely possible that a man, for instance, could have passed between the six unbroken hairs; for no one would ever have noticed them, entering the room that way, you see; but just walked through them, ignorant of their very existence.

"I removed the other hairs, and the seals. Then I looked up the chimney. It went up straight, and I could see blue sky at the top. It was a big, open flue, and free from any suggestion of hiding places, or corners. Yet, of course, I did not trust to any such casual examination, and after breakfast, I put on my overalls, and climbed to the very top, sounding all the way; but I found nothing.

"Then I came down, and went over the whole of the room—floor, ceiling, and walls, mapping them out in six-inch squares, and sounding with both hammer and probe. But there was nothing unusual.

"Afterwards, I made a three-weeks' search of the whole castle, in the same thorough way; but found nothing. I went even further, then;

for at night, when the whistling commenced, I made a microphone test. You see, if the whistling were mechanically produced, this test would have made evident to me the working of the machinery, if there were any such concealed within the walls. It certainly was an up-to-date method of examination, as you must allow.

"Of course, I did not think that any of Tassoc's rivals had fixed up any mechanical contrivance; but I thought it just possible that there had been some such thing for producing the whistling, made away back in the years, perhaps with the intention of giving the room a reputation that would insure its being free of inquisitive folk. You see what I mean? Well, of course, it was just possible, if this were the case, that someone knew the secret of the machinery, and was utilising the knowledge to play this devil of a prank on Tassoc. The microphone test of the walls would certainly have made this known to me, as I have said; but there was nothing of the sort in the castle; so that I had practically no doubt at all now, but that it was a genuine case of what is popularly termed 'haunting.'

"All this time, every night, and sometimes most of each night, the hooning whistling of the Room was intolerable. It was as if an Intelligence there, knew that steps were being taken against it, and piped and hooned in a sort of mad, mocking contempt. I tell you, it was as extraordinary as it was horrible. Time after time, I went along—tip-toeing noiselessly on stockinged feet—to the sealed door (for I always kept the Room sealed). I went at all hours of the night, and often the whistling, inside, would seem to change to a brutally jeering note, as though the half-animate monster saw me plainly through the shut door. And all the time, as I would stand, watching, the hooning of the whistling would seem to fill the whole corridor, so that I used to feel a precious lonely chap, messing about there with one of Hell's mysteries.

"And every morning, I would enter the room, and examine the different hairs and seals. You see, after the first week, I had stretched parallel hairs all along the walls of the room, and along the ceiling; but over the floor, which was of polished stone, I had set out little, colourless wafers, tacky-side uppermost. Each wafer was numbered, and they were arranged after a definite plan, so that I should be able to trace the exact movements of any living thing that went across.

"You will see that no material being or creature could possibly have entered that room, without leaving many signs to tell me about it. But nothing was ever disturbed, and I began to think that I should have to risk an attempt to stay a night in the room, in the Electric Pentacle. Mind you, I *knew* that it would be a crazy thing to do; but I was getting stumped, and ready to try anything.

"Once, about midnight, I did break the seal on the door, and have a quick look in; but, I tell you, the whole Room gave one mad yell, and seemed to come towards me in a great belly of shadows, as if the walls had bellied in towards me. Of course, that must have been fancy. Anyway, the yell was sufficient, and I slammed the door, and locked it, feeling a bit weak down my spine. I wonder whether you know the feeling.

"And then, when I had got to that state of readiness for anything, I made what, at first, I thought was something of a discovery:

"It was about one in the morning, and I was walking slowly round the castle, keeping in the soft grass. I had come under the shadow of the East Front, and far above me, I could hear the vile, hooning whistling of the Room, up in the darkness of the unlit wing. Then, suddenly, a little in front of me, I heard a man's voice, speaking low, but evidently in glee:

"'By George! You Chaps; but I wouldn't care to bring a wife home to that!' it said, in the tone of the cultured Irish.

"Someone started to reply; but there came a sharp exclamation, and then a rush, and I heard footsteps running in all directions. Evidently, the men had spotted me.

"For a few seconds, I stood there, feeling an awful ass. After all, *they* were at the bottom of the haunting! Do you see what a big fool it made me seem? I had no doubt but that they were some of Tassoc's rivals; and here I had been feeling in every bone that I had hit a genuine Case! And then, you know, there came the memory of hundreds of details, that made me just as much in doubt, again. Anyway, whether it was natural, or ab-natural, there was a great deal yet to be cleared up.

"I told Tassoc, next morning, what I had discovered, and through the whole of every night, for five nights, we kept a close watch round the East Wing; but there was never a sign of anyone prowling about; and all the time, almost from evening to dawn, that grotesque whistling would hoon incredibly, far above us in the darkness.

"On the morning after the fifth night, I received a wire from here, which brought me home by the next boat. I explained to Tassoc that I was simply bound to come away for a few days; but told him to keep up the watch round the castle. One thing I was very careful to do, and that was to make him absolutely promise never to go into the Room, between sunset and sunrise. I made it clear to him that we knew nothing definite yet, one way or the other; and if the room were what I had first thought it to be, it might be a lot better for him to die first, than enter it after dark.

"When I got here, and had finished my business, I thought you chaps would be interested; and also I wanted to get it all spread out clear in my mind; so I rang you up. I am going over again tomorrow, and when I get back, I ought to have something pretty extraordinary to tell you. By the way, there is a curious thing I forgot to tell you. I tried to get a phonographic record of the whistling; but it simply produced no impression on the wax at all. That is one of the things that has made me feel queer.

"Another extraordinary thing is that the microphone will not magnify the sound—will not even transmit it; seems to take no account of it, and acts as if it were non-existent. I am absolutely and utterly stumped, up to the present. I am a wee bit curious to see whether any of your dear clever heads can make daylight of it. *I* cannot—not yet."

He rose to his feet.

"Good-night, all," he said, and began to usher us out abruptly, but without offence, into the night.

A fortnight later, he dropped us each a card, and you can imagine that I was not late this time. When we arrived, Carnacki took us straight into dinner, and when we had finished, and all made ourselves comfortable, he began again, where he had left off:

"Now just listen quietly; for I have got something very queer to tell you. I got back late at night, and I had to walk up to the castle, as I had not warned them that I was coming. It was bright moonlight; so that the walk was rather a pleasure, than otherwise. When I got there, the whole place was in darkness, and I thought I would go round outside, to see whether Tassoc or his brother was keeping watch. But I could not find them anywhere, and concluded that they had got tired of it, and gone off to bed.

"As I returned across the lawn that lies below the front of the East Wing, I caught the hooning whistling of the Room, coming down strangely clear through the stillness of the night. It had a peculiar note in it, I remember—low and constant, queerly meditative. I looked up at the window, bright in the moonlight, and got a sudden thought to bring a ladder from the stable-yard, and try to get a look into the Room, from the outside.

"With this notion, I hunted round at the back of the castle, among the straggle of offices, and presently found a long, fairly light ladder; though it was heavy enough for one, goodness knows! I thought at first that I should never get it reared. I managed at last, and let the ends rest very quietly against the wall, a little below the sill of the larger window. Then, going silently, I went up the ladder. Presently, I had my face above the sill, and was looking in, alone with the moonlight.

"Of course, the queer whistling sounded louder up there; but it still conveyed that peculiar sense of something whistling quietly to itself—can you understand? Though, for all the meditative lowness of the note, the horrible, gargantuan quality was distinct—a mighty parody of the human; as if I stood there and listened to the whistling from the lips of a monster with a man's soul.

"And then, you know, I saw something. The floor in the middle of the huge, empty room, was puckered upwards in the centre into a strange, soft-looking mound, parted at the top into an everchanging hole, that pulsated to that great, gentle hooning. At times, as I watched, I saw the heaving of the indented mound, gap across with a queer, inward suction, as with the drawing of an enormous breath; then the thing would dilate and pout once more to the incredible melody. And suddenly, as I stared, dumb, it came to me that the thing was living. I was looking at two enormous, blackened lips, blistered and brutal, there in the pale moonlight...

"Abruptly, they bulged out to a vast, pouting mound of force and sound, stiffened and swollen, and hugely massive and clean-cut in the moonbeams. And a great sweat lay heavy on the vast upper-lip. In the same moment of time, the whistling had burst into a mad screaming note, that seemed to stun me, even where I stood, outside of the window. And then, the following moment, I was staring blankly at the solid, undisturbed floor of the room—smooth, polished stone flooring, from wall to wall. And there was an absolute silence.

"You can picture me staring into the quiet Room, and knowing what I knew. I felt like a sick, frightened child, and I wanted to slide *quietly* down the ladder, and run away. But in that very instant, I heard Tassoc's voice calling to me from within the Room, for help, *help*. My God! but I got such an awful dazed feeling; and I had a vague, bewildered notion that, after all, it was the Irishmen who had got him in there, and were taking it out of him. And then the call came again, and I burst the window, and jumped in to help him. I had a confused idea that the call had come from within the shadow of the great fireplace, and I raced across to it; but there was no one there.

"'Tassoc!' I shouted, and my voice went empty-sounding round the great apartment; and then, in a flash, *I knew that Tassoc had never called*. I whirled round, sick with fear, towards the window, and as I did so, a frightful, exultant whistling scream burst through the Room. On my left, the end wall had bellied-in towards me, in a pair of gargantuan lips, black and utterly monstrous, to within a yard of my face. I fumbled for a mad instant at my revolver; not for *it*, but myself; for the danger was a thousand times worse than death. And then, suddenly, the Unknown Last Line of the Saaamaaa Ritual was whispered quite audibly in the room. Instantly, the thing happened that I have known once before. There came a sense as of dust falling continually and monotonously, and I knew that my life hung uncertain and suspended for a flash, in a brief, reeling vertigo of unseeable things. Then *that* ended, and I knew that I might live. My soul and body blended again, and life and power came to me. I dashed furiously at the window, and hurled myself out head-foremost; for I can tell you that I had stopped being afraid of death. I crashed down on to the ladder, and slithered, grabbing and grabbing; and so came some way or other alive to the bottom. And there I sat in the soft, wet grass, with the moonlight all about me; and far above, through the broken window of the Room, there was a low whistling.

"That is the chief of it. I was not hurt, and I went round to the front, and knocked Tassoc up. When they let me in, we had a long yarn, over some good whisky—for I was shaken to pieces—and I explained things as much as I could. I told Tassoc that the room would have to come down, and every fragment of it be burned in a blast-furnace, erected within a pentacle. He nodded. There was nothing to say. Then I went to bed.

"We turned a small army on to the work, and within ten days, that lovely thing had gone up in smoke, and what was left was calcined, and clean.

"It was when the workmen were stripping the panelling, that I got hold of a sound notion of the beginnings of that beastly development. Over the great fireplace, after the great oak panels had been torn down, I found that there was let into the masonry a scrollwork of stone, with on it an old inscription, in ancient Celtic, that here in this room was burned Dian Tiansay, Jester of King Alzof, who made the Song of Foolishness upon King Ernore of the Seventh Castle.

"When I got the translation clear, I gave it to Tassoc. He was tremendously excited; for he knew the old tale, and took me down to the library to look at an old parchment that gave the story in detail. Afterwards, I found that the incident was well-known about the countryside; but always regarded more as a legend, than as history. And no one seemed ever to have dreamt that the old East Wing of Iastrae Castle was the remains of the ancient Seventh Castle.

"From the old parchment, I gathered that there had been a pretty dirty job done, away back in the years. It seems that King Alzof and

King Ernore had been enemies by birthright, as you might say truly; but that nothing more than a little raiding had occurred on either side for years, until Dian Tiansay made the Song of Foolishness upon King Ernore, and sang it before King Alzof; and so greatly was it appreciated that King Alzof gave the jester one of his ladies, to wife.

"Presently, all the people of the land had come to know the song, and so it came at last to King Ernore, who was so angered that he made war upon his old enemy, and took and burned him and his castle; but Dian Tiansay, the jester, he brought with him to his own place, and having torn his tongue out because of the song which he had made and sung, he imprisoned him in the Room in the East Wing (which was evidently used for unpleasant purposes), and the jester's wife, he kept for himself, having a fancy for her prettiness.

"But one night, Dian Tiansay's wife was not to be found, and in the morning they discovered her lying dead in her husband's arms, and he sitting, whistling the Song of Foolishness, for he had no longer the power to sing it.

"Then they roasted Dian Tiansay, in the great fireplace—probably from that selfsame 'gallows-iron' which I have already mentioned. And until he died, Dian Tiansay 'ceased not to whistle' the Song of Foolishness, which he could no longer sing. But afterwards, 'in that room' there was often heard at night the sound of something whistling; and there 'grew a power in that room,' so that none dared to sleep in it.

"And presently, it would seem, the King went to another castle; for the whistling troubled him.

"There you have it all. Of course, that is only a rough rendering of the translation from the parchment. It's a bit quaint! Don't you think so?"

*

"Yes," I said, answering for the lot. "But how did the thing grow to such a tremendous manifestation?"

"One of those cases of continuity of thought producing a positive action upon the immediate surrounding material," replied Carnacki. "The development must have been going forward through centuries, to have produced such a monstrosity. It was a true instance of Saiitii manifestation, which I can best explain by likening it to a living spiritual fungus, which involves the very structure of the aether-fibre itself, and, of course, in so doing, acquires an essential control over the 'material-substance' involved in it. It is impossible to make it plainer in a few words."

"What broke the seventh hair?" asked Taylor.

But Carnacki did not know. He thought it was probably nothing but being too severely tensioned. He also explained that they found out that the men who had run away, had not been up to mischief; but had come over secretly, merely to hear the whistling, which, indeed, had suddenly become the talk of the whole countryside.

"One other thing," said Arkright, "have you any idea what governs the use of the Unknown Last Line of the Saaamaaa Ritual? I know, of course, that it was used by the Ab-human Priests in the Incantation of Raaaee; but what used it on your behalf, and what made it?"

"You had better read Harzam's Monograph, and my Addenda to it, on Astral and 'Astarral' Co-ordination and Interference," said Carnacki. "It is an extraordinary subject, and I can only say here that the human-vibration may not be insulated from the 'astarral' (as is always believed to be the case, in interferences by the Ab-human), without immediate action being taken by those Forces which govern the spinning of the outer circle. In other words, it is being proved, time after time, that there is some inscrutable Protective Force constantly intervening between the human-soul (not the body, mind you), and the Outer Monstrosities. Am I clear?"

"Yes, I think so," I replied. "And you believe that the Room had become the material expression of the ancient Jester—that his soul, rotted with hatred, had bred into a monster—eh?" I asked.

"Yes," said Carnacki, nodding. "I think you've put my thought rather neatly. It is a queer coincidence that Miss Donnehue is supposed to be descended (so I have heard since) from the same King Ernore. It makes one think some rather curious thoughts, doesn't it? The marriage coming on, and the Room waking to fresh life. If she had gone into that room, ever... eh? IT had waited a long time. Sins of the fathers. Yes, I've thought of that. They're to be married next week, and I am to be best man, which is a thing I hate. And he won his bets, rather! Just think, *if* ever she had gone into that room. Pretty horrible, eh?"

He nodded his head, grimly, and we four nodded back. Then he rose and took us collectively to the door, and presently thrust us forth in friendly fashion on to the Embankment, and into the fresh night air.

"Good-night," we all called back, and went to our various homes.

If she had, eh? If she had? That is what I kept thinking.

—1912—

THE DERELICT

"It's the *Material*," said the old ship's doctor... "The *Material*, plus the Conditions; and, maybe," he added slowly, "a third factor—yes, a third factor; but there, there..." He broke off his half-meditative sentence, and began to charge his pipe.

"Go on, Doctor," we said, encouragingly, and with more than a little expectancy. We were in the smoke-room of the *Sand-a-lea*, running across the North Atlantic, and the Doctor was a character. He concluded the charging of his pipe, and lit it; then settled himself, and began to express himself more fully:

"The *Material*," he said, with conviction, "is inevitably the medium of expression of the Life-Force—the fulcrum, as it were; lacking which, it is unable to exert itself, or, indeed, to express itself in any form or fashion that would be intelligible or evident to us.

"So potent is the share of the *Material* in the production of that thing which we name Life, and so eager the Life-Force to express itself, that I am convinced it would, if given the right Conditions, make itself manifest even through so hopeless-seeming a medium as a simple block of sawn wood; for I tell you, gentlemen, the Life-Force is both as fiercely urgent and as indiscriminate as Fire—the Destructor; yet which some are now growing to consider the very essence of Life rampant... There is a quaint seeming paradox there," he concluded, nodding his old grey head.

"Yes, Doctor," I said. "In brief, your argument is that Life is a thing, state, fact, or element, call-it-what-you-like, which requires the *Material* through which to manifest itself, and that given the *Material*, plus the Conditions, the result is Life. In other words, that Life is an evolved product, manifested through Matter and bred of Conditions—eh?"

"As we understand the word," said the old Doctor. "Though, mind you, there *may* be a third factor. But, in my heart, I believe that it is a matter of chemistry; Conditions and a suitable medium; but given the Conditions, the Brute is so almighty that it will seize upon anything through which to manifest itself. It is a Force generated by Conditions; but nevertheless this does not bring us one iota nearer to its *explanation*, any more than to the explanation of Electricity or Fire. They are, all three, of the Outer Forces—Monsters of the Void. Nothing we can do will *create* any one of them; our power is merely to be able, by providing the Conditions, to make each one of them manifest to our physical senses. Am I clear?"

"Yes, Doctor, in a way you are," I said. "But I don't agree with you; though I think I understand you. Electricity and Fire are both what I might call natural things; but Life is an abstract something—a kind of all-permeating Wakefulness. Oh, I can't explain it; who could! But it's spiritual; not just a thing bred out of a Condition, like Fire, as you say, or Electricity. It's a horrible thought of yours. Life's a kind of spiritual mystery..."

"Easy, my boy!" said the old Doctor, laughing gently to himself; "or else I may be asking you to demonstrate the spiritual mystery of life of the limpet, or the crab, shall we say."

He grinned at me, with ineffable perverseness. "Anyway," he continued, "as I suppose you've all guessed, I've a yarn to tell you in support of my impression that Life is no more a mystery or a miracle than Fire or Electricity. But, please to remember, gentlemen, that because we've succeeded in naming and making good use of these two Forces, they're just as much mysteries, fundamentally, as ever. And, anyway, the thing I'm going to tell you, won't explain the mystery of Life; but only give you one of my pegs on which I hang my feeling that Life is, as I have said, a Force made manifest through Conditions (that is to say, natural Chemistry), and that it can take for its purpose and Need, the most incredible and unlikely Matter; for without Matter, it cannot come into existence—it cannot become manifest..."

"I don't agree with you, Doctor," I interrupted. "Your theory would destroy all belief in life after death. It would..."

"Hush, sonny," said the old man, with a quiet little smile of comprehension. "Hark to what I've to say first; and, anyway, what objection have you to material life, after death; and if you object to a material framework, I would still have you remember that I am speaking of Life, as we understand the word in this our life. Now do be a quiet lad, or I'll never be done:

"It was when I was a young man, and that is a good many years ago, gentlemen. I had passed my examinations; but was so run down with overwork, that it was decided that I had better take a trip to sea. I was by no means well off, and very glad, in the end, to secure a nominal post as Doctor in a sailing passenger-clipper, running out to China.

"The name of the ship was the *Bheotpte*, and soon after I had got all my gear aboard, she cast off, and we dropped down the Thames, and next day were well away out in the Channel.

"The Captain's name was Gannington, a very decent man; though quite illiterate. The First Mate, Mr. Berlies, was a quiet, sternish, reserved man, very well-read. The Second Mate, Mr. Selvern, was, perhaps, by birth and upbringing, the most socially cultured of the three; but he lacked the stamina and indomitable pluck of the two others. He was more of a sensitive; and emotionally and even mentally, the most alert man of the three.

"On our way out, we called at Madagascar, where we landed some of our passengers; then we ran Eastward, meaning to call at North West Cape; but about a hundred degrees East, we encountered very dreadful weather, which carried away all our sails and sprung the jibboom and fore t'gallant mast.

"The storm carried us Northward for several hundred miles, and when it dropped us finally, we found ourselves in a very bad state. The ship had been strained, and had taken some three feet of water through her seams; the main top-mast had been sprung, in addition to the jibboom and fore t'gallant mast; two of our boats had gone, as also one of the pigsties (with three fine pigs), this latter having been washed overboard but some half hour before the wind began to ease, which it did quickly; though a very ugly sea ran for some hours after.

"The wind left us just before dark, and when morning came, it brought splendid weather; a calm, mildly undulating sea, and a brilliant sun, with no wind. It showed us also that we were not alone; for about two miles away to the Westward, was another vessel, which Mr. Selvern, the Second Mate, pointed out to me.

"'That's a pretty rum-looking packet, Doctor,' he said, and handed me his glass. I looked through it, at the other vessel, and saw what he meant; at least, I thought I did.

"'Yes, Mr. Selvern,' I said, 'she's got a pretty old-fashioned look about her.'

"He laughed at me, in his pleasant way.

"'It's easy to see you're not a sailor, Doctor,' he remarked. 'There's a dozen rum things about her. She's a derelict, and has been floating round, by the look of her, for many a score of years. Look at the shape of her counter, and the bows and cutwater. She's as old as the hills, as you might say, and ought to have gone down to Davy Jones a long time ago. Look at the growths on her, and the thickness of her standing rigging; that's all salt encrustations, I fancy, if you notice the white colour. She's been a small barque; but don't you see she's not a yard left aloft. They've all dropped out of the slings; everything rotted away; wonder the standing rigging hasn't gone too. I wish the Old Man would let us take the boat, and have a look at her; she'd be well worth it.'

"There seemed little chance, however, of this; for all hands were turned-to and kept hard at it all day long, repairing the damage to the masts and gear, and this took a long while, as you may think. Part of the time, I gave a hand, heaving on one of the deck-capstans; for the exercise was good for my liver. Old Captain Gannington approved, and I persuaded him to come along and try some of the same medicine, which he did; and we grew very chummy over the job.

"We got talking about the derelict, and he remarked how lucky we were not to have run full tilt on to her, in the darkness; for she lay right away to leeward of us, according to the way that we had been drifting in the storm. He also was of the opinion that she had a strange look about her, and that she was pretty old; but on this latter point, he plainly had far less knowledge than the Second Mate; for he was, as I have said, an illiterate man, and knew nothing of sea-craft, beyond what experience had taught him. He lacked the book-knowledge which the Second Mate had, of vessels previous to his day, which it appeared the derelict was.

"'She's an old 'un, Doctor,' was the extent of his observations in this direction.

"Yet, when I mentioned to him that it would be interesting to go aboard, and give her a bit of an overhaul, he nodded his head, as if the idea had been already in his mind, and accorded with his own inclinations.

"'When the work's over, Doctor,' he said. 'Can't spare the men now, ye know. Got to get all shipshape an' ready as smart as we can. But we'll take my gig, an' go off in the Second Dog Watch. The glass is steady, an' it'll be a bit of gam for us.'

"That evening, after tea, the Captain gave orders to clear the gig and get her overboard. The Second Mate was to come with us, and the Skipper gave him word to see that two or three lamps were put into the boat, as it would soon fall dark. A little later, we were pulling across the calmness of the sea, with a crew of six at the oars, and making very good speed of it.

"Now, gentlemen, I have detailed to you with great exactness, all the facts, both big and little, so that you can follow step by step each incident in this extraordinary affair; and I want you now to pay the closest attention.

"I was sitting in the stern-sheets, with the Second Mate, and the Captain, who was steering; and as we drew nearer and nearer to the stranger, I studied her with an ever growing attention, as, indeed, did Captain Gannington and the Second Mate. She was, as you know, to the Westward of us, and the sunset was making a great flame of red light to the back of her, so that she showed a little blurred and indistinct, by reason of the halation of the light, which almost defeated the eye in any attempt to see her rotting spars and standing-rigging, submerged as they were in the fiery glory of the sunset.

"It was because of this effect of the sunset, that we had come quite close, comparatively, to the derelict, before we saw that she was all surrounded by a sort of curious scum, the colour of which was difficult to decide upon, by reason of the red light that was in the atmosphere; but which afterwards we discovered to be brown. This scum spread all about the old vessel for many hundreds of yards, in a huge, irregular patch, a great stretch of which reached out to the Eastward, upon our starboard side, some score, or so, fathoms away.

"'Queer stuff,' said Captain Gannington, leaning to the side, and looking over. 'Something in the cargo as 'as gone rotten an' worked out through 'er seams.'

"'Look at her bows and stern,' said the Second Mate; 'just look at the growth on her.'

"There were, as he said, great clumpings of strange-looking sea-fungi under the bows and the short counter astern. From the stump of her jibboom and her cutwater, great beards of rime and marine-growths hung downward into the scum that held her in. Her blank starboard side was presented to us, all a dead, dirtyish white, streaked and mottled vaguely with dull masses of heavier colour.

"'There's a steam or haze rising off her,' said the Second Mate, speaking again; 'you can see it against the light. It keeps coming and going. Look!'

"I saw then what he meant—a faint haze or steam, either suspended above the old vessel, or rising from her; and Captain Gannington saw it also:

"'Spontaneous combustion!' he exclaimed. 'We'll 'ave to watch w'en we lift the 'atches; 'nless it's some poor devil that's got aboard of 'er; but that ain't likely.'

"We were now within a couple of hundred yards of the old derelict, and had entered into the brown scum. As it poured off the lifted oars, I heard one of the men mutter to himself: 'dam treacle!' and, indeed, it was something like it. As the boat continued to forge nearer and nearer to the old ship, the scum grew thicker and thicker; so that, at last, it perceptibly slowed us.

"'Give way, lads! Put some beef to it!' sung out Captain Gannington; and thereafter there was no sound, except the panting of the men, and the faint, reiterated suck, suck, of the sullen brown scum upon the oars, as the boat was forced ahead. As we went, I was conscious of a peculiar smell in the evening air, and whilst I had no doubt that the puddling of the scum, by the oars, made it rise, I felt that in some way, it was vaguely familiar; yet I could give it no name.

"We were now very close to the old vessel, and presently she was high above us, against the dying light. The Captain called out then to: 'in with the bow oars, and stand-by with the boat-hook,' which was done.

"'Aboard there! Ahoy! Aboard there! Ahoy!' shouted Captain Gannington; but there came no answer, only the flat sound of his voice going lost into the open sea, each time he sung out.

"'Ahoy! Aboard there! Ahoy!' he shouted, time after time; but there was only the weary silence of the old hulk that answered us; and, somehow as he shouted, the while that I stared up half expectantly at her, a queer little sense of oppression, that amounted almost to nervousness, came upon me. It passed; but I remember how I was suddenly aware that it was growing dark. Darkness comes fairly rapidly in the tropics; though not so quickly as many fiction-writers seem to think; but it was not that the coming dusk had perceptibly deepened in that brief time, of only a few moments, but rather that my nerves had made me suddenly a little hyper-sensitive. I mention my state particularly; for I am not a nervy man, normally; and my abrupt touch of nerves is significant, in the light of what happened.

"'There's no one aboard there!' said Captain Gannington. 'Give way, men!' For the boat's crew had instinctively rested on their oars, as the Captain hailed the old craft. The man gave way again; and then the Second Mate called out excitedly: 'Why, look there, there's our pigsty! See, it's got *Bheotpte* painted on the end. It's drifted down here, and the scum's caught it. What a blessed wonder!'

"It was, as he had said, our pigsty that had been washed overboard in the storm; and most extraordinary to come across it there.

"'We'll tow it off with us, when we go,' remarked the Captain, and shouted to the crew to get-down to their oars; for they were hardly moving the boat, because the scum was so thick, close in around the old ship, that it literally clogged the boat from going ahead. I remember that it struck me, in a half-conscious sort of way, as curious that the pigsty, containing our three dead pigs, had managed to drift in so far, unaided, whilst we could scarcely manage to *force* the boat in, now that we had come right into the scum. But the thought passed from my mind; for so many things happened within the next few minutes.

"The men managed to bring the boat in alongside, within a couple of feet of the derelict, and the man with the boat-hook, hooked on.

"''Ave ye got 'old there, forrard?' asked Captain Gannington.

"'Yessir!' said the bow-man; and as he spoke, there came a queer noise of tearing.

"'What's that?' asked the Captain.

"'It's tore, Sir. Tore clean away!' said the man; and his tone showed that he had received something of a shock.

"'Get a hold again then!' said Captain Gannington, irritably. 'You don't s'pose this packet was built yesterday! Shove the hook into the main chains.' The man did so, gingerly, as you might say; for it seemed to me, in the growing dusk, that he put no strain on to the hook; though, of course, there was no need; you see, the boat could not go very far, of herself, in the stuff in which she was embedded. I remember thinking this, also, as I looked up at the bulging side of the old vessel. Then I heard Captain Gannington's voice:

"'Lord! but she's old! An' what a colour, Doctor! She don't half want paint, do she!… Now then, somebody, one of them oars.'

"An oar was passed to him, and he leant it up against the ancient, bulging side; then he paused, and called to the Second Mate to light a couple of the lamps, and stand-by to pass them up; for darkness had settled down now upon the sea.

"The Second Mate lit two of the lamps, and told one of the men to light a third, and keep it handy in the boat; then he stepped across, with a lamp in each hand, to where Captain Gannington stood by the oar against the side of the ship.

"'Now, my lad,' said the Captain, to the Mate who had pulled stroke, 'up with you, an we'll pass ye up the lamps.'

"The man jumped to obey; caught the oar, and put his weight upon it, and as he did so, something seemed to give a little.

"'Look!' cried out the Second Mate, and pointed, lamp in hand... 'It's sunk in!'

"This was true. The oar had made quite an indentation into the bulging, somewhat slimy side of the old vessel.

"'Mould, I reckon,' said Captain Gannington, bending towards the derelict, to look. Then, to the man:

"'Up you go, my lad, and be smart... Don't stand there waitin'!'

"At that, the man, who had paused a moment as he felt the oar give beneath his weight, began to shin up, and in a few seconds he was aboard, and leant out over the rail for the lamps. These were passed up to him, and the Captain called to him to steady the oar. Then Captain Gannington went, calling to me to follow, and after me the Second Mate.

"As the Captain put his face over the rail, he gave a cry of astonishment:

"'Mould, by gum! Mould... Tons of it!... Good Lord!'

"As I heard him shout that, I scrambled the more eagerly after him, and in a moment or two, I was able to see what he meant— Everywhere that the light from the two lamps struck, there was nothing but smooth great masses and surfaces of a dirty-white mould.

"I climbed over the rail, with the Second Mate close behind, and stood upon the mould-covered decks. There might have been no planking beneath the mould, for all that our feet could feel. It gave under our tread, with a spongy, puddingy feel. It covered the deck-furniture of the old ship, so that the shape of each article and fitment was often no more than suggested through it.

"Captain Gannington snatched a lamp from the man, and the Second Mate reached for the other. They held the lamps high, and we all stared. It was most extraordinary, and, somehow, most abominable. I can think of no other word, gentlemen, that so much describes the predominant feeling that affected me at the moment.

"'Good Lord!' said Captain Gannington, several times. 'Good Lord!' But neither the Second Mate nor the man said anything, and for my part I just stared, and at the same time began to smell a little at the air; for there was again a vague odour of something half familiar, that somehow brought to me a sense of half-known fright.

"I turned this way and that, staring, as I have said. Here and there, the mould was so heavy as to entirely disguise what lay beneath; converting the deck-fittings into indistinguishable mounds of mould, all dirty-white, and blotched and veined with irregular, dull purplish markings.

"There was a strange thing about the mould, which Captain Gannington drew attention to—it was that our feet did not crush into it and break the surface, as might have been expected; but merely indented it.

"'Never seen nothin' like it before!... Never!' said the Captain, after having stooped with his lamp to examine the mould under our feet. He stamped with his heel, and the stuff gave out a dull, puddingy sound. He stooped again, with a quick movement, and stared, holding the lamp close to the deck. 'Blest, if it ain't a reg'lar skin to it!' he said.

"The Second Mate and the man and I all stooped, and looked at it. The Second Mate progged it with his forefinger, and I remember I rapped it several times with my knuckles, listening to the dead sound it gave out, and noticing the close, firm texture of the mould.

"'Dough!' said the Second Mate. 'It's just like blessed dough!... Pouf!' He stood up with a quick movement. 'I could fancy it stinks a bit,' he said.

"As he said this, I knew suddenly what the familiar thing was, in the vague odour that hung about us— It was that the smell had something animal-like in it; something of the same smell, only *heavier*, that you will smell in any place that is infested with mice. I began to look about with a sudden very real uneasiness... There might be vast numbers of hungry rats aboard... They might prove exceedingly dangerous, if in a starving condition; yet, as you will understand, somehow I hesitated to put forward my idea as a reason for caution; it was too fanciful.

"Captain Gannington had begun to go aft, along the mould-covered maindeck, with the Second Mate; each of them holding his lamp high up, so as to cast a good light about the vessel. I turned quickly and followed them, the man with me keeping close to my heels, and plainly uneasy. As we went, I became aware that there was a feeling of moisture in the air, and I remembered the slight mist, or smoke, above the hulk, which had made Captain Gannington suggest spontaneous combustion, in explanation.

"And always, as we went, there was that vague, animal smell; and, suddenly, I found myself wishing we were well away from the old vessel.

"Abruptly, after a few paces, the Captain stopped and pointed at a row of mould-hidden shapes on either side of the maindeck... 'Guns,' he said. 'Been a privateer in the old days, I guess; maybe worse! We'll 'ave a look below, Doctor; there may be something worth touchin'. She's older than I thought. Mr. Selvern thinks she's about three hundred year old; but I scarce think it.'

"We continued our way aft, and I remember that I found myself walking as lightly and gingerly as possible; as if I were subconsciously afraid of treading through the rotten, mould-hid decks. I think the others had a touch of the same feeling, from the way that they walked. Occasionally, the soft mould would grip our heels, releasing them with a little, sullen suck.

"The Captain forged somewhat ahead of the Second Mate; and I know that the suggestion he had made himself, that perhaps there might be something below, worth the carrying away, had stimulated his imagination. The Second Mate was, however, beginning to feel somewhat the same way that I did; at least, I have that impression. I think, if it had not been for what I might truly describe as Captain Gannington's sturdy courage, we should all of us have just gone back over the side very soon; for there was most certainly an unwholesome feeling abroad, that made one feel queerly lacking in pluck; and you will soon perceive that this feeling was justified.

"Just as the Captain reached the few, mould-covered steps, leading up on to the short half-poop, I was suddenly aware that the feeling of moisture in the air had grown very much more definite. It was perceptible now, intermittently, as a sort of thin, moist, fog-like vapour, that came and went oddly, and seemed to make the decks a little indistinct to the view, this time and that. Once, an odd puff of it beat up suddenly from somewhere, and caught me in the face, carrying a queer, sickly, heavy odour with it, that somehow frightened me strangely, with a suggestion of a waiting and half-comprehended danger.

"We had followed Captain Gannington up the three, mould-covered steps, and now went slowly aft along the raised after-deck.

"By the mizzen-mast, Captain Gannington paused, and held his lantern near to it...

"'My word, Mister,' he said to the Second Mate, 'it's fair thickened up with the mould; why, I'll g'antee it's close on four foot thick.' He shone the light down to where it met the deck. 'Good Lord!' he said, 'look at the sea-lice on it!' I stepped up; and it was as he had said; the sea-lice were thick upon it, some of them huge; not less than the size of large beetles, and all a clear, colourless shade, like water, except where there were little spots of grey in them, evidently their internal organisms.

"'I've never seen the like of them, 'cept on a live cod!' said Captain Gannington, in an extremely puzzled voice. 'My word! but they're whoppers!' Then he passed on; but a few paces farther aft, he stopped again, and held his lamp near to the mould-hidden deck.

"'Lord bless me, Doctor!' he called out, in a low voice, 'did ye ever see the like of that? Why, it's a foot long, if it's a hinch!'

"I stooped over his shoulder, and saw what he meant; it was a clear, colourless creature, about a foot long, and about eight inches high, with a curved back that was extraordinarily narrow. As we stared, all in a group, it gave a queer little flick, and was gone.

"'Jumped!' said the Captain. 'Well, if that ain't a giant of all the sea-lice that ever I've seen! I guess it's jumped twenty-foot clear.' He straightened his back, and scratched his head a moment, swinging the lantern this way and that with the other hand, and staring about us. 'Wot are *they* doin' aboard 'ere!' he said. 'You'll see 'em (little things) on fat cod, an' such-like... I'm blowed, Doctor, if I understand.'

"He held his lamp towards a big mound of the mould, that occupied part of the after portion of the low poop-deck, a little foreside of where there came a two-foot high 'break' to a kind of second and loftier poop, that ran away aft to the taffrail. The mound was pretty big, several feet across, and more than a yard high. Captain Gannington walked up to it:

"'I reck'n this 's the scuttle,' he remarked, and gave it a heavy kick. The only result was a deep indentation into the huge, whitish hump of mould, as if he had driven his foot into a mass of some doughy substance. Yet; I am not altogether correct in saying that this was the only result; for a certain other thing happened— From a place made by the Captain's foot, there came a little gush of a purplish fluid, accompanied by a peculiar smell, that was, and was not, half-familiar. Some of the mould-like substance had stuck to the toe of the Captain's boot, and from this, likewise, there issued a sweat, as it were, of the same colour.

"'Well!' said Captain Gannington, in surprise; and drew back his foot to make another kick at the hump of mould; but he paused, at an exclamation from the Second Mate:

"'Don't, Sir!' said the Second Mate.

"I glanced at him, and the light from Captain Gannington's lamp showed me that his face had a bewildered, half-frightened look, as if he were suddenly and unexpectedly half-afraid of something, and as if his tongue had given away his sudden fright, without any intention on his part to speak.

"The Captain also turned and stared at him:

"'Why, Mister?' he asked, in a somewhat puzzled voice, through which there sounded just the vaguest hint of annoyance. 'We've got to shift this muck, if we're to get below.'

"I looked at the Second Mate, and it seemed to me that, curiously enough, he was listening less to the Captain, than to some other sound.

"Suddenly, he said in a queer voice: 'Listen, everybody!'

"Yet, we heard nothing, beyond the faint murmur of the men talking together in the boat alongside.

"'I don't hear nothin',' said Captain Gannington, after a short pause. 'Do you, Doctor?'

"'No,' I said.

"'Wot was it you thought you heard?' asked the Captain, turning again to the Second Mate. But the Second Mate shook his head, in a curious, almost irritable way; as if the Captain's question interrupted his listening. Captain Gannington stared a moment at him; then held his lantern up, and glanced about him, almost uneasily. I know I felt a queer sense of strain. But the light showed nothing, beyond the greyish dirty-white of the mould in all directions.

"'Mister Selvern,' said the Captain at last, looking at him, 'don't get fancying things. Get hold of your bloomin' self. Ye know ye heard nothin'?'

"'I'm quite sure I heard something, Sir!' said the Second Mate. 'I seemed to hear—' He broke off sharply, and appeared to listen, with an almost painful intensity.

"'What did it sound like?' I asked.

"'It's all right, Doctor,' said Captain Gannington, laughing gently. 'Ye can give him a tonic when we get back. I'm goin' to shift this stuff.'

"He drew back, and kicked for the second time at the ugly mass, which he took to hide the companionway. The result of his kick was startling; for the whole thing wobbled sloppily, like a mound of unhealthy-looking jelly.

"He drew his foot out of it, quickly, and took a step backward, staring, and holding his lamp towards it:

"'By gum!' he said; and it was plain that he was genuinely startled, 'the blessed thing's gone soft!'

"The man had run back several steps from the suddenly flaccid mound, and looked horribly frightened. Though, of what, I am sure he had not the least idea. The Second Mate stood where he was, and stared. For my part, I know I had a most hideous uneasiness upon me. The Captain continued to hold his light towards the wobbling mound, and stare:

"'It's gone squashy all through!' he said. 'There's no scuttle there. There's no bally woodwork inside that lot! Phoo! what a rum smell!'

"He walked round to the after-side of the strange mound, to see whether there might be some signs of an opening into the hull at the back of the great heap of mould-stuff. And then:

"'Listen!' said the Second Mate, again, in the strangest sort of voice.

"Captain Gannington straightened himself upright, and there succeeded a pause of the most intense quietness, in which there was not even the hum of talk from the men alongside in the boat. We all heard it—a kind of dull, soft Thud! Thud! Thud! Thud! somewhere in the hull under us; yet so vague that I might have been half doubtful I heard it, only that the others did so, too.

"Captain Gannington turned suddenly to where the man stood:

"'Tell them—' he began. But the fellow cried out something, and pointed. There had come a strange intensity into his somewhat unemotional face; so that the Captain's glance followed his action instantly. I stared, also, as you may think. It was the great mound, at which the man was pointing. I saw what he meant.

"From the two gapes made in the mould-like stuff by Captain Gannington's boot, the purple fluid was jetting out in a queerly regular fashion, almost as if it were being forced out by a pump. My word! but I stared! And even as I stared, a larger jet squirted out, and splashed as far as the man, spattering his boots and trouser-legs.

"The fellow had been pretty nervous before, in a stolid, ignorant sort of way; and his funk had been growing steadily; but, at this, he simply let out a yell, and turned about to run. He paused an instant, as if a sudden fear of the darkness that held the decks, between him and the boat, had taken him. He snatched at the Second Mate's lantern; tore it out of his hand, and plunged heavily away over the vile stretch of mould.

"Mr. Selvern, the Second Mate, said not a word; he was just standing, staring at the strange-smelling twin streams of dull purple, that were jetting out from the wobbling mound. Captain Gannington, however, roared an order to the man to come back; but the man plunged on and on across the mould, his feet seeming to be clogged by the stuff, as if it had grown suddenly soft. He zigzagged, as he ran, the lantern swaying in wild circles, as he wrenched his feet free, with a constant plop, plop; and I could hear his frightened gasps, even from where I stood.

"'Come back with that lamp!' roared the Captain again; but still the man took no notice, and Captain Gannington was silent an instant, his lips working in a queer, inarticulate fashion; as if he were stunned momentarily by the very violence of his anger at the man's insubordination. And in the silence, I heard the sounds again: Thud! Thud! Thud! Thud! Quite distinctly now, beating, it seemed suddenly to me, right down under my feet, but deep.

"I stared down at the mould on which I was standing, with a quick, disgusting sense of the terrible all about me; then I looked at the Captain, and tried to say something, without appearing frightened. I saw that he had turned again to the mound, and all the anger had gone out of his face. He had his lamp out towards the mound, and was listening. There was a further moment of absolute silence; at least, I know that I was not conscious of any sound at all, in all the world, except that extraordinary Thud! Thud! Thud! Thud! down somewhere in the huge bulk under us.

"The Captain shifted his feet, with a sudden, nervous movement; and as he lifted them, the mould went plop! plop! He looked quickly at me, trying to smile, as if he were not thinking anything very much about it: 'What do you make of it, Doctor?' he said.

"'I think—' I began. But the Second Mate interrupted with a single word; his voice pitched a little high, in a tone that made us both stare instantly at him:

"'Look!' he said, and pointed at the mound. The thing was all of a slow quiver. A strange ripple ran outward from it, along the deck, like you will see a ripple run inshore out of a calm sea. It reached a mound a little fore-side of us, which I had supposed to be the cabin-skylight; and in a moment, the second mound sank nearly level with the surrounding decks, quivering floppily in a most extraordinary fashion. A sudden, quick tremor took the mould, right under the Second Mate, and he gave out a hoarse little cry, and held his arms out on each side of him, to keep his balance. The tremor in the mould, spread, and Captain Gannington swayed, and spread his feet, with a sudden curse of fright. The Second Mate jumped across to him, and caught him by the wrist:

"'The boat, Sir!' he said, saying the very thing that I had lacked the pluck to say. 'For God's sake—'

"But he never finished; for a tremendous, hoarse scream cut off his words. They hove themselves round, and looked. I could see without turning. The man who had run from us, was standing in the waist of the ship, about a fathom from the starboard bulwarks. He was swaying from side to side, and screaming in a dreadful fashion. He appeared to be trying to lift his feet, and the light from his swaying lantern showed an almost incredible sight. All about him the mould was in active movement. His feet had sunk out of sight. The stuff appeared to be *lapping* at his legs; and abruptly his bare flesh showed. The hideous stuff had rent his trouser-legs away, as if they were paper. He gave out a simply sickening scream, and, with a vast effort, wrenched one leg free. It was partly destroyed. The next instant he pitched face downward, and the stuff heaped itself upon him, as if it were actually alive, with a dreadful savage life. It was simply infernal. The man had gone from sight. Where he had fallen was now a writhing, elongated mound, in constant and horrible increase, as the mould appeared to move towards it in strange ripples from all sides.

"Captain Gannington and the Second Mate were stone silent, in amazed and incredulous horror; but I had begun to reach towards a grotesque and terrific conclusion, both helped and hindered by my professional training.

"From the men in the boat alongside, there was a loud shouting, and I saw two of their faces appear suddenly above the rail. They showed clearly, a moment, in the light from the lamp which the man had snatched from Mr. Selvern; for, strangely enough, this lamp was standing upright and unharmed on the deck, a little way fore-side of that dreadful, elongated, growing mound, that still swayed and writhed with an incredible horror. The lamp rose and fell on the passing ripples of the mould, just—for all the world—as you will see a boat rise and fall on little swells. It is of some interest to me now, psychologically, to remember how that rising and falling lantern brought home to me, more than anything, the incomprehensible, dreadful strangeness of it all.

"The men's faces disappeared, with sudden yells, as if they had slipped, or been suddenly hurt; and there was a fresh uproar of shouting from the boat. The men were calling to us to come away; to come away. In the same instant, I felt my left boot drawn suddenly and forcibly downward, with a horrible, painful gripe. I wrenched it free, with a yell of angry fear. Forrard of us, I saw that the vile surface was all a-move; and abruptly I found myself shouting in a queer frightened voice:

"'The boat, Captain! The boat, Captain!'

"Captain Gannington stared round at me, over his right shoulder, in a peculiar, dull way, that told me he was utterly dazed with bewilderment and the incomprehensibleness of it all. I took a quick, clogged, nervous step towards him, and gripped his arm and shook it fiercely.

"'The boat!' I shouted at him. 'The boat! For God's sake, tell the men to bring the boat aft!'

"Then the mould must have drawn his feet down; for, abruptly, he bellowed fiercely with terror, his momentary apathy giving place to furious energy. His thick-set, vastly muscular body doubled and writhed with his enormous effort, and he struck out madly, dropping the lantern. He tore his feet free, something ripping as he did so. The *reality* and necessity of the situation had come upon him, brutishly real, and he was roaring to the men in the boat:

"'Bring the boat aft! Bring 'er aft! Bring 'er aft!'

"The Second Mate and I were shouting the same thing, madly.

"'For God's sake be smart, lads!' roared the Captain, and stooped quickly for his lamp, which still burned. His feet were gripped again, and he hove them out, blaspheming breathlessly, and leaping a yard high with his effort. Then he made a run for the side, wrenching his feet free at each step. In the same instant, the Second Mate cried out something, and grabbed at the Captain:

"'It's got hold of my feet! It's got hold of my feet!' he screamed. His feet had disappeared up to his boot-tops; and Captain Gannington caught him round the waist with his powerful left arm, gave a mighty heave, and the next instant had him free; but both his boot-soles had almost gone.

"For my part, I jumped madly from foot to foot, to avoid the plucking of the mould; and suddenly I made a run for the ship's side. But before I could get there, a queer gape came in the mould, between us and the side, at least a couple of feet wide; and how deep I don't know. It closed up in an instant; and all the mould, where the gape had been, went into a sort of flurry of horrible ripplings, so that I ran back from it; for I did not dare to put my foot upon it. Then the Captain was shouting to me:

"'Aft, Doctor! Aft, Doctor! This way, Doctor! Run!' I saw then that he had passed me, and was up on the after, raised portion of the poop. He had the Second Mate thrown like a sack, all loose and quiet, over his left shoulder; for Mr. Selvern had fainted, and his long legs flogged, limp and helpless, against the Captain's massive knees as the Captain ran. I saw, with a queer, unconscious noting of minor details, how the torn soles of the Second Mate's boots flapped and jigged, as the Captain staggered aft.

"'Boat ahoy! Boat ahoy! Boat ahoy!' shouted the Captain; and then I was beside him, shouting also. The men were answering with loud yells of encouragement, and it was plain they were working desperately to force the boat aft, through the thick scum about the ship.

"We reached the ancient, mould-hid taffrail, and slewed about, breathlessly, in the half-darkness, to see what was happening. Captain Gannington had left his lantern by the big mound, when he picked up the Second Mate; and as we stood, gasping, we discovered suddenly that all the mould between us and the light was full of movement. Yet, the part on which we stood, for about six or eight feet forrard of us, was still firm.

"Every couple of seconds, we shouted to the men to hasten, and they kept on calling to us that they would be with us in an instant. And all the time, we watched the deck of that dreadful hulk, feeling, for my part, literally sick with mad suspense, and ready to jump overboard into that filthy scum all about us.

"Down somewhere in the huge bulk of the ship, there was all the time that extraordinary, dull, ponderous Thud! Thud! Thud! Thud! growing ever louder. I seemed to feel the whole hull of the derelict beginning to quiver and thrill with each dull beat. And to me, with the grotesque and monstrous suspicion of what made that noise, it was, at once, the most dreadful and incredible sound I have ever heard.

"As we waited desperately for the boat, I scanned incessantly so much of the grey-white bulk as the lamp showed. The whole of the decks seemed to be in strange movement. Forrard of the lamp, I could see, indistinctly, the moundings of the mould swaying and nodding hideously, beyond the circle of the brightest rays. Nearer, and full in the glow of the lamp, the mound which should have indicated the skylight, was swelling steadily. There were ugly, purple veinings on it, and as it swelled, it seemed to me that the veinings and mottlings on it, were becoming plainer—rising, as though embossed upon it, like you will see the veins stand out on the body of a powerful, full-blooded horse. It was most extraordinary. The mound that we had supposed to cover the companionway, had sunk flat with the surrounding mould, and I could not see that it jetted out any more of the purplish fluid.

"A quaking movement of the mould began, away forrard of the lamp, and came flurrying away aft towards us; and at the sight of that, I climbed up on to the spongy-feeling taffrail, and yelled afresh for the boat. The men answered with a shout, which told me they were nearer; but the beastly scum was so thick that it was evidently a fight to move the boat at all. Beside me, Captain Gannington was shaking the Second Mate furiously, and the man stirred and began to moan. The Captain shook him again.

"'Wake up! Wake up, Mister!' he shouted.

"The Second Mate staggered out of the Captain's arms, and collapsed suddenly, shrieking: 'My feet! Oh, God! My feet!' The Captain and I lugged him up off the mould, and got him into a sitting position upon the taffrail, where he kept up a continual moaning.

"'Hold 'im, Doctor,' said the Captain, and whilst I did so, he ran forrard a few yards, and peered down over the starboard quarter rail. 'For God's sake, be smart, lads! Be smart! Be smart!' he shouted down to the men; and they answered him, breathless, from close at hand; yet still too far away for the boat to be any use to us on the instant.

"I was holding the moaning, half-unconscious officer, and staring forrard along the poop decks. The flurrying of the mould was coming aft, slowly and noiselessly. And then, suddenly, I saw something closer:

"'Look out, Captain!' I shouted; and even as I shouted, the mould near to him gave a sudden peculiar slobber. I had seen a ripple stealing towards him through the horrible stuff. He gave an enormous, clumsy leap, and landed near to us on the sound part of the mould; but the movement followed him. He turned and faced it, swearing fiercely. All about his feet there came abruptly little gapings, which made horrid sucking noises.

"'Come *back*, Captain!' I yelled. 'Come back, *quick*!'

"As I shouted, a ripple came at his feet—lipping at them; and he stamped insanely at it, and leaped back, his boot torn half off his foot. He swore madly with pain and anger, and jumped swiftly for the taffrail.

"'Come on, Doctor! Over we go!' he called. Then he remembered the filthy scum, and hesitated; roaring out desperately to the men to hurry. I stared down, also.

"'The Second Mate?' I said.

"'I'll take charge, Doctor,' said Captain Gannington, and caught hold of Mr. Selvern. As he spoke, I thought I saw something beneath us, outlined against the scum. I leaned out over the stern, and peered. There was something under the port quarter.

"'There's something down there, Captain!' I called, and pointed in the darkness.

"He stooped far over, and stared.

"'A boat, by Gum! A BOAT!' he yelled, and began to wriggle swiftly along the taffrail, dragging the Second Mate after him. I followed.

"'A boat it is, sure!' he exclaimed, a few moments later; and, picking up the Second Mate clear of the rail, he hove him down into the boat, where he fell with a crash into the bottom.

"'Over ye go, Doctor!' he yelled at me, and pulled me bodily off the rail, and dropped me after the officer. As he did so, I felt the whole of the ancient, spongy rail give a peculiar, sickening quiver, and begin to wobble. I fell on to the Second Mate, and the Captain came after, almost in the same instant; but fortunately, he landed clear of us, onto the fore thwart, which broke under his weight, with a loud crack and splintering of wood.

"'Thank God!' I heard him mutter. 'Thank God!... I guess that was a mighty near thing to goin' to hell.'

"He struck a match, just as I got to my feet, and between us we got the Second Mate straightened out on one of the after thwarts. We shouted to the men in the boat, telling them where we were, and saw the light of their lantern shining round the starboard counter of the derelict. They called back to us, to tell us they were doing their best; and then, whilst we waited, Captain Gannington struck another match, and began to overhaul the boat we had dropped into. She was a modern, two-bowed boat, and on the stern, there was painted

'Cyclone Glasgow.' She was in pretty fair condition, and had evidently drifted into the scum and been held by it.

"Captain Gannington struck several matches, and went forrard towards the derelict. Suddenly he called to me, and I jumped over the thwarts to him.

"'Look, Doctor,' he said; and I saw what he meant—a mass of bones, up in the bows of the boat. I stooped over them, and looked. There were the bones of at least three people, all mixed together, in an extraordinary fashion, and quite clean and dry. I had a sudden thought concerning the bones; but I said nothing; for my thought was vague, in some ways, and concerned the grotesque and incredible suggestion that had come to me, as to the cause of that ponderous, dull Thud! Thud! Thud! Thud! that beat on so infernally within the hull, and was plain to hear even now that we had got off the vessel herself. And all the while, you know, I had a sick, horrible, mental-picture of that frightful wriggling mound aboard the hulk.

"As Captain Gannington struck a final match, I saw something that sickened me, and the Captain saw it in the same instant. The match went out, and he fumbled clumsily for another, and struck it. We saw the thing again. We had not been mistaken... A great lip of grey-white was protruding in over the edge of the boat—a great lappet of the mould was coming stealthily towards us; a live mass of *the very hull itself.* And suddenly Captain Gannington yelled out, in so many words, the grotesque and incredible thing I was thinking:

"'SHE'S ALIVE!'

"I never heard such a sound of *comprehension* and terror in a man's voice. The very horrified assurance of it, made actual to me the thing that, before, had only lurked in my subconscious mind. I knew he was right; I knew that the explanation, my reason and my training, both repelled and reached towards, was the true one... I wonder whether anyone can possibly understand our feelings in that moment... The unmitigable horror of it, and the *incredibleness*.

"As the light of the match burned up fully, I saw that the mass of living matter, coming towards us, was streaked and veined with purple, the veins standing out, enormously distended. The whole thing quivered continuously to each ponderous Thud! Thud! Thud! Thud! of that gargantuan organ that pulsed within the huge grey-white bulk. The flame of the match reached the Captain's fingers, and there came to me a little sickly whiff of burned flesh; but he seemed unconscious of any pain. Then the flame went out, in a brief sizzle; yet at the last moment, I had seen an extraordinary raw look, become visible upon the end of that monstrous, protruding lappet. It had become dewed with a hideous, purplish sweat. And with the darkness, there came a sudden charnel-like stench.

"I heard the match-box split in Captain Gannington's hands, as he wrenched it open. Then he swore, in a queer frightened voice; for he had come to the end of his matches. He turned clumsily in the darkness, and tumbled over the nearest thwart, in his eagerness to get to the stern of the boat; and I after him; for we knew that thing was coming towards us through the darkness; reaching over that piteous mingled heap of human bones, all jumbled together in the bows. We shouted madly to the men, and for answer saw the bows of the boat emerge dimly into view, round the starboard counter of the derelict.

"'Thank God!' I gasped out; but Captain Gannington yelled to them to show a light. Yet this they could not do; for the lamp had just been stepped on, in their desperate efforts to force the boat round to us.

"'Quick! Quick!' I shouted.

"'For God's sake be smart, men!' roared the Captain; and both of us faced the darkness under the port counter, out of which we knew (but could not see) the thing was coming towards us.

"'An oar! Smart now; pass me an oar!' shouted the Captain; and reached out his hands through the gloom towards the oncoming boat. I saw a figure stand up in the bows, and hold something out to us, across the intervening yards of scum. Captain Gannington swept his hands through the darkness, and encountered it.

"'I've got it. Let go there!' he said, in a quick, tense voice.

"In the same instant, the boat we were in, was pressed over suddenly to starboard by some tremendous weight. Then I heard the Captain shout: 'Duck y'r head, Doctor;' and directly afterwards he swung the heavy, fourteen-foot ash oar round his head, and struck into the darkness. There came a sudden squelch, and he struck again, with a savage grunt of fierce energy. At the second blow, the boat righted, with a slow movement, and directly afterwards the other boat bumped gently into ours.

"Captain Gannington dropped the oar, and springing across to the Second Mate, hove him up off the thwart, and pitched him with knee and arms clear in over the bows among the men; then he shouted to me to follow, which I did, and he came after me, bringing the oar with him. We carried the Second Mate aft, and the Captain shouted to the men to back the boat a little; then they got her bows clear of the boat we had just left, and so headed out through the scum for the open sea.

"'Where's Tom 'Arrison?' gasped one of the men, in the midst of his exertions. He happened to be Tom Harrison's particular chum; and Captain Gannington answered him, briefly enough:

"'Dead! Pull! Don't talk!'

"Now, difficult as it had been to force the boat through the scum to our rescue, the difficulty to get clear seemed tenfold. After some five minutes pulling, the boat seemed hardly to have moved a fathom, if so much; and a quite dreadful fear took me afresh; which one of the panting men put suddenly into words:

"'It's got us!' he gasped out; 'same as poor Tom!' It was the man who had inquired where Harrison was.

"'Shut y'r mouth an' *pull*!' roared the Captain. And so another few minutes passed. Abruptly, it seemed to me that the dull, ponderous Thud! Thud! Thud! Thud! came more plainly through the dark, and I stared intently over the stern. I sickened a little; for I could almost swear that the dark mass of the monster was actually *nearer*… that it was coming nearer to us through the darkness. Captain Gannington must have had the same thought; for after a brief look into the darkness, he made one jump to the stroke-oar, and began to double-bank it.

"'Get forrid under the thwarts, Doctor!' he said to me, rather breathlessly. 'Get in the bows, an' see if you can't free the stuff a bit round the bows.'

"I did as he told me, and a minute later I was in the bows of the boat, puddling the scum from side to side with the boat-hook, and trying to break up the viscid, clinging muck. A heavy, almost animal-like odour rose off it, and all the air seemed full of the deadening smell. I shall never find words to tell anyone the whole horror of it all—the threat that seemed to hang in the very air around us; and, but a little astern, that incredible thing, coming, as I firmly believe, nearer, and the scum holding us like half melted glue.

"The minutes passed in a deadly, eternal fashion, and I kept staring back astern into the darkness; but never ceasing to puddle that filthy scum, striking at it and switching it from side to side, until I sweated.

"Abruptly, Captain Gannington sang out:

"'We're gaining, lads. Pull!' And I felt the boat forge ahead perceptibly, as they gave way, with renewed hope and energy. There was soon no doubt of it; for presently that hideous Thud! Thud! Thud! Thud! had grown quite dim and vague somewhere astern, and I could no longer see the derelict; for the night had come down tremendously dark, and all the sky was thick overset with heavy clouds. As we drew nearer and nearer to the edge of the scum, the boat moved more and more freely, until suddenly we emerged with a clean, sweet, fresh sound, into the open sea.

"'Thank God!' I said aloud, and drew in the boat-hook, and made my way aft again to where Captain Gannington now sat once more at the tiller. I saw him looking anxiously up at the sky, and across to where the lights of our vessel burned, and again he would seem to listen intently; so that I found myself listening also.

"'What's that, Captain?' I said sharply; for it seemed to me that I heard a sound far astern, something between a queer whine and a low whistling. 'What's that?'

"'It's wind, Doctor,' he said, in a low voice. 'I wish to God we were aboard.'

"Then, to the men: 'Pull! Put y'r backs into it, or ye'll never put y'r teeth through good bread again!'

"The men obeyed nobly, and we reached the vessel safely, and had the boat safely stowed, before the storm came, which it did in a furious white smother out of the West. I could see it for some minutes beforehand, tearing the sea, in the gloom, into a wall of phosphorescent foam; and as it came nearer, that peculiar whining, piping sound, grew louder and louder, until it was like a vast steam whistle, rushing towards us across the sea.

"And when it did come, we got it very heavy indeed; so that the morning showed us nothing but a welter of white seas; and that grim derelict was many a score of miles away in the smother, lost as utterly as our hearts could wish to lose her.

"When I came to examine the Second Mate's feet, I found them in a very extraordinary condition. The soles of them had the appearance of having been partly digested. I know of no other word that so exactly describes their condition; and the agony the man suffered, must have been dreadful.

"Now," concluded the Doctor, "that is what I call a case in point. If we could know exactly what that old vessel had originally been loaded with, and the juxtaposition of the various articles of her cargo, plus the heat and time she had endured, plus one or two other only guessable quantities, we should have solved the chemistry of the Life-Force, gentlemen. Not necessarily the *origin*, mind you; but, at least, we should have taken a big step on the way. I've often regretted that gale, you know—in a way, that is, in a way! It was a most amazing discovery; but, at the time, I had nothing but thankfulness to be rid of it… A most amazing chance. I often think of the way the monster woke out of its torpor… And that scum… The dead pigs caught in it… I fancy that was, a grim kind of a net, gentlemen… It caught many things… It…"

The old Doctor sighed and nodded.

"If I could have had her bill of lading," he said, his eyes full of regret. "If— It might have told me something to help. But, anyway…" He began to fill his pipe again… "I suppose," he ended, looking round at us gravely, "I s'pose we humans are an ungrateful lot of beggars, at the best!… But… but what a chance! What a chance—eh?"

—1916—

THE THING IN THE WEEDS

I

THIS IS AN EXTRAORDINARY TALE. WE HAD COME UP FROM THE Cape, and owing to the Trades heading us more than usual, we had made some hundreds of miles more westing than I ever did before or since.

I remember the particular night of the happening perfectly. I suppose what occurred stamped it solid into my memory, with a thousand little details that, in the ordinary way, I should never have remembered an hour. And, of course, we talked it over so often among ourselves that this, no doubt, helped to fix it all past any forgetting.

I remember the Mate and I had been pacing the weather side of the poop and discussing various old shellbacks' superstitions. I was Third Mate, and it was between four and five bells in the first watch, i.e. between ten and half-past. Suddenly he stopped in his walk and lifted his head and sniffed several times.

"My word, Mister," he said, "there's a rum kind of stink somewhere about. Don't you smell it?"

I sniffed once or twice at the light airs that were coming in on the beam; then I walked to the rail and leaned over, smelling again at the slight breeze. And abruptly I got a whiff of it, faint and sickly, yet vaguely suggestive of something I had once smelt before.

"I can smell something, Mr. Lammart," I said. "I could almost give it name; and yet somehow I can't." I stared away into the dark to windward. "What do you seem to smell?" I asked him.

"I can't smell anything now," he replied, coming over and standing beside me. "It's gone again. No! By Jove! There it is again. My goodness! Phoo!"

The smell was all about us now, filling the night air. It had still that indefinable familiarity about it, and yet it was curiously strange; and, more than anything else, it was certainly simply beastly.

The stench grew stronger, and presently the Mate asked me to go forrard and see whether the look-out man noticed anything. When I reached the break of the fo'c'sle head I called up to the man, to know whether he smelled anything.

"Smell anythin', Sir?" he sang out. "Jumpin' larks! I sh'u'd think I do. I'm fair p'isoned with it."

I ran up the weather steps, and stood beside him. The smell was certainly very plain up there; and after savouring it for a few moments, I asked him whether he thought it might be a dead whale. But he was very emphatic that this could not be the case; for, as he said, he had been nearly fifteen years in whaling ships, and knew the smell of a dead whale, "like as you would the smell of bad whisky, Sir," as he put it. "'Tain't no whale yon; but the Lord He knows what 'tis. I'm thinking it's Davy Jones come up for a breather."

I stayed with him some minutes, staring out into the darkness, but could see nothing; for, even had there been something big close to us, I doubt whether I could have seen it, so black a night it was, without a visible star, and with a vague, dull haze breeding an indistinctness all about the ship.

I returned to the Mate, and reported that the look-out complained of the smell; but that neither he nor I had been able to see anything in the darkness, to account for it.

By this time the queer, disgusting odour seemed to be in all the air about us, and the Mate told me to go below and shut all the ports, so as to keep the beastly smell out of the cabins and the saloon.

When I returned he suggested that we should shut the companion doors; and after that we commenced to pace the poop again, discussing the extraordinary smell, and stopping from time to time to stare through our night-glasses out into the night about the ship.

"I'll tell you what it smells like, Mister," the Mate remarked, once, "and that's like a mighty old derelict I once went aboard in the North Atlantic. She was a proper old-timer, an' she gave us all the creeps. There was just this funny, dank, rummy sort of smell about her, sort of century-old bilge-water and dead men an' seaweed. I can't stop thinkin' we're nigh some lonesome old packet out there; an' a good thing we've not much way on us!"

"Do you notice how almighty quiet everything's gone the last half hour or so?" I said, a little later. "It must be the mist thickening down."

"It is the mist," said the Mate, going to the rail and staring out. "Good Lord, what's that?" he added.

Something had knocked his hat from his head, and it fell with a sharp rap at my feet. And suddenly, you know, I got a premonition of something horrid.

"Come away from the rail, Sir!" I said sharply, and gave one jump, and caught him by the shoulders and dragged him back. "Come away from the side!"

"What's up, Mister?" he growled at me, and twisted his shoulders free. "What's wrong with you? Was it you knocked off my cap?" He stooped and felt around for it, and as he did so I *heard* something unmistakably fiddling away at the rail which the Mate had just left.

"My God, Sir!" I said, "there's something there. Hark!"

The Mate stiffened up, listening; then he heard it. It was, for all the world, as if something was feeling and rubbing the rail, there in the darkness, not two fathoms away from us.

"Who's there?" said the Mate quickly. Then, as there was no answer: "What the devil's this hanky-panky? Who's playing the goat there?" He made a swift step through the darkness towards the rail, but I caught him by the elbow.

"Don't go, Mister!" I said, hardly above a whisper. "It's not one of the men. Let me get a light."

"Quick, then!" he said; and I turned and ran aft to the binnacle and snatched out the lighted lamp. As I did so I heard the Mate shout something out of the darkness, in a strange voice. There came a sharp, loud, rattling sound, and then a crash, and immediately the Mate roaring to me to hasten with the light. His voice changed, even whilst he shouted, and gave out something that was nearer a scream than anything else. There came two loud, dull blows, and an extraordinary gasping sound; and then, as I raced along the poop, there was a tremendous smashing of glass, and an immediate silence.

"Mr. Lammart!" I shouted. "Mr. Lammart!" And then I had reached the place where I had left the Mate, not forty seconds before; but he was not there.

"Mr. Lammart!" I shouted again, holding the light high over my head, and turning quickly to look behind me. As I did so my foot glided on some slippery substance, and I went headlong to the deck, with a tremendous thud, smashing the lamp and putting out the light.

I was on my feet again in an instant. I groped a moment for the lamp, and as I did so I heard the men singing out from the main-deck, and the noise of their feet as they came running aft. I found the broken lamp and realised it was useless; then I jumped for the companionway, and in half a minute I was back, with the big saloon lamp glaring bright in my hands.

I ran forrard again, shielding the upper edge of the glass chimney from the draught of my running, and the blaze of the big lamp seemed to make the weather side of the poop as bright as day, except for the mist, that gave something of a vagueness to things.

Where I had left the Mate there was blood upon the deck, but nowhere any signs of the man himself. I ran to the weather rail, and held the lamp to it. There was blood upon it; and the rail itself seemed to have been wrenched by some huge force. I put out my hand and found that I could shake it. Then I leaned outboard, and held the lamp at arm's length, staring down over the ship's side.

"Mr. Lammart!" I shouted into the night and the thick mist. "Mr. Lammart! Mr. Lammart!" But my voice seemed to go, lost and muffled and infinitely small, away into the billowy darkness.

I heard the men snuffling and breathing, waiting to leeward of the poop. I whirled round to them, holding the lamp high.

"We heard somethin', Sir," said Tarpley, the leading seaman in our watch. "Is anythin' wrong, Sir?"

"The Mate's gone," I said blankly. "We heard something, and I went for the binnacle lamp. Then he shouted, and I heard a sound of things smashing, and when I got back he'd gone clean." I turned and held the light out again over the unseen sea; and the men crowded round along the rail, and stared, bewildered.

"Blood, Sir," said Tarpley, pointing. "There's somethin' almighty queer out there." He waved a huge hand into the darkness. "That's what stinks—"

He never finished; for, suddenly, one of the men cried out something in a frightened voice: "Look out, Sir! Look out, Sir!"

I saw, in one brief flash of sight, something come in with an infernal flicker of movement; and then, before I could form any notion of what I had seen, the lamp was dashed to pieces across the poop deck. In that instant my perceptions cleared, and I saw the incredible folly of what we were doing; for there we were, standing up against the blank, unknowable night; and out there in the darkness there surely lurked some Thing of monstrousness; and we were at its mercy. I seemed to feel it hovering, hovering over us; so that I felt the sickening creep of gooseflesh all over me.

"Stand back from the rail!" I shouted. "Stand back from the rail!" There was a rush of feet as the men obeyed, in sudden apprehension of their danger; and I gave back with them. Even as I did so I felt some invisible thing brush my shoulder; and an indescribable smell was in my nostrils, from something that moved over me in the dark.

"Down into the saloon, everyone!" I shouted. "Down with you all! Don't wait a moment!"

There was a rush along the dark weather deck, and then the men went helter-skelter down the companion steps into the saloon, falling and cursing over one another in the darkness. I sang out to the man at the wheel to join them, and then I followed.

I came upon the men huddled at the foot of the stairs and filling up the passage, all crowding each other in the darkness. The Skipper's voice was filling the saloon, and he was demanding in violent adjectives the cause of so tremendous a noise. From the steward's berth there came also a voice, and the splutter of a match; and then the glow of a lamp in the saloon itself.

I pushed my way through the men and found the Captain in the saloon, in his sleeping gear, looking both drowsy and angry; though perhaps bewilderment topped every other feeling. He held his cabin lamp in his hand, and shone the light over the huddle of men.

I hurried to explain, and told him of the incredible disappearance of the Mate, and of my conviction that some extraordinary thing was lurking near the ship, out in the mist and the darkness. I mentioned the curious smell, and told how the Mate had suggested that we had drifted down near some old-time, sea-rotted derelict. And, you know, even as I put it into awkward words, my imagination began to awaken to horrible discomforts; a thousand dreadful impossibilities of the sea became suddenly possible.

The Captain (Jeldy was his name) did not stop to dress, but ran back into his cabin, and came out in a few moments with a couple of revolvers and a handful of cartridges. The Second Mate had come running out of his cabin at the noise, and had listed intently to what I had to say. Now he jumped back into his berth and brought out his own lamp and a large Smith and Wesson, which was evidently ready loaded.

Captain Jeldy pushed one of his revolvers into my hands, with some of the cartridges, and we began hastily to load the weapons. Then the Captain caught up his lamp and made for the stairway, ordering the men into the saloon out of his way.

"Shall you want them, Sir?" I asked.

"No," he said. "It's no use their running any unnecessary risks." He threw a word over his shoulder: "Stay quiet here, men; if I want you, I'll give you a shout; then come spry!"

"i, i, Sir," said the watch in a chorus; and then I was following the Captain up the stairs, with the Second Mate close behind.

We came up through the companionway on to the silence of the deserted poop. The mist had thickened up, even during the brief time that I had been below, and there was not a breath of wind. The mist was so dense that it seemed to press in upon us, and the two lamps made a kind of luminous halo in the mist, which seemed to absorb their light in a most peculiar way.

"Where was he?" the Captain asked me, almost in a whisper.

"On the port side, Sir," I said, "a little foreside the charthouse, and about a dozen feet in from the rail. I'll show you the exact place."

We went forrard along what had been the weather side, going quietly and watchfully; though, indeed, it was little enough that we could see, because of the mist. Once, as I led the way, I thought I heard a vague sound somewhere in the mist; but was all unsure because of the slow creak, creak of the spars and gear as the vessel rolled slightly upon an odd, oily swell. Apart from this slight sound, and the far-up rustle of the canvas, slatting gently against the masts, there was no sound at all throughout the ship. I assure you, the silence seemed to me to be almost menacing, in the tense, nervous state in which I was.

"Hereabouts is where I left him," I whispered to the Captain, a few seconds later. "Hold your lamp low, Sir. There's blood on the deck."

Captain Jeldy did so, and made a slight sound with his mouth at what he saw. Then, heedless of my hurried warning, he walked across to the rail, holding his lamp high up. I followed him; for I could not let him go alone; and the Second Mate came too, with his lamp. They leaned over the port rail, and held their lamps out into the mist and the unknown darkness beyond the ship's side. I remember how the lamps made just two yellow glares in the mist, ineffectual, yet serving somehow to make extraordinarily plain the vastitude of the night and the *possibilities of the dark.* Perhaps that is a queer way to put it, but it gives you the effect of that moment upon my feelings. And all the time, you know, there was upon me the brutal, frightening expectancy of something reaching in at us from out of that everlasting darkness and mist that held all the sea and the night, so that we were just three mist-shrouded, hidden figures, peering nervously.

The mist was now so thick that we could not even see the surface of the water overside; and fore and aft of us the rail vanished away into the fog and the dark. And then, as we stood here staring, I heard something moving down on the maindeck. I caught Captain Jeldy by the elbow.

"Come away from the rail, Sir," I said, hardly above a whisper; and he, with the swift premonition of danger, stepped back and allowed me to urge him well inboard. The Second Mate followed, and the three of us stood there in the mist, staring round about us and holding our revolvers handy, and the dull waves of the mist beating in slowly upon the lamps in vague wreathings and swirls of fog.

"What was it you heard, Mister?" asked the Captain after a few moments.

"Ssst!" I muttered. "There it is again. There's something moving down on the maindeck!"

Captain Jeldy heard it himself, now; and the three of us stood listening intensely. Yet it was hard to know what to make of the sounds. And then, suddenly, there was the rattle of a deck ringbolt, and then again, as if something or someone were fumbling and playing with it.

"Down there on the maindeck!" shouted the Captain, abruptly, his voice seeming hoarse close to my ear, yet immediately smothered by the fog. "Down there on the maindeck! Who's there?"

But there came never an answering sound. And the three of us stood there, looking quickly this way and that, and listening. Abruptly the Second Mate muttered something:

"The look-out, Sir! The look-out!"

Captain Jeldy took the hint, on the instant.

"On the look-out, there!" he shouted.

And then, far away and muffled-sounding, there came the answering cry of the look-out man, from the fo'c'sle head:

"Sir-r-r?" A little voice, long drawn out, through unknowable alleys of fog.

"Go below into the fo'c'sle and shut both doors, an' don't stir out till you're told!" sung out Captain Jeldy, his voice going lost into the mist. And then the man's answering "i, i, Sir!" coming to us faint and mournful. And directly afterwards the clang of a steel door, hollow-sounding and remote; and immediately the sound of another.

"That puts them safe for the present, anyway," said the Second Mate. And even as he spoke, there came again that indefinite noise, down upon the maindeck, of something moving with an incredible and unnatural stealthiness.

"On the maindeck there!" shouted Captain Jeldy, sternly. "If there is anyone there, answer, or I shall fire!"

The reply was both amazing and terrifying; for suddenly, a tremendous blow was stricken upon the deck, and then there came the dull, rolling sound of some enormous weight going hollowly across the maindeck. And then an abominable silence.

"My God!" said Captain Jeldy, in a low voice; "what was *that?*" And he raised his pistol; but I caught him by the wrist. "Don't shoot, Sir!" I whispered. "It'll be no good. That—that—whatever it is I—mean it's something enormous, Sir. I—I really wouldn't shoot—" I found it impossible to put my vague idea into words; but I felt there was a Force aboard, down on the maindeck, that it would be futile to attack with so ineffectual a thing as a puny revolver bullet.

And then, as I held Captain Jeldy's wrist, and he hesitated, irresolute, there came a sudden bleating of sheep, and the sound of lashings being burst and the cracking of wood; and the next instant a huge crash, followed by crash after crash, and the anguished m-aa-a-a-ing of sheep.

"My God!" said the Second Mate, "the sheep-pen's being beaten to pieces against the deck. Good God! What sort of thing could do that?"

The tremendous beating ceased, and there was a splashing overside; and after that a silence so profound that it seemed as if the whole atmosphere of the night was full of an unbearable, tense quietness. And then the damp slatting of a sail, far up in the night, that made me start—a lonesome sound to break suddenly through that infernal silence, upon my raw nerves.

"Get below, both of you. Smartly now!" muttered Captain Jeldy. "There's something run either aboard us or alongside; and we can't do anything till daylight."

We went below, and shut the doors of the companionway, and there we lay in the wide Atlantic, without wheel or look-out or officer in charge, and something incredible down on the dark maindeck.

II

For some hours we sat in the Captain's cabin, talking the matter over, whilst the watch slept, sprawled in a dozen attitudes on the floor of the saloon. Captain Jeldy and the Second Mate still wore their pyjamas, and our loaded revolvers lay handy on the cabin table. And so we watched anxiously through the hours for the dawn to come in.

As the light strengthened, we endeavoured to get some view of the sea, from the ports; but the mist was so thick about us that it was exactly like looking out into a grey nothingness, that became presently white, as the day came.

"Now," said Captain Jeldy, "we're going to look into this."

He went out through the saloon, to the companion stairs. At the top he opened the two doors, and the mist rolled in on us, white and impenetrable. For a little while we stood there, the three of us, absolutely silent and listening, with our revolvers handy; but never a sound came to us except the odd, vague slatting of a sail, or the slight creaking of the gear as the ship lifted on some slow, invisible swell.

Presently the Captain stepped cautiously out on to the deck; he was in his cabin slippers, and therefore made no sound. I was wearing gum-boots, and followed him silently, and the Second Mate after me, in his bare feet. Captain Jeldy went a few paces along the deck, and the mist hid him utterly. "Phoo!" I heard him mutter, "the stink's worse than ever!" His voice came odd and vague to me through the wreathing of the mist.

"The sun'll soon eat up all this fog," said the Second Mate, at my elbow, in a voice little above a whisper.

We stepped after the Captain, and found him a couple of fathoms away, standing shrouded in the mist, in an attitude of tense listening.

"Can't hear a thing!" he whispered. "We'll go forrard to the break, as quiet as you like. Don't make a sound."

We went forward, like three shadows, and suddenly Captain Jeldy kicked his shin against something, and pitched headlong over it, making a tremendous noise. He got up quickly, swearing grimly, and the three of us stood there in silence, waiting lest any infernal thing should come upon us out of all that white invisibility. Once, I felt sure I saw something coming towards me, and I raised my revolver; but saw in a moment that there was nothing. The tension of imminent, nervous expectancy eased from us, and Captain Jeldy stooped over the object on the deck.

"The port hencoop's been shifted out here!" he muttered. "It's all stove!"

"That must be what I heard last night, when the Mate went," I whispered. "There was a loud crash, just before he sang out to me to hurry with the lamp."

Captain Jeldy left the smashed hencoop, and the three of us tiptoed silently to the rail across the break of the poop. Here we leaned over and stared down into the blank whiteness of the mist that hid everything.

"Can't see a thing," whispered the Second Mate; yet, as he spoke, I could fancy that I heard a slight, indefinite, slurring noise somewhere below us; and I caught them each by an arm to draw them back.

"There's something down there," I muttered. "For goodness' sake, come back from the rail."

We gave back a step or two, and then stopped to listen; and even as we did so there came a slight air playing through the mist. "The breeze is coming," said the Second Mate. "Look, the mist is clearing already."

He was right. Already the look of white impenetrability had gone; and suddenly we could see the corner of the after-hatch coamings through the thinning fog. Within a minute we could see as far forrard as the mainmast, and then the stuff blew away from us, clear of the vessel, like a great wall of whiteness, that dissipated as it went.

"*Look!*" we all exclaimed together. The whole of the vessel was now clear to our sight; but it was not at the ship herself that we looked, for, after one quick glance along the empty maindeck, we had seen something beyond the ship's side. All around the vessel there lay a submerged spread of weed, for, maybe, a good quarter of a mile upon every side.

"Weed!" sang out Captain Jeldy in a voice of comprehension. "Weed! Look! By Jove, I guess I know now what got the Mate!"

He turned and ran to the port side and looked over. And suddenly he stiffened and beckoned silently over his shoulder to us to come and see. We had followed, and now we stood, one on each side of him, staring.

"Look!" whispered the Captain, pointing. "See the great brute! Do you see it? There! Look!"

At first I could see nothing except the submerged spread of the weed, into which we had evidently run after dark. Then, as I stared intently, my gaze began to separate from the surrounding weed a leathery-looking something that was somewhat darker in hue than the weed itself.

"My God!" said Captain Jeldy. "What a monster! What a monster! Just look at the brute! Look at the thing's eyes! That's what got the Mate. What a creature out of hell itself!"

I saw it plainly now; three of the massive feelers lay twined in and out among the clumpings of the weed; and then, abruptly, I realised that the two extraordinary round disks, motionless and inscrutable, were the creature's eyes, just below the surface of the water. It appeared to be staring, expressionless, up at the steel side of the vessel. I traced, vaguely, the shapeless monstrosity of what must be termed its head. "My God!" I muttered. "It's an enormous squid of some kind! What an awful brute! What—"

The sharp report of the Captain's revolver came at that moment. He had fired at the thing; and instantly there was a most awful commotion alongside. The weed was hove upward, literally in tons. An enormous quantity was thrown aboard us by the thrashing of the monster's great feelers. The sea seemed almost to boil, in one great cauldron of weed and water, all about the brute, and the steel side of the ship resounded with the dull, tremendous blows that the creature gave in its struggle. And into all that whirling boil of tentacles, weed, and seawater the three of us emptied our revolvers as fast as we could fire and reload. I remember the feeling of fierce satisfaction I had in thus aiding to avenge the death of the Mate.

Suddenly the Captain roared out to us to jump back; and we obeyed on the instant. As we did so the weed rose up into a great mound, over twenty feet in height, and more than a ton of it slopped aboard. The next instant three of the monstrous tentacles came in over the side, and the vessel gave a slow, sullen roll to port, as the weight came upon her; for the monster had literally hove itself almost free of the sea against our port side, in one vast, leathery shape, all wreathed with weed-fronds, and seeming drenched with blood and curious black liquid.

The feelers that had come inboard thrashed round, here and there, and suddenly one of them curled in the most hideous, snake-like fashion around the base of the mainmast. This seemed to attract it, for immediately it curled the two others about the mast, and forthwith wrenched upon it with such hideous violence that the whole towering length of spars, through all their height of a hundred and fifty feet, were shaken visibly, whilst the vessel herself vibrated with the stupendous efforts of the brute.

"It'll have the mast down, Sir!" said the Second Mate, with a gasp. "My God! It'll strain her side open! My—"

"One of those blasting cartridges!" I said to Jeldy, almost in a shout, as the inspiration took me. "Blow the brute to pieces!"

"Get one, quick!" said the Captain, jerking his thumb towards the companion. "You know where they are."

In thirty seconds I was back with the cartridge. Captain Jeldy took out his knife and cut the fuse dead short; then, with a steady hand, he lit the fuse, and calmly held it, until I backed away, shouting to him to throw it, for I knew it must explode in another couple of seconds.

Captain Jeldy threw the thing, like one throws a quoit, so that it fell into the sea just on the outward side of the vast bulk of the monster. So well had he timed it that it burst, with a stunning report, just as it struck the water. The effect upon the squid was amazing. It seemed literally to collapse. The enormous tentacles released themselves from the mast and curled across the deck helplessly, and were drawn inertly over the rail, as the enormous bulk sank away from the ship's side, out of sight, into the weed. The ship rolled slowly to starboard, and then steadied. "Thank God!" I muttered, and looked at the two others. They were pallid and sweating, and I must have been the same.

"Here's the breeze again," said the Second Mate, a minute later. "We're moving." He turned, without another word, and raced aft to the wheel, whilst the vessel slid over and through the weed-field.

Meanwhile, Captain Jeldy had sung out to the men, who had opened the port fo'c'sle door, to keep under cover until he told them to come out. Then he turned to have a look at the vessel itself.

"Look where that brute broke up the sheep-pen!" he cried, pointing. "And here's the skylight of the sail-locker smashed to bits!"

He walked across to it, and glanced down. And suddenly he let out a thunderous shout of astonishment:

"Here's the Mate, down here!" he shouted. "He's not overboard at all! He's *here*!"

He dropped himself down through the skylight on to the sails, and I after him; and, surely, there was the Mate, lying all huddled and insensible on a hummock of spare sails. In his right hand he held a drawn sheath-knife, which he was in the habit of carrying, A.B. fashion, whilst his left hand was all caked with dried blood, where he had been badly cut. Afterwards, we concluded he had cut himself in slashing at one of the tentacles of the squid, which had caught him round the left wrist, the tip of the tentacle being still curled, cruelly tight, about his arm, just as it had been when he hacked it through. For the rest, he was not seriously damaged, the creature having obviously flung him violently away, as he slashed at it, so that he had crashed through the framework of the skylight, and so had fallen in a stunned condition on to the pile of sails.

We got him on deck, and down into his bunk, where we left the steward to attend to him. When we returned to the poop the vessel had drawn clear of the weed-field, and the Captain and I stopped for a few moments to stare astern over the taffrail. The Second Mate turned also, as he stood at the wheel, and the three of us looked in a silence at that Death Patch lying now so quiet and sullen in the dawn.

As we stood and looked, something wavered up out of the heart of the weed—a long, tapering, sinuous thing, that curled and wavered against the dawn-light, and presently sank back again into the demure weed—a veritable spider of the deep, waiting in the great web that Dame Nature had spun for it, in the eddy of her tides and currents.

And we sailed away northwards, with strengthening Trades, and left that patch of monstrousness to the loneliness of the sea.

—1947—

THE HOG

I

WE HAD FINISHED DINNER AND CARNACKI HAD DRAWN HIS big chair up to the fire, and started his pipe.

Jessop, Arkright, Taylor and I had each of us taken up our favourite positions, and waited for Carnacki to begin.

"What I'm going to tell you about happened in the next room," he said, after drawing at his pipe for a while. "It has been a terrible experience. Doctor Witton first brought the case to my notice. We'd been chatting over a pipe at the Club one night about an article in the *Lancet*, and Witton mentioned having just such a similar case in a man called Bains. I was interested at once. It was one of those cases of a gap or flaw in a man's protection barrier, I call it. A failure to be what I might term efficiently insulated—spiritually—from the outer monstrosities.

"From what I knew of Witton, I knew he'd be no use. You all know Witton. A decent sort, hard-headed, practical, stand-no-kind-of-nonsense sort of man, all right at his own job when that job's a fractured leg or a broken collarbone; but he'd never have made anything of the Bains case."

For a space Carnacki puffed meditatively at his pipe, and we waited for him to go on with his tale.

"I told Witton to send Bains to me," he resumed, "and the following Saturday he came up. A little sensitive man. I liked him as soon as

I set eyes on him. After a bit, I got him to explain what was troubling him, and questioned him about what Doctor Witton had called his 'dreams.'

"'They're more than dreams,' he said, 'they're so real that they're actual experiences to me. They're simply horrible. And yet there's nothing very definite in them to tell you about. They generally come just as I am going off to sleep. I'm hardly over before suddenly I seem to have got down into some deep, vague place with some inexplicable and frightful horror all about me. I can never understand what it is, for I never see anything, only I always get a sudden knowledge like a warning that I have got down into some terrible place—a sort of hellplace I might call it, where I've no business ever to have wandered; and the warning is always insistent—even imperative—that I must get out, get out, or some enormous horror will come at me.'

"'Can't you pull yourself back?' I asked him. 'Can't you wake up?'

"'No,' he told me. 'That's just what I can't do, try as I will. I can't stop going along this labyrinth-of-hell as I call it to myself, towards some dreadful unknown Horror. The warning is repeated, ever so strongly—almost as if the live me of my waking moments was awake and aware. Something seems to warn me to wake up, that whatever I do I must wake, wake, and then my consciousness comes suddenly alive and I know that my body is there in the bed, but my essence or spirit is still down there in that hell, wherever it is, in a danger that is both unknown and inexpressible; but so overwhelming that my whole spirit seems sick with terror.

"'I keep saying to myself all the time that I must wake up,' he continued, 'but it is as if my spirit is still down there, and as if my consciousness knows that some tremendous invisible Power is fighting against me. I know that if I do not wake then, I shall never wake up again, but go down deeper and deeper into some stupendous horror of soul destruction. So then I fight. My body lies in the bed there, and pulls. And the power down there in that labyrinth exerts itself too so that a feeling of despair, greater than any I have ever known on this earth, comes on me. I know that if I give way and cease to fight, and do not wake, then I shall pass out—out to that monstrous Horror which seems to be silently calling my soul to destruction.

"'Then I make a final stupendous effort,' he continued, 'and my brain seems to fill my body like the ghost of my soul. I can even open my eyes and see with my brain, or consciousness, out of my own eyes. I can see the bedclothes, and I know just how I am lying in the bed; yet the real me is down in that hell in terrible danger. Can you get me?' he asked.

"'Perfectly,' I replied.

"'Well, you know,' he went on, 'I fight and fight. Down there in that great pit my very soul seems to shrink back from the call of some brooding horror that impels it silently a little further, always a little further round a visible corner, which if I once pass I know I shall never return again to this world. Desperately I fight; brain and consciousness fighting together to help it. The agony is so great that I could scream were it not that I am rigid and frozen in the bed with fear.

"'Then, just when my strength seems almost gone, soul and body win, and blend slowly. And I lie there worn out with this terrible extraordinary fight. I have still a sense of a dreadful horror all about me, as if out of that horrible place some brooding monstrosity had followed me up, and hangs still and silent and invisible over me, threatening me there in my bed. Do I make it clear to you?' he asked. 'It's like some monstrous Presence.'

"'Yes,' I said. 'I follow you.'

"The man's forehead was actually covered with sweat, so keenly did he live again through the horrors he had experienced.

"After a while he continued:

"'Now comes the most curious part of the dream or whatever it is,' he said. 'There's always a sound I hear as I lie there exhausted in the bed. It comes while the bedroom is still full of the sort of atmosphere of monstrosity that seems to come up with me when I get out of that place. I hear the sound coming up out of that enormous depth, and it is always the noise of pigs—pigs grunting, you know. It's just simply dreadful. The dream is always the same. Sometimes I've had it every single night for a week, until I fight not to go to sleep; but, of course, I have to sleep sometimes. I think that's how a person might go mad, don't you?' he finished.

"I nodded, and looked at his sensitive face. Poor beggar! He had been through it, and no mistake.

"'Tell me some more,' I said. 'The grunting—what does it sound like exactly?'

"'It's just like pigs grunting,' he told me again. 'Only much more awful. There are grunts, and squeals and pig howls, like you hear when their food is being brought to them at a pig farm. You know those large pig farms where they keep hundreds of pigs. All the grunts, squeals and howls blend into one brutal chaos of sound—only it isn't a chaos. It all blends in a queer horrible way. I've heard it. A sort of swinish, clamouring melody that grunts and roars and shrieks in chunks of grunting sounds, all tied together with squealings and shot through with pig howls. I've sometimes thought there was a definite beat in it; for every now and again there comes a gargantuan GRUNT, breaking through the million pig-voiced roaring—a stupendous GRUNT that comes in with a beat. Can you understand me? It seems to shake everything... It's like a spiritual earthquake. The howling, squealing, grunting, rolling clamour of swinish noise coming up out of that place, and then the monstrous GRUNT rising up through it all, an ever-recurring beat out of the depth—the voice of the swine-mother of monstrosity beating up from below through that chorus of mad swine-hunger... It's no use! I can't explain it. No one ever could. It's just terrible! And I'm afraid you're saying to yourself that I'm in a bad way; that I want a change or a tonic; that I must buck up or I'll land myself in a madhouse. If only you could understand! Doctor Witton seemed to half understand, I thought; but I know he's only sent me to you as a sort of last hope. He thinks I'm booked for the asylum. I could tell it.'

"'Nonsense!' I said. 'Don't talk such rubbish. You're as sane as I am. Your ability to think clearly what you want to tell me, and then to transmit it to me so well that you compel my mental retina to see something of what you have seen, stands sponsor for your mental balance.

"'I am going to investigate your case, and if it is what I suspect, one of those rare instances of a "flaw" or "gap" in your protective barrier (what I might call your spiritual insulation from the Outer Monstrosities) I've no doubt we can end the trouble. But we've got to go properly into the matter first, and there will certainly be danger in doing so.'

"'I'll risk it,' replied Bains. 'I can't go on like this any longer.'

"'Very well,' I told him. 'Go out now, and come back at five o'clock. I shall be ready for you then. And don't worry about your sanity. You're all right, and we'll soon make things safe for you again. Just keep cheerful and don't brood about it.'"

II

"I put in the whole afternoon preparing my experimenting room, across the landing there, for his case. When he returned at five o'clock I was ready for him and took him straight into the room.

"It gets dark now about six-thirty, as you know, and I had just enough time before it grew dusk to finish my arrangements. I prefer always to be ready before the dark comes.

"Bains touched my elbow as we walked into the room.

"'There's something I ought to have told you,' he said, looking rather sheepish. 'I've somehow felt a bit ashamed of it.'

"'Out with it,' I replied.

"He hesitated a moment, then it came out with a jerk.

"'I told you about the grunting of the pigs,' he said. 'Well, I grunt too. I know it's horrible. When I lie there in bed and hear those sounds after I've come up, I just grunt back as if in reply. I can't stop myself. I just do it. Something makes me. I never told Doctor Witton that. I couldn't. I'm sure now you think me mad,' he concluded.

"He looked into my face, anxious and queerly ashamed.

"'It's only the natural sequence of the abnormal events, and I'm glad you told me,' I said, slapping him on the back. 'It follows logically on what you had already told me. I have had two cases that in some way resembled yours.'

"'What happened?' he asked me. 'Did they get better?'

"'One of them is alive and well today, Mr. Bains,' I replied. 'The other man lost his nerve, and fortunately for all concerned, he is dead.'

"I shut the door and locked it as I spoke, and Bains stared round, rather alarmed, I fancy, at my apparatus.

"'What are you going to do?' he asked. 'Will it be a dangerous experiment?'

"'Dangerous enough,' I answered, 'if you fail to follow my instructions absolutely in everything. We both run the risk of never leaving this room alive. Have I your word that I can depend on you to obey me whatever happens?'

"He stared round the room and then back at me.

"'Yes,' he replied. And, you know, I felt he would prove the right kind of stuff when the moment came.

"I began now to get things finally in train for the night's work. I told Bains to take off his coat and his boots. Then I dressed him entirely from head to foot in a single thick rubber combination-overall, with rubber gloves, and a helmet with ear-flaps of the same material attached.

"I dressed myself in a similar suit. Then I began on the next stage of the night's preparations.

"First I must tell you that the room measures thirty-nine feet by thirty-seven, and has a plain board floor over which is fitted a heavy, half-inch rubber covering.

"I had cleared the floor entirely, all but the exact centre where I had placed a glass-legged, upholstered table, a pile of vacuum tubes and batteries, and three pieces of special apparatus which my experiment required.

"'Now Bains,' I called, 'come and stand over here by this table. Don't move about. I've got to erect a protective "barrier" round us, and on no account must either of us cross over it by even so much as a hand or foot, once it is built.'

"We went over to the middle of the room, and he stood by the glass-legged table while I began to fit the vacuum tubing together round us.

"I intended to use the new spectrum 'defence' which I have been perfecting lately. This, I must tell you, consists of seven glass vacuum circles with the red on the outside, and the colour circles lying inside it, in the order of orange, yellow, green, blue, indigo and violet.

"The room was still fairly light, but a slight quantity of dusk seemed to be already in the atmosphere, and I worked quickly.

"Suddenly, as I fitted the glass tubes together I was aware of some vague sense of nerve-strain, and glancing round at Bains, who was standing there by the table, I noticed him staring fixedly before him. He looked absolutely drowned in uncomfortable memories.

"'For goodness' sake stop thinking of those horrors,' I called out to him. 'I shall want you to think hard enough about them later; but in this specially constructed room it is better not to dwell on things of that kind till the barriers are up. Keep your mind on anything normal or superficial—the theatre will do—think about that last piece you saw at the Gaiety. I'll talk to you in a moment.'

"Twenty minutes later the 'barrier' was completed all round us, and I connected up the batteries. The room by this time was greying with the coming dusk, and the seven differently coloured circles shone out with extraordinary effect, sending out a cold glare.

"'By Jove!' cried Bains, 'that's very wonderful—very wonderful!'

"My other apparatus which I now began to arrange consisted of a specially made camera, a modified form of phonograph with earpieces instead of a horn, and a glass disk composed of many fathoms of glass vacuum tubes arranged in a special way. It had two wires leading to an electrode constructed to fit round the head.

"By the time I had looked over and fixed up these three things, night had practically come, and the darkened room shone most strangely in the curious upward glare of the seven vacuum tubes.

"'Now, Bains,' I said, 'I want you to lie on this table. Now put your hands down by your sides and lie quiet and think. You've just got two things to do,' I told him. 'One is to lie there and concentrate your thoughts on the details of the dream you are always having, and the other is not to move off this table whatever you see or hear, or whatever happens, unless I tell you. You understand, don't you?'

"'Yes,' he answered, 'I think you may rely on me not to make a fool of myself. I feel curiously safe with you somehow.'

"'I'm glad of that,' I replied. 'But I don't want you to minimise the possible danger too much. There may be horrible danger. Now, just let me fix this band on your head,' I added, as I adjusted the electrode. I gave him a few more instructions, telling him to concentrate his thoughts particularly upon the noises he heard just as he was waking, and I warned him again not to let himself fall asleep. 'Don't talk,' I said, 'and don't take any notice of me. If you find I disturb your concentration keep your eyes closed.'

"He lay back and I walked over to the glass disk arranging the camera in front of it on its stand in such a way that the lens was opposite the centre of the disk.

"I had scarcely done this when a ripple of greenish light ran across the vacuum tubes of the disk. This vanished, and for maybe a minute there was complete darkness. Then the green light rippled once more across it—rippled and swung round, and began to dance in varying shades from a deep heavy green to a rank ugly shade; back and forward, back and forward.

"Every half second or so there shot across the varying greens a flicker of yellow, an ugly, heavy repulsive yellow, and then abruptly there came sweeping across the disk a great beat of muddy red. This died as quickly as it came, and gave place to the changing greens shot through by the unpleasant and ugly yellow hues. About every seventh second the disk was submerged, and the other colours momentarily blotted out by the great beat of heavy, muddy red which swept over everything.

"'He's concentrating on those sounds,' I said to myself, and I felt queerly excited as I hurried on with my operations. I threw a word over my shoulder to Bains.

"'Don't get scared, whatever happens,' I said. 'You're all right!'

"I proceeded now to operate my camera. It had a long roll of specially prepared paper ribbon in place of a film or plates. By turning the handle the roll passed through the machine, exposing the ribbon.

"It took about five minutes to finish the roll, and during all that time the green lights predominated; but the dull heavy beat of muddy red never ceased to flow across the vacuum tubes of the disk at every seventh second. It was like a recurrent beat in some unheard and somehow displeasing melody.

"Lifting the exposed spool of paper ribbon out of the camera I laid it horizontally in the two 'rests' that I had arranged for it on my modified gramophone. Where the paper had been acted upon by the varying coloured lights which had appeared on the disk, the prepared surface had risen in curious, irregular little waves.

"I unrolled about a foot of the ribbon and attached the loose end to an empty spool-roller (on the opposite side of the machine) which I had geared to the driving clockwork mechanism of the gramophone. Then I took the diaphragm and lowered it gently into place above the ribbon. Instead of the usual needle, the diaphragm was fitted with a beautifully made metal-filament brush, about an inch broad, which just covered the whole breadth of the ribbon. This fine and fragile brush rested lightly on the prepared surface of the paper, and when I started the machine the ribbon began to pass under the brush; and as it passed, the delicate metal-filament 'bristles' followed every minute inequality of those tiny, irregular wave-like excrescences on the surface.

"I put the ear-pieces to my ears, and instantly I knew that I had succeeded in actually recording what Bains had heard in his sleep. In fact, I was even then hearing 'mentally' by means of his effort of memory. I was listening to what appeared to be the faint, far-off squealing and grunting of countless swine. It was extraordinary, and at the same time exquisitely horrible and vile. It frightened me, with a sense of my having come suddenly and unexpectedly too near to something foul and most abominably dangerous.

"So strong and imperative was this feeling that I twitched the ear-pieces out of my ears, and sat awhile staring round the room trying to steady my sensations back to normality.

"The room looked strange and vague in the dull glow of light from the circles, and I had a feeling that a taint of monstrosity was all about me in the air. I remembered what Bains had told me of the feeling he'd always had after coming up out of 'that place'—as if some horrible atmosphere had followed him up and filled his bedroom. I understood him perfectly now—so much so that I had mentally used almost his exact phrase in explaining to myself what I felt.

"Turning round to speak to him I saw there was something curious about the centre of the 'defence.'

"Now, before I tell you fellows any more I must explain that there are certain, what I call 'focussing,' qualities about this new 'defence' I've been trying.

"The Sigsand manuscript puts it something like this: 'Avoid diversities of colour; nor stand ye within the barrier of the colour lights; for in colour hath Satan a delight. Nor can he abide in the Deep if ye adventure against him armed with red purple. So be warned. Neither forget that in blue, which is God's colour in the Heavens, ye have safety.'

"You see, from that statement in the Sigsand manuscript I got my first notion for this new 'defence' of mine. I have aimed to make it a 'defence' and yet have 'focussing' or 'drawing' qualities such as the Sigsand hints at. I have experimented enormously, and I've proved that reds and purples—the two extreme colours of the spectrum—are fairly dangerous; so much so that I suspect they actually 'draw' or 'focus' the outside forces. Any action or 'meddling' on the part of the experimentalist is tremendously enhanced in its effect if the action is taken within barriers composed of these colours, in certain proportions and tints.

"In the same way blue is distinctly a 'general defence.' Yellow appears to be neutral, and green a wonderful protection within limits. Orange, as far as I can tell, is slightly attractive and indigo is dangerous by itself in a limited way, but in certain combinations with the other colours it becomes a very powerful 'defence.' I've not yet discovered a tenth of the possibilities of these circles of mine. It's a kind of colour organ upon which I seem to play a tune of colour combinations that can be either safe or infernal in its effects. You know I have a keyboard with a separate switch to each of the colour circles.

"Well, you fellows will understand now what I felt when I saw the curious appearance of the floor in the middle of the 'defence.' It looked exactly as if a circular shadow lay, not just on the floor, but a few inches above it. The shadow seemed to deepen and blacken at the centre even while I watched it. It appeared to be spreading from the centre outwardly, and all the time it grew darker.

"I was watchful, and not a little puzzled; for the combination of lights that I had switched on approximated a moderately safe 'general defence.' Understand, I had no intention of making a focus until I had learnt more. In fact, I meant that first investigation not to go beyond a tentative inquiry into the kind of thing I had got to deal with.

"I knelt down quickly and felt the floor with the palm of my hand, but it was quite normal to the feel, and that reassured me that there was no Saaaiti mischief abroad; for that is a form of danger which can involve, and make use of, the very material of the 'defence' itself. It can materialise out of everything except fire.

"As I knelt there I realised all at once that the legs of the table on which Bains lay were partly hidden in the ever-blackening shadow, and my hands seemed to grow vague as I felt at the floor.

"I got up and stood away a couple of feet so as to see the phenomenon from a little distance. It struck me then that there was something different about the table itself. It seemed unaccountably lower.

"'It's the shadow hiding the legs,' I thought to myself. 'This promises to be interesting; but I'd better not let things go too far.'

"I called out to Bains to stop thinking so hard. 'Stop concentrating for a bit,' I said; but he never answered, and it occurred to me suddenly that the table appeared to be still lower.

"'Bains,' I shouted, 'stop thinking a moment.' Then in a flash I realised it. 'Wake up, man! Wake up!' I cried.

"He had fallen over asleep—the very last thing he should have done; for it increased the danger twofold. No wonder I had been getting such good results! The poor beggar was worn out with his sleepless nights. He neither moved nor spoke as I strode across to him.

"'Wake up!' I shouted again, shaking him by the shoulder.

"My voice echoed uncomfortably round the big empty room; and Bains lay like a dead man.

"As I shook him again I noticed that I appeared to be standing up to my knees in the circular shadow. It looked like the mouth of a pit. My legs, from the knees downwards, were vague. The floor under my feet felt solid and firm when I stamped on it; but all the same I had a feeling that things were going a bit too far, so striding across to the switchboard I switched on the 'full defence.'

"Stepping back quickly to the table I had a horrible and sickening shock. The table had sunk quite unmistakably. Its top was within a couple of feet of the floor, and the legs had that fore-shortened appearance that one sees when a stick is thrust into water. They looked vague and shadowy in the peculiar circle of dark shadows which had such an extraordinary resemblance to the black mouth of a pit. I could see only the top of the table plainly with Bains lying motionless on it; and the whole thing was going down, as I stared, into that black circle."

III

"There was not a moment to lose, and like a flash I caught Bains round his neck and body and lifted him clean up into my arms off the table. And as I lifted him he grunted like a great swine in my ear.

"The sound sent a thrill of horrible funk through me. It was just as though I held a hog in my arms instead of a human. I nearly dropped him. Then I held his face to the light and stared down at him. His eyes were half opened, and he was looking at me apparently as if he saw me perfectly.

"Then he grunted again. I could feel his small body quiver with the sound.

"I called out to him. 'Bains,' I said, 'can you hear me?'

"His eyes still gazed at me; and then, as we looked at each other, he grunted like a swine again.

"I let go one hand, and hit him across the cheek, a stinging slap.

"'Wake up, Bains!' I shouted. 'Wake up!' But I might have hit a corpse. He just stared up at me. And suddenly I bent lower and looked into his eyes more closely. I never saw such a fixed, intelligent, mad horror as I saw there. It knocked out all my sudden disgust. Can you understand?

"I glanced round quickly at the table. It stood there at its normal height; and, indeed, it was in every way normal. The curious shadow that had somehow suggested to me the black mouth of the pit had vanished. I felt relieved; for it seemed to me that I had entirely broken up any possibility of a partial 'focus' by means of the full 'defence' which I had switched on.

"I laid Bains on the floor, and stood up to look round and consider what was best to do. I dared not step outside of the barriers, until any 'dangerous tensions' there might be in the room had been dissipated. Nor was it wise, even inside the full 'defence,' to have him sleeping the kind of sleep he was in; not without certain preparations having been made first, which I had not made.

"I can tell you, I felt beastly anxious. I glanced down at Bains, and had a sudden fresh shock; for the peculiar circular shadow was forming all round him again, where he lay on the floor. His hands and face showed curiously vague, and distorted, as they might have looked through a few inches of faintly stained water. But his eyes were somehow clear to see. They were staring up, mute and terrible, at me, through that horrible darkening shadow.

"I stopped, and with one quick lift, tore him up off the floor into my arms, and for the third time he grunted like a swine, there in my arms. It was damnable.

"I stood up, in the barrier, holding Bains, and looked about the room again; then back at the floor. The shadow was still thick round about my feet, and I stepped quickly across to the other side of the table. I stared at the shadow, and saw that it had vanished; then I glanced down again at my feet, and had another shock; for the shadow was showing faintly again, all round where I stood.

"I moved a pace, and watched the shadow become invisible; and then, once more, like a slow stain, it began to grow about my feet.

"I moved again, a pace, and stared round the room, meditating a break for the door. And then, in that instant, I saw that this would be certainly impossible; for there was something indefinite in the atmosphere of the room—something that moved, circling slowly about the barrier.

"I glanced down at my feet, and saw that the shadow had grown thick about them. I stepped a pace to the right, and as it disappeared, I stared again round the big room and somehow it seemed tremendously big and unfamiliar. I wonder whether you can understand.

"As I stared I saw again the indefinite something that floated in the air of the room. I watched it steadily for maybe a minute. It went twice completely round the barrier in that time. And, suddenly, I saw it more distinctly. It looked like a small puff of black smoke.

"And then I had something else to think about; for all at once I was aware of an extraordinary feeling of vertigo, and in the same moment, a sense of sinking—I was sinking bodily. I literally sickened as I glanced down, for I saw in that moment that I had gone down, almost up to my thighs, into what appeared to be actually the shadowy, but quite unmistakable, mouth of a pit. Do you understand? I was sinking down into this thing, with Bains in my arms.

"A feeling of furious anger came over me, and I swung my right boot forward with a fierce kick. I kicked nothing tangible, for I went clean through the side of the shadowy thing, and fetched up against the table, with a crash. I had come through something that made all my skin creep and tingle—an invisible, vague something which resembled an electric tension. I felt that if it had been stronger, I might not have been able to charge through as I had. I wonder if I make it clear to you?

"I whirled round, but the beastly thing had gone; yet even as I stood there by the table, the slow greying of a circular shadow began to form again about my feet.

"I stepped to the other side of the table, and leaned against it for a moment: for I was shaking from head to foot with a feeling of extraordinary horror upon me, that was in some way different from any kind of horror I have ever felt. It was as if I had in that one moment been near something no human has any right to be near, for his soul's sake. And abruptly, I wondered whether I had not felt just one brief touch of the horror that the rigid Bains was even then enduring as I held him in my arms.

"Outside of the barrier there were now several of the curious little clouds. Each one looked exactly like a little puff of black smoke. They increased as I watched them, which I did for several minutes; but all the time as I watched, I kept moving from one part to another of the 'defence,' so as to prevent the shadow forming round my feet again.

"Presently, I found that my constant changing of position had resolved into a slow monotonous walk round and round, inside the 'defence'; and all the time I had to carry the unnaturally rigid body of poor Bains.

"It began to tire me; for though he was small, his rigidity made him dreadfully awkward and tiring to hold, as you can understand; yet I could not think what else to do; for I had stopped shaking him, or trying to wake him, for the simple reason that he was as wide awake as I was mentally; though but physically inanimate, through one of those partial spiritual disassociations which he had tried to explain to me.

"Now I had previously switched out the red, orange, yellow and green circles, and had on the full defence of the blue end of the spectrum—I knew that one of the repelling vibrations of each of the three colours: blue, indigo and violet were beating out protectingly into space; yet they were proving insufficient, and I was in the position of having either to take some desperate action to stimulate Bains to an even greater effort of will than I judged him to be making, or else to risk experimenting with fresh combinations of the defensive colours.

"You see, as things were at that moment, the danger was increasing steadily; for plainly, from the appearance of the air of the room outside the barrier, there were some mighty dangerous tensions generating. While inside the danger was also increasing; the steady recurrence of the shadow proving that the 'defence' was insufficient.

"In short, I feared that Bains in his peculiar condition was literally a 'doorway' into the 'defence'; and unless I could wake him or find out the correct combinations of circles necessary to set up stronger repelling vibrations against that particular danger, there were very ugly possibilities ahead. I felt I had been incredibly rash not to have foreseen the possibility of Bains falling asleep under the hypnotic effect of deliberately paralleling the associations of sleep.

"Unless I could increase the repulsion of the barriers or wake him there was every likelihood of having to chose between a rush for the door—which the condition of the atmosphere outside the barrier showed to be practically impossible—or of throwing him outside the barrier, which, of course, was equally not possible.

"All this time I was walking round and round inside the barrier, when suddenly I saw a new development of the danger which threatened us. Right in the centre of the 'defence' the shadow had formed into an intensely black circle, about a foot wide.

"This increased as I looked at it. It was horrible to see it grow. It crept out in an ever-widening circle till it was quite a yard across.

"Quickly I put Bains on the floor. A tremendous attempt was evidently going to be made by some outside force to enter the 'defence,' and it was up to me to make a final effort to help Bains to 'wake up.' I took out my lancet, and pushed up his left coat sleeve.

"What I was going to do was a terrible risk, I knew, for there is no doubt that in some extraordinary fashion blood attracts.

"The Sigsand mentions it particularly in one passage which runs something like this: 'In blood there is the Voice which calleth through all space. Ye Monsters in ye Deep hear, and hearing, they lust. Likewise hath it a greater power to reclaim backward ye soul that doth wander foolish adrift from ye body in which it doth have natural abiding. But woe unto him that doth spill ye blood in ye deadly hour; for there will be surely Monsters that shall hear ye Blood Cry.'

"That risk I had to run. I knew that the blood would call to the outer forces; but equally I knew that it should call even more loudly to that portion of Bains' 'Essence' that was adrift from him, down in those depths.

"Before lancing him, I glanced at the shadow. It had spread out until the nearest edge was not more than two feet away from Bains' right shoulder; and the edge was creeping nearer, like the blackening edge of burning paper, even while I stared. The whole thing had a less shadowy, less ghostly appearance than at any time before. And it looked simply and literally like the black mouth of a pit.

"'Now, Bains,' I said, 'pull yourself together, man. Wake up!' And at the same time as I spoke to him, I used my lancet quickly but superficially.

"I watched the little red spot of blood well up, then trickle round his wrist and fall to the floor of the 'defence.' And in the moment that it fell the thing that I had feared happened. There was a sound like a low peal of thunder in the room, and curious deadly-looking flashes of light rippled here and there along the floor outside the barrier.

"Once more I called to him, trying to speak firmly and steadily as I saw that the horrible shadowy circle had spread across every inch of the floor space of the centre of the 'defence,' making it appear as if both Bains and I were suspended above an unutterable black void—the black void that stared up at me out of the throat of that shadowy pit. And yet, all the time I could feel the floor solid under my knees as I knelt beside Bains holding his wrist.

"'Bains!' I called once more, trying not to shout madly at him. 'Bains, wake up! Wake up, man! Wake up!'

"But he never moved, only stared up at me with eyes of quiet horror that seemed to be looking at me out of some dreadful eternity."

IV

"By this time the shadow had blackened all around us, and I felt that strangely terrible vertigo coming over me again. Jumping to my feet I caught up Bains in my arms and stepped over the first of the protective circles—the violet, and stood between it and the indigo circle, holding Bains as close to me as possible so as to prevent any portion of his helpless body from protruding outside the indigo and blue circles.

"From the black shadowy mouth which now filled the whole of the centre of the 'defence' there came a faint sound—not near but seeming to come up at me out of unknown abysses. Very, very faint and lost it sounded, but I recognised it as unmistakably the infinitely remote murmur of countless swine.

"And that same moment Bains, as if answering the sound, grunted like a swine in my arms.

"There I stood between the glass vacuum tubes of the circles, gazing dizzily into that black shadowy pit-mouth, which seemed to drop sheer into hell from below my left elbow.

"Things had gone so utterly beyond all that I had thought of, and it had all somehow come about so gradually and yet so suddenly, that I was really a bit below my natural self. I felt mentally paralysed, and could think of nothing except that not twenty feet away was the door and the outer natural world; and here was I face to face with some unthought-of danger, and all adrift, what to do to avoid it.

"You fellows will understand this better when I tell you that the bluish glare from the three circles showed me that there were now hundreds and hundreds of those small smoke-like puffs of black cloud circling round and round outside the barrier in an unvarying, unending procession.

"And all the time I was holding the rigid body of Bains in my arms, trying not to give way to the loathing that got me each time he grunted. Every twenty or thirty seconds he grunted, as if in answer to the sounds which were almost too faint for my normal hearing. I can tell you, it was like holding something worse than a corpse in my arms, standing there balanced between physical death on the one side and soul destruction on the other.

"Abruptly, from out of the deep that lay so close that my elbow and shoulder overhung it, there came again a faint, marvellously faint murmur of swine, so utterly far away that the sound was as remote as a lost echo.

"Bains answered it with a pig-like squeal that set every fibre in me protesting in sheer human revolt, and I sweated coldly from head to foot. Pulling myself together I tried to pierce down into the mouth of the great shadow when, for the second time, a low peal of thunder sounded in the room, and every joint in my body seemed to jolt and burn.

"In turning to look down the pit I had allowed one of Bains' heels to protrude for a moment slightly beyond the blue circle, and a fraction of the 'tension' outside the barrier had evidently discharged through Bains and me. Had I been standing directly inside the 'defence' instead of being 'insulated' from it by the violet circle, then no doubt things might have been much more serious. As it was, I had, psychically, that dreadful soiled feeling which the healthy human always experiences when he comes too closely in contact with certain Outer Monstrosities. Do you fellows remember how I had just the same feeling when the Hand came too near me in the 'Gateway' case?

"The physical effects were sufficiently interesting to mention; for Bains' left boot had been ripped open, and the leg of his trousers was charred to the knee, while all around the leg were numbers of bluish marks in the form of irregular spirals.

"I stood there holding Bains, and shaking from head to foot. My head ached and each joint had a queer numbish feeling; but my physical pains were nothing compared with my mental distress. I felt that we were done! I had no room to turn or move for the space between the violet circle which was the innermost, and the blue circle which was the outermost of those in use was thirty-one inches, including the one inch of the indigo circle. So you see I was forced to stand there like an image, fearing each moment lest I should get another shock, and quite unable to think what to do.

"I daresay five minutes passed in this fashion. Bains had not grunted once since the 'tension' caught him, and for this I was just simply thankful; though at first I must confess I had feared for a moment that he was dead.

"No further sounds had come up out of the black mouth to my left, and I grew steady enough again to begin to look about me, and think a bit. I leant again so as to look directly down into the shadowy pit. The edge of the circular mouth was now quite defined, and had a curious solid look, as if it were formed out of some substance like black glass.

"Below the edge, I could trace the appearance of solidity for a considerable distance, though in a vague sort of way. The centre of this extraordinary phenomenon was simple and unmitigated blackness—an utter velvety blackness that seemed to soak the very light out of the room down into it. I could see nothing else, and if anything else came out of it except a complete silence, it was the atmosphere of frightening suggestion that was affecting me more and more every minute.

"I turned away slowly and carefully, so as not to run any risks of allowing either Bains or myself to expose any part of us over the blue circle. Then I saw that things outside of the blue circle had developed considerably; for the odd, black puffs of smoke-like cloud had increased enormously and blent into a great, gloomy, circular wall of tufted cloud, going round and round and round eternally, and hiding the rest of the room entirely from me.

"Perhaps a minute passed, while I stared at this thing; and then, you know, the room was shaken slightly. This shaking lasted for three or four seconds, and then passed; but it came again in about half a minute, and was repeated from time to time. There was a queer oscillating quality in the shaking, that made me think suddenly of that *Jarvee* Haunting case. You remember it?

"There came again the shaking, and a ripple of deadly light seemed to play round the outside of the barrier; and then, abruptly, the room was full of a strange roaring—a brutish enormous yelling, grunting storm of swine-sounds.

"They fell away into a complete silence, and the rigid Bains grunted twice in my arms, as if answering. Then the storm of swine noise came again, beating up in a gigantic riot of brute sound that roared through the room, piping, squealing, grunting, and howling. And as it sank with a steady declination, there came a single gargantuan grunt out of some dreadful throat of monstrousness, and in one beat, the crashing chorus of unknown millions of swine came thundering and raging through the room again.

"There was more in that sound than mere chaos—there was a mighty devilish rhythm in it. Suddenly, it swept down again into a multitudinous swinish whispering and minor gruntings of unthinkable millions; and then with a rolling, deafening bellow of sound came the single vast grunt. And, as if lifted upon it, the swine roar of the millions of the beasts beat up through the room again; and at every seventh second, as I knew well enough without the need of the watch on my wrist, came the single storm beat of the great grunt out of the throat of unknowable monstrosity—and in my arms, Bains, the human, grunted in time to the swine melody—a rigid grunting monster there in my two arms.

"I tell you from head to foot I shook and sweated. I believe I prayed; but if I did I don't know what I prayed. I have never before felt or endured just what I felt, standing there in that thirty-one-inch space, with that grunting thing in my arms, and the hell melody beating up out of the great Deeps: and to my right, 'tensions' that would have torn me into a bundle of blazing tattered flesh, if I had jumped out over the barriers.

"And then, with an effect like a clap of unexpected thunder, the vast storm of sound ceased; and the room was full of silence and an unimaginable horror.

"This silence continued. I want to say something which may sound a bit silly; but the silence seemed to *trickle* round the room. I don't know why I felt it like that; but my words give you just what I seemed to feel, as I stood there holding the softly grunting body of Bains.

"The circular, gloomy wall of dense black cloud enclosed the barrier as completely as ever, and moved round and round and round, with a slow, 'eternal' movement. And at the back of that black wall of circling cloud, a dead silence went trickling round the room, out of my sight. Do you understand at all?...

"It seemed to me to show very clearly the state of almost insane mental and psychic tension I was enduring... The way in which my brain insisted that the silence was *trickling* round the room, interests me enormously; for I was either in a state approximating a phase of madness, or else I was, psychically, tuned to some abnormal pitch of awaredness and sensitiveness in which silence had ceased to be an abstract quality, and had become to me a definite concrete element, much as (to use a stupidly crude illustration), the invisible moisture of the atmosphere becomes a visible and concrete element when it becomes deposited as water. I wonder whether this thought attracts you as it does me?

"And then, you know, a slow awaredness grew in me of some further horror to come. This sensation or knowledge or whatever it should be named, was so strong that I had a sudden feeling of suffocation... I felt that I could bear no more; and that if anything else happened, I should just pull out my revolver and shoot Bains through the head, and then myself, and so end the whole dreadful business.

"This feeling, however, soon passed; and I felt stronger and more ready to face things again. Also, I had the first, though still indefinite, idea of a way in which to make things a bit safer; but I was too dazed to see how to 'shape' to help myself efficiently.

"And then a low, far-off whining stole up into the room, and I knew that the danger was coming. I leant slowly to my left, taking care not to let Bains' feet stick over the blue circle, and stared down into the blackness of the pit that dropped sheer into some Unknown, from under my left elbow.

"The whining died; but far down in the blackness, there was something—just a remote luminous spot. I stood in a grim silence for maybe ten long minutes, and looked down at the thing. It was increasing in size all the time, and had become much plainer to see; yet it was still lost in the far, tremendous Deep.

"Then, as I stood and looked, the low whining sound crept up to me again, and Bains, who had lain like a log in my arms all the time, answered it with a long animal-like whine, that was somehow newly abominable.

"A very curious thing happened then; for all around the edge of the pit, that looked so peculiarly like black glass, there came a sudden, luminous glowing. It came and went oddly, smouldering queerly round and round the edge in an opposite direction to the circling of the wall of black, tufted cloud on the outside of the barrier.

"This peculiar glowing finally disappeared, and, abruptly, out of the tremendous Deep, I was conscious of a dreadful quality or 'atmosphere' of monstrousness that was coming up out of the pit. If I said there had been a sudden waft of it, this would very well describe the actuality of it; but the spiritual sickness of distress that it caused me to feel, I am simply stumped to explain to you. It was something that made me feel I should be soiled to the very core of me, if I did not beat it off from me with my will.

"I leant sharply away from the pit towards the outer of the burning circles. I meant to see that no part of my body should overhang the pit whilst that disgusting power was beating up out of the unknown depths.

"And thus it was, facing so rigidly away from the centre of the 'defence,' I saw presently a fresh thing; for there was something, many things, I began to think, on the other side of the gloomy wall that moved everlastingly around the outside of the barrier.

"The first thing I noticed was a queer disturbance of the ever circling cloud-wall. This disturbance was within eighteen inches of the floor, and directly before me. There was a curious, 'puddling' action in the misty wall; as if something were meddling with it. The area of this peculiar little disturbance could not have been more than a foot across, and it did not remain opposite to me; but was taken round by the circling of the wall.

"When it came past me again, I noticed that it was bulging slightly inwards towards me; and as it moved away from me once more, I saw another similar disturbance, and then a third and a fourth, all in different parts of the slowly whirling black wall; and all of them were no more than about eighteen inches from the floor.

"When the first one came opposite me again, I saw that the slight bulge had grown into a very distinct protuberance towards me.

"All around the moving wall, there had now come these curious swellings. They continued to reach inwards, and to elongate; and all the time they kept in a constant movement.

"Suddenly, one of them broke, or opened, at the apex, and there protruded through, for an instant, the tip of a pallid, but unmistakable *snout*. It was gone at once, but I had seen the thing distinctly; and within a minute, I saw another one poke suddenly through the wall, to my right, and withdraw as quickly. I could not look at the base of the strange, black, moving circle about the barrier without seeing a swinish snout peep through momentarily, in this place or that.

"I stared at these things in a very peculiar state of mind. There was so great a weight of the abnormal about me, before and behind and every way, that to a certain extent it bred in me a sort of antidote to fear. Can you understand? It produced in me a temporary dazedness in which things and the horror of things became less real. I stared at them, as a child stares out from a fast train at a quickly passing night-landscape, oddly hit by the furnaces of unknown industries. I want you to try to understand.

"In my arms Bains lay quiet and rigid; and my arms and back ached until I was one dull ache in all my body; but I was only partly conscious of this when I roused momentarily from my psychic to my physical awaredness, to shift him to another position, less intolerable temporarily to my tired arms and back.

"There was suddenly a fresh thing—a low but enormous, solitary grunt came rolling, vast and brutal, into the room. It made the still body of Bains quiver against me, and he grunted thrice in return, with the voice of a young pig.

"High up in the moving wall of the barrier, I saw a fluffing out of the black tufted clouds; and a pig's hoof and leg, as far as the knuckle, came through and pawed a moment. This was about nine or ten feet above the floor. As it gradually disappeared I heard a low grunting from the other side of the veil of clouds, which broke out suddenly into a diapason of brute-sound, grunting, squealing and swine-howling; all formed into a sound that was the essential melody of the brute—a grunting, squealing, howling roar that rose, roar by roar, howl by howl, and squeal by squeal to a crescendo of horrors—the bestial growths, longings, zests and acts of some grotto of hell... It is no use, I can't give it to you. I get dumb with the failure of my command over speech to tell you what that grunting, howling, roaring melody conveyed to me. It had in it something so inexplicably *below* the horizons of the soul in its monstrousness and fearfulness that the ordinary simple fear of death itself, with all its attendant agonies and terrors and sorrows, seemed like a thought of something peaceful and infinitely holy compared with the fear of those unknown elements in that dreadful roaring melody. And the sound was with me *inside* the room—there right in the room with me. Yet I seemed not to be aware of confining walls, but of echoing spaces of gargantuan corridors. Curious! I had in my mind those two words—gargantuan corridors.

As the rolling chaos of swine melody beat itself away on every side, there came booming through it a single grunt, the single recurring grunt of the HOG; for I knew now that I was actually and without any doubt hearing the beat of monstrosity, the HOG.

"In the Sigsand the thing is described something like this: 'Ye Hogge which ye Almighty alone hath power upon. If in sleep or in ye hour of danger ye hear the voice of ye Hogge, cease ye to meddle. For ye Hogge doth be of ye outer Monstrous Ones, nor shall any human come nigh him nor continue meddling when ye hear his voice, for in ye earlier life upon the world did the Hogge have power, and shall again in ye end. And in that ye Hogge had once a power upon ye earth, so doth he crave sore to come again. And dreadful shall be ye harm to ye soul if ye continue to meddle, and to let ye beast come nigh. And I say unto all, if ye have brought this dire danger upon ye, have memory of ye cross, for of all sign hath ye Hogge a horror.'

"There's a lot more, but I can't remember it all and that is about the substance of it.

"There was I holding Bains, who was all the time howling that dreadful grunt out with the voice of a swine. I wonder I didn't go mad. It was, I believe, the antidote of dazedness produced by the strain which helped me through each moment.

"A minute later, or perhaps five minutes, I had a sudden new sensation, like a warning cutting through my dulled feelings. I turned my head; but there was nothing behind me, and bending over to my left I seemed to be looking down into that black depth which fell away sheer under my left elbow. At that moment the roaring bellow of swine-noise ceased and I seemed to be staring down into miles of black aether at something that hung there—a pallid face floating far down and remote—a great swine face.

"And as I gazed I saw it grow bigger. A seemingly motionless, pallid swine-face rising upward out of the depth. And suddenly I realised that I was actually looking at the Hog."

V

"For perhaps a full minute I stared down through the darkness at that thing swimming like some far-off, dead-white planet in the stupendous void. And then I simply woke up bang, as you might say, to the possession of my faculties. For just a certain over-degree of strain had brought about the dumbly helpful anaesthesia of dazedness, so this sudden overwhelming supreme fact of horror produced, in turn, its reaction from inertness to action. I passed in one moment from listlessness to a fierce efficiency.

"I knew that I had, through some accident, penetrated beyond all previous 'bounds,' and that I stood where no human soul had any right to be, and that in but a few of the puny minutes of earth's time I might be dead.

"Whether Bains had passed beyond the 'lines of retraction' or not, I could not tell. I put him down carefully but quickly on his side, between the inner circles—that is, the violet circle and the indigo circle—where he lay grunting slowly. Feeling that the dreadful moment had come I drew out my automatic. It seemed best to make sure of our end before that thing in the depth came any nearer: for once Bains in his present condition came within what I might term the 'inductive forces' of the monster, he would cease to be human. There would happen, as in that case of Aster who stayed outside the pentacles in the Black Veil Case, what can only be described as a pathological, spiritual change—literally in other words, soul destruction.

"And then something seemed to be telling me not to shoot. This sounds perhaps a bit superstitious; but I meant to kill Bains in that moment, and what stopped me was a distinct message from the outside.

"I tell you, it sent a great thrill of hope through me, for I knew that the forces which govern the spinning of the outer circle were intervening. But the very fact of the intervention proved to me afresh the enormous spiritual peril into which we had stumbled; for that inscrutable Protective Force only intervenes between the human soul and the Outer Monstrosities.

"The moment I received that message I stood up like a flash and turned towards the pit, stepping over the violet circle slap into the mouth of darkness. I had to take the risk in order to get at the switch board which lay on the glass shelf under the table top in the centre. I could not shake free from the horror of the idea that I might fall down through that awful blackness. The floor felt solid enough under me; but I seemed to be walking on nothing above a black void, like an inverted starless night, with the face of the approaching Hog rising up from far down under my feet—a silent, incredible thing out of the abyss—a pallid, floating swine-face, framed in enormous blackness.

"Two quick, nervous strides took me to the table standing there in the centre with its glass legs apparently resting on nothing. I grabbed out the switch board, sliding out the vulcanite plate which carried the switch-control of the blue circle. The battery which fed this circle was the right-hand one of the row of seven, and each battery was marked with the letter of its circle painted on it, so that in an emergency I could select any particular battery in a moment.

"As I snatched up the B switch I had a grim enough warning of the unknown dangers that I was risking in that short journey of two steps; for that dreadful sense of vertigo returned suddenly and for one horrible moment I saw everything through a blurred medium as if I were trying to look through water.

"Below me, far away down between my feet, I could see the Hog; which, in some peculiar way, looked different dearer and much nearer, and enormous. I felt it had got nearer to me all in a moment. And suddenly I had the impression I was descending bodily.

"I had a sense of a tremendous force being used to push me over the side of that pit, but with every shred of will power I had in me I hurled myself into the smoky appearance that hid everything, and reached the violet circle where Bains lay in front of me.

"Here I crouched down on my heels, and with my two arms out before me I slipped the nails of each forefinger under the vulcanite base of the blue circle, which I lifted very gently so that when the base was far enough from the floor I could push the tips of my fingers underneath. I took care to keep from reaching farther under than the inner edge of the glowing tube which rested on the two-inch-broad foundation of vulcanite.

"Very slowly I stood upright, lifting the side of the blue circle with me. My feet were between the indigo and the violet circles, and only the blue circle between me and sudden death; for if it had snapped with the unusual strain I was putting upon it by lifting it like that, I knew that I should in all probability go west pretty quickly.

"So you fellows can imagine what I felt like. I was conscious of a disagreeable faint prickling that was strongest in the tips of my fingers and wrists, and the blue circle seemed to vibrate strangely as if minute particles of something were impinging upon it in countless millions. Along the shining glass tubes for a couple of feet on each side of my hands, a queer haze of tiny sparks boiled and whirled in the form of an extraordinary halo.

"Stepping forward over the indigo circle I pushed the blue circle out against the slowly moving wall of black cloud, causing a ripple of tiny pale flashes to curl in over the circle. These flashes ran along the vacuum tube until they came to the place where the blue circle crossed the indigo, and there they flicked off into space with sharp cracks of sound.

"As I advanced slowly and carefully with the blue circle a most extraordinary thing happened, for the moving wall of cloud gave from it in a great belly of shadow, and appeared to thin away from before it. Lowering my edge of the circle to the floor I stepped over Bains and right into the mouth of the pit, lifting the other side of the circle over the table. It creaked as if it were about to break in half as I lifted it, but eventually it came over safely.

"When I looked again into the depth of that shadow, I saw below me the dreadful pallid head of the Hog floating in a circle of night. It struck me that it glowed very slightly—just a vague luminosity. And quite near—comparatively. No one could have judged distances in that black void.

"Picking up the edge of the blue circle again as I had done before, I took it out further till it was half clear of the indigo circle. Then I picked up Bains and carried him to that portion of the floor guarded by the part of the blue circle which was clear of the 'defence.' Then I lifted the circle and started to move it forward as quickly as I dared, shivering each time the joints squeaked as the whole fabric of it groaned with the strain I was putting upon it. And all the time the moving wall of tufted clouds gave from the edge of the blue circle, bellying away from it in a marvellous fashion as if blown by an unheard wind.

"From time to time little flashes of light had begun to flick in over the blue circle, and I began to wonder whether it would be able to hold out the 'tension' until I had dragged it clear of the 'defence.'

"Once it was clear I hoped the abnormal stress would cease from about us, and concentrate chiefly around the 'defence' again, and the attractions of the negative 'tension.'

"Just then I heard a sharp tap behind me, and the blue circle jarred somewhat, having now ridden completely over the violet and indigo circles, and dropped clear on to the floor. The same instant there came a low rolling noise as of thunder, and a curious roaring. The black circling wall had thinned away from around us and the room showed clearly once more, yet nothing was to be seen, except that now and then a peculiar bluish flicker of light would ripple across the floor.

"Turning to look at the 'defence' I noticed it was surrounded by the circling wall of black cloud, and looked strangely extraordinary seen from the outside. It resembled a slightly swaying squat funnel of whirling black mist reaching from the floor to the ceiling, and through it I could see glowing, sometimes vague and sometimes plain, the indigo and violet circles. And then as I watched, the whole room seemed suddenly filled with an awful presence which pressed upon me with a weight of horror that was the very essence of spiritual deathliness.

"Kneeling there in the blue circle by Bains, my initiative faculties stupefied and temporarily paralysed, I could form no further plan of escape, and indeed I seemed to care for nothing at the moment. I felt I had already escaped from immediate destruction and I was strung up to an amazing pitch of indifference to any minor horrors.

"Bains all this while had been quietly lying on his side. I rolled him over and looked closely at his eyes, taking care on account of his condition not to gaze *into* them; for if he had passed beyond the 'line of retraction' he would be dangerous. I mean, if the 'wandering' part of his essence had been assimilated by the Hog, then Bains would be spiritually accessible and might be even then no more than the outer form of the man, charged with radiation of the monstrous ego of the Hog, and therefore capable of what I might term, for want of a more exact phrase, a psychically *infective* force; such force being more readily transmitted through the eyes than any other way, and capable of producing a brain storm of an extremely dangerous character.

"I found Bains, however, with both eyes with an extraordinary distressed, interned quality; not the eyeballs, remember, but a reflex action transmitted from the 'mental eye' to the physical eye, and giving to the physical eye an expression of thought instead of sight. I wonder whether I make this clear to you?

"Abruptly, from every part of the room there broke out the noise of those hoofs again, making the place echo with the sound as if a thousand swine had started suddenly from an absolute immobility into a mad charge. The whole riot of animal sound seemed to heave itself in one wave towards the oddly swaying and circling funnel of black cloud which rose from floor to ceiling around the violet and indigo circles.

"As the sounds ceased I saw something was rising up through the middle of the 'defence.' It rose with a slow steady movement. I saw it pale and huge through the swaying, whirling funnel of cloud—a monstrous, pallid snout rising out of that unknowable abyss… It rose higher like a huge pale mound. Through a thinning of the cloud curtain I saw one small eye… I shall never see a pig's eye again without feeling something of what I felt then. A pig's eye with a sort of hell-light of vile understanding shining at the back of it."

VI

"And then suddenly a dreadful terror came over me, for I saw the beginning of the end that I had been dreading all along—I saw through the slow whirl of the cloud curtains that the violet circle had begun to leave the floor. It was being taken up on the spread of the vast snout.

"Straining my eyes to see through the swaying funnel of clouds I saw that the violet circle had melted and was running down the pale sides of the snout in streams of violet-coloured fire. And as it melted there came a change in the atmosphere of the room. The black funnel shone with a dull gloomy red, and a heavy red glow filled the room.

"The change was such as one might experience if one had been looking through a protective glass at some light and the glass had been suddenly removed. But there was a further change that I realised directly through my feelings. It was as if the horrible presence in the room had come closer to my own soul. I wonder if I am making it at all clear to you. Before, it had oppressed me somewhat as a death on a very gloomy and dreary day beats down upon one's spirit. But now there was a savage menace, and the actual feeling of a foul thing close up against me. It was horrible, simply horrible.

"And then Bains moved. For the first time since he went to sleep the rigidity went out of him, and rolling suddenly over on to his stomach he fumbled up in a curious animal-like fashion, on to his hands and feet. Then he charged straight across the blue circle towards the thing in the 'defence.'

"With a shriek I jumped to pull him back; but it was not my voice that stopped him. It was the blue circle. It made him give back from it as though some invisible hand had jerked him backwards. He threw up his head like a hog, squealing with the voice of a swine, and started off round the inside of the blue circle. Round and round it he went, twice attempting to bolt across it to the horror in that swaying funnel of cloud. Each time he was thrown back, and each time he squealed like a great swine, the sounds echoing round the room in a horrible fashion as though they came from somewhere a long way off.

"By this time I was fairly sure that Bains had indeed passed the 'line of retraction,' and the knowledge brought a fresh and more hopeless horror and pity to me, and a grimmer fear for myself. I knew that if it were so, it was not Bains I had with me in the circle but a monster, and that for my own last chance of safety I should have to get him outside of the circle.

"He had ceased his tireless running round and round, and now lay on his side grunting continually and softly in a dismal kind of way. As the slowly whirling clouds thinned a little I saw again that pallid face with some clearness. It was still rising, but slowly, very slowly, and again a hope grew in me that it might be checked by the 'defence.' Quite plainly I saw that the horror was looking at Bains, and at that moment I saved my own life and soul by looking down. There, close to me on the floor was the thing that looked like Bains, its hands stretched out to grip my ankles. Another second, and I should have been tripped outwards. Do you realise what that would have meant?

"It was no time to hesitate. I simply jumped and came down crash with my knees on top of Bains. He lay quiet enough after a short struggle; but I took off my braces and lashed his hands up behind him. And I shivered with the very touch of him, as though I was touching something monstrous.

"By the time I had finished I noticed that the reddish glow in the room had deepened quite considerably, and the whole room was darker. The destruction of the violet circle had reduced the light perceptibly; but the darkness that I am speaking of was something more than that. It seemed as if something now had come into the atmosphere of the room—a sort of gloom; and in spite of the shining of the blue circle and the indigo circle inside the funnel of cloud, there was now more red light than anything else.

"Opposite me the huge, cloud-shrouded monster in the indigo circle appeared to be motionless. I could see its outline vaguely all the time, and only when the cloud funnel thinned could I see it plainly—a vast, snouted mound, faintly and whitely luminous, one gargantuan side turned towards me, and near the base of the slope a minute slit out of which shone one whitish eye.

"Presently through the thin gloomy red vapour I saw something that killed the hope in me, and gave me a horrible despair; for the indigo circle, the final barrier of the defence, was being slowly lifted into the air—the Hog had begun to rise higher. I could see its dreadful snout rising upwards out of the cloud. Slowly, very slowly, the snout rose up, and the indigo circle went up with it.

"In the dead stillness of that room I got a strange sense that all eternity was tense and utterly still as if certain powers knew of this horror I had brought into the world... And then I had an awareness of something coming... something from far, far away. It was as if some hidden unknown part of my brain knew it. Can you understand? There was, somewhere in the heights of space, a light that was coming near. I seemed to hear it coming. I could just see the body of Bains on the floor, huddled and shapeless and inert. Within the swaying veil of cloud the monster showed as a vast pale, faintly luminous mound, hugely snouted—an infernal hillock of monstrosity, pallid and deadly amid the redness that hung in the atmosphere of the room.

"Something told me that it was making a final effort against the help that was coming. I saw the indigo circle was now some inches from the floor, and every moment I expected to see it flash into streams of indigo fire running down the pale slopes of the snout. I could see the circle beginning to move upward at a perceptible speed. The monster was triumphing.

"Out in some realm of space a low continuous thunder sounded. The thing in the great heights was coming fast, but it could never come in time. The thunder grew from a low, far mutter into a deep steady rolling of sound... It grew louder and louder, and as it grew I saw the indigo circle, now shining through the red gloom of the room, was a whole foot off the floor. I thought I saw a faint splutter of indigo light… The final circle of the barrier was beginning to melt.

"That instant the thunder of the thing in flight which my brain heard so plainly, rose into a crashing, a world-shaking bellow of speed, making the room rock and vibrate to an immensity of sound. A strange flash of blue flame ripped open the funnel of cloud momentarily from top to base, and I saw for one brief instant the pallid monstrosity of the Hog, stark and pale and dreadful.

"Then the sides of the funnel joined again, hiding the thing from me as the funnel became submerged quickly into a dome of silent blue light—God's own colour! All at once it seemed the cloud had gone, and from floor to ceiling of the room, in awful majesty, like a living Presence, there appeared that dome of blue fire banded with three rings of green light at equal distances. There was no sound or movement, not even a flicker, nor could I see anything in the light: for looking into it was like looking into the cold blue of the skies. But I felt sure that there had come to our aid one of those inscrutable forces which govern the spinning of the outer circle, for the dome of blue light, banded with three green bands of silent fire, was the outward or visible sign of an enormous force, undoubtedly of a defensive nature.

"Through ten minutes of absolute silence I stood there in the blue circle watching the phenomenon. Minute by minute I saw the heavy, repellent red driven out of the room as the place lightened quite noticeably. And as it lightened, the body of Bains began to resolve out of a shapeless length of shadow, detail by detail, until I could see the braces with which I had lashed his wrists together.

"And as I looked at him his body moved slightly, and in a weak but perfectly sane voice he said:

"'I've had it again! My God! I've had it again!'"

VII

"I knelt down quickly by his side and loosened the braces from his wrists, helping him to turn over and sit up. He gripped my arm a little crazily with both hands.

"'I went to sleep after all,' he said. 'And I've been down there again. My God! It nearly had me. I was down in that awful place and it seemed to be just round a great corner, and I was stopped from coming back. I seemed to have been fighting for ages and ages. I felt I was going mad. Mad! I've been nearly down into a hell. I could hear you calling down to me from some awful height. I could hear your voice echoing along yellow passages. They were yellow. I know they were. And I tried to come and I couldn't.'

"'Did you see me?' I asked him when he stopped, gasping.

"'No,' he answered, leaning his head against my shoulder. 'I tell you it nearly got me that time. I shall never dare go to sleep again as long as I live. Why didn't you wake me?'

"'I did,' I told him. 'I had you in my arms most of the time. You kept looking up into my eyes as if you knew I was there.'

"'I know,' he said. 'I remember now; but you seemed to be up at the top of a frightful hole, miles and miles up from me, and those horrors were grunting and squealing and howling, and trying to catch me and keep me down there. But I couldn't see anything—only the yellow walls of those passages. And all the time there was something round the corner.'

"'Anyway, you're safe enough now,' I told him. 'And I'll guarantee you shall be safe in the future.'

"The room had grown dark save for the light from the blue circle. The dome had disappeared, the whirling funnel of black cloud had gone, the Hog had gone, and the light had died out of the indigo circle. And the atmosphere of the room was safe and normal again as I proved by moving the switch, which was near me, so as to lessen the defensive power of the blue circle and enable me to 'feel' the outside tension. Then I turned to Bains.

"'Come along,' I said. 'We'll go and get something to eat, and have a rest.'

"But Bains was already sleeping like a tired child, his head pillowed on his hand. 'Poor little devil!' I said as I picked him up in my arms. 'Poor little devil!'

"I walked across to the main switchboard and threw over the current so as to throw the 'V' protective pulse out of the four walls and the door; then I carried Bains out into the sweet wholesome normality of everything. It seemed wonderful, coming out of that chamber of horrors, and it seemed wonderful still to see my bedroom door opposite, wide open, with the bed looking so soft and white as usual—so ordinary and human. Can you chaps understand?

"I carried Bains into the room and put him on the couch; and then it was I realised how much I'd been up against, for when I was getting myself a drink I dropped the bottle and had to get another.

"After I had made Bains drink a glass I laid him on the bed.

"'Now,' I said, 'look into my eyes fixedly. Do you hear me? You are going off to sleep safely and soundly, and if anything troubles you, obey me and wake up. Now, sleep—sleep—sleep!'

"I swept my hands down over his eyes half a dozen times, and he fell over like a child. I knew that if the danger came again he would obey my will and wake up. I intend to cure him, partly by hypnotic suggestion, partly by a certain electrical treatment which I am getting Doctor Witton to give him.

"That night I slept on the couch, and when I went to look at Bains in the morning I found him still sleeping, so leaving him there

I went into the test room to examine results. I found them very surprising.

"Inside the room I had a queer feeling, as you can imagine. It was extraordinary to stand there in that curious bluish light from the 'treated' windows, and see the blue circle lying, still glowing, where I had left it; and further on, the 'defence,' lying circle within circle, all 'out'; and in the centre the glass-legged table standing where a few hours before it had been submerged in the horrible monstrosity of the Hog. I tell you, it all seemed like a wild and horrible dream as I stood there and looked. I have carried out some curious tests in there before now, as you know, but I've never come nearer to a catastrophe.

"I left the door open so as not to feel shut in, and then I walked over to the 'defence.' I was intensely curious to see what had happened physically under the action of such a force as the Hog. I found unmistakable signs that proved the thing had been indeed a Saaitii manifestation, for there had been no psychic or physical illusion about the melting of the violet circle. There remained nothing of it except a ring of patches of melted glass. The gutta base had been fused entirely, but the floor and everything was intact. You see, the Saaitii forms can often attack and destroy, or even make use of, the very defensive material used against them.

"Stepping over the outer circle and looking closely at the indigo circle I saw that it was melted clean through in several places. Another fraction of time and the Hog would have been free to expand as an invisible mist of horror and destruction into the atmosphere of the world. And then, in that very moment of time, salvation had come. I wonder if you can get my feelings as I stood there staring down at the destroyed barrier."

Carnacki began to knock out his pipe, which is always a sign that he has ended his tale, and is ready to answer any questions we may want to ask.

Taylor was first in. "Why didn't you use the Electric Pentacle as well as your new spectrum circles?" he asked.

"Because," replied Carnacki, "the pentacle is simply 'defensive' and I wished to have the power to make a 'focus' during the early part of the experiment, and then, at the critical moment, to change the combination of the colours so as to have a 'defence' against the results of the 'focus.' You follow me.

"You see," he went on, seeing we hadn't grasped his meaning, "there can be no 'focus' within a pentacle. It is just of a 'defensive' nature. Even if I had switched the current out of the Electric Pentacle I should still have had to contend with the peculiar and undoubtedly 'defensive' power that its form seems to exert, and this would have been sufficient to 'blur' the focus.

"In this new research work I'm doing, I'm bound to use a 'focus' and so the pentacle is barred. But I'm not sure it matters. I'm convinced this new spectrum 'defence' of mine will prove absolutely invulnerable when I've learnt how to use it; but it will take me some time. This last case has taught me something new. I had never thought of combining green with blue; but the three bands of green in the blue of that dome has set me thinking. If only I knew the right combinations! It's the combinations I've got to learn. You'll understand better the importance of these combinations when I remind you that green by itself is, in a very limited way, more deadly than red itself—and red is the danger colour of all."

"Tell us, Carnacki," I said, "what is the Hog? Can you? I mean what kind of monstrosity is it? Did you *really* see it, or was it all some horrible, dangerous kind of dream? How do you know it was one of the outer monsters? And what is the difference between that sort of danger and the sort of thing you saw in the Gateway of the Monster case? And what...?"

"Steady!" laughed Carnacki. "One at a time! I'll answer all your questions; but I don't think I'll take them quite in your order. For instance, speaking about actually seeing the Hog, I might say that, speaking generally, things seen of a 'ghostly' nature are not seen with the eyes; they are seen with the mental eye which has this psychic quality, not always developed to a useable state, in addition to its 'normal' duty of revealing to the brain what our physical eyes record.

"You will understand that when we see 'ghostly' things it is often the 'mental' eye performing simultaneously the duty of revealing to the brain what the physical eye sees as well as what it sees itself. The two sights blending their functions in such a fashion gives us the impression that we are actually seeing through our physical eyes the whole of the 'sight' that is being revealed to the brain.

"In this way we get an impression of seeing with our physical eyes both the material and the immaterial parts of an 'abnormal' scene; for each part being received and revealed to the brain by machinery suitable to the particular purpose appears to have equal value of reality that is, it appears to be equally material. Do you follow me?"

We nodded our assent, and Carnacki continued:

"In the same way, were anything to threaten our psychic body we should have the impression, generally speaking, that it was our physical body that had been threatened, because our psychic sensations and impressions would be super-imposed upon our physical, in the same way that our psychic and our physical sight are super-imposed.

"Our sensations would blend in such a way that it would be impossible to differentiate between what we felt physically and what we felt psychically. To explain better what I mean. A man may seem to himself, in a 'ghostly' adventure, to fall *actually*. That is, to be falling in a physical sense; but all the while it may be his psychic entity, or being—call it what you will—that is falling. But to his brain there is presented the sensation of falling all together. Do you get me?

"At the same time, please remember that the danger is none the less because it is his psychic body that falls. I am referring to the sensation I had of falling during the time of stepping across the mouth of that pit. My physical body could walk over it easily and feel the floor solid under me; but my psychic body was in very real danger of falling. Indeed, I may be said to have literally *carried* my psychic body over, held within me by the pull of my life-force. You see, to my psychic body the pit was as real and as actual as a coal pit would have been to my physical body. It was merely the pull of my life-force which prevented my psychic body from falling *out* of me, rather like a plummet, down through the everlasting depths in obedience to the giant pull of the monster.

"As you will remember, the pull of the Hog was too great for my life-force to withstand, and, psychically, I began to fall. Immediately on my brain was recorded a sensation identical with that which would have been recorded on it had my actual physical body been falling. It was a mad risk I took, but as you know, I had to take it to get to the switch and the battery. When I had that physical sense of falling and seemed to see the black misty sides of the pit all around me, it was my mental eye recording upon the brain what it was seeing. My psychic body had actually begun to fall and was really below the edge of the pit but still in contact with me. In other words my physical magnetic and psychic 'haloes' were still mingled. My physical body was still standing firmly upon the floor of the room, but if I had not each time by effort or will forced my physical body across to the side, my psychic body would have fallen completely out of 'contact' with me, and gone like some ghostly meteorite, obedient to the pull of the Hog.

"The curious sensation I had of forcing myself through an obstructing medium was not a physical sensation at all, as we understand that word, but rather the psychic sensation of forcing my entity to re-cross the 'gap' that had already formed between my falling psychic body now below the edge of the pit and my physical body standing on the floor of the room. And that 'gap' was full of a force that strove to prevent my body and soul from rejoining. It was a terrible experience. Do you remember how I could still see with my brain through the eyes of my psychic body, though it had already fallen some distance out of me? That is an extraordinary thing to remember.

"However, to get ahead, all 'ghostly' phenomena are extremely diffuse in a normal state. They become actively physically dangerous in all cases where they are concentrated. The best off-hand illustration I can think of is the all-familiar electricity—a force which, by the way, we are too prone to imagine we understand because we've named and harnessed it, to use a popular phrase. But we don't understand it at all! It is still a complete fundamental mystery. Well, electricity when diffused is an 'imagined and unpictured something', but when concentrated it is sudden death. Have you got me in that?

"Take, for instance, that explanation, as a very, very crude sort of illustration of what the Hog is. The Hog is one of those million-mile-long clouds of 'nebulosity' lying in the Outer Circle. It is because of this that I term those clouds of force the Outer Monsters.

"What they are exactly is a tremendous question to answer. I sometimes wonder whether Dodgson there realises just how impossible it is to answer some of his questions," and Carnacki laughed.

"But to make a brief attempt at it. There is around this planet, and presumably others, of course, circles of what I might call 'emanations.'

This is an extremely light gas, or shall I say ether. Poor ether, it's been hard worked in its time!

"Go back one moment to your school-days, and bear in mind that at one time the earth was just a sphere of extremely hot gases. These gases condensed in the form of materials and other 'solid' matters; but there are some that are not yet solidified—air, for instance. Well, we have an earth-sphere of solid matter on which to stamp as solidly as we like; and round about that sphere there lies a ring of gases, the constituents of which enter largely into all life, as we understand life—that is, air.

"But this is not the only circle of gas which is floating round us. There are, as I have been forced to conclude, larger and more attenuated 'gas' belts lying, zone on zone, far up and around us. These compose what I have called the inner circles. They are surrounded in turn by a circle or belt of what I have called, for want of a better word, 'emanations.'

"This circle which I have named the Outer Circle cannot lie less than a hundred thousand miles off the earth, and has a thickness which I have presumed to be anything between five and ten million miles. I believe, but I cannot prove, that it does not spin with the earth but in the opposite direction, for which a plausible cause might be found in the study of the theory upon which a certain electrical machine is constructed.

"I have reason to believe that the spinning of this, the Outer Circle, is disturbed from time to time through causes which are quite unknown to me, but which I believe are based in physical phenomena. Now, the Outer Circle is the psychic circle, yet it is also physical. To illustrate what I mean I must again instance electricity, and say that just as electricity discovered itself to us as something quite different from any of our previous conceptions of matter, so is the Psychic or Outer Circle different from any of our previous conceptions of matter. Yet it is none the less physical in its origin, and in the sense that electricity is physical, the Outer or Psychic Circle is physical in its constituents. Speaking pictorially it is, physically, to the Inner Circle, what the Inner Circle is to the upper strata of the air, and what the air—as we know that intimate gas—is to the waters and the waters to the solid world. You get my line of suggestion?"

We all nodded, and Carnacki resumed.

"Well, now let me apply all this to what I am leading up to. I suggest that these million-mile-long clouds of monstrosity which float in the Psychic or Outer Circle, are bred of the elements of that circle. They are tremendous psychic forces, bred out of its elements just as an octopus or shark is bred out of the sea, or a tiger or any other physical force is bred out of the elements of its earth-and-air surroundings.

"To go further, a physical man is composed entirely from the constituents of earth and air, by which terms I include sunlight and water and 'condiments'! In other words without earth and air he could not *BE*! Or to put it another way, earth and air breed within themselves the materials of the body and the brain, and therefore, presumably, the machine of intelligence.

"Now apply this line of thought to the Psychic or Outer Circle which though so attenuated that I may crudely presume it to be approximate to our conception of aether, yet contains all the elements for the production of certain phases of force and intelligence. But these elements are in a form as little like matter as the emanations of scent are like the scent itself. Equally, the force-and-intelligence-producing capacity of the Outer Circle no more approximates to the life-and-intelligence-producing capacity of the earth and air, than the results of the Outer Circle constituents resemble the results of earth and air. I wonder whether I make it clear.

"And so it seems to me we have the conception of a huge psychic world, bred out of the physical, lying far outside of this world and completely encompassing it, except for the doorways about which I hope to tell you some other evening. This enormous psychic world of the Outer Circle 'breeds' if I may use the term, its own psychic forces and intelligences, monstrous and otherwise; just as this world produces its own physical forces and intelligences—beings, animals, insects, etc., monstrous and otherwise.

"The monstrosities of the Outer Circle are malignant towards all that we consider most desirable, just in the same way a shark or a tiger may be considered malignant, in a physical way, to all that we consider desirable. They are predatory—as all positive force is predatory. They have desires regarding us which are incredibly more dreadful to our minds when comprehended than an intelligent sheep would consider our desires towards its own carcass. They plunder and destroy to satisfy lusts and hungers exactly as other forms of existence plunder and destroy to satisfy their lusts and hungers. And the desire of these monsters is chiefly, if not always, for the psychic entity of the human.

"But that's as much as I can tell you tonight. Some evening I want to tell you about the tremendous mystery of the Psychic Doorways. In the meantime, have I made things a bit clearer to you, Dodgson?"

"Yes, and no," I answered. "You've been a brick to make the attempt, but there are still about ten thousand other things I want to know."

Carnacki stood up. "Out you go!" he said using the recognised formula in friendly fashion. "Out you go! I want a sleep."

And shaking him by the hand we strolled out onto the quiet Embankment.

—*1973*—

THE RIVEN NIGHT

CAPTAIN RONALDSON HAD LOST HIS WIFE. THIS MUCH WE KNEW, and when the stern-visaged gloomy man came aboard to take command, it was I, the eldest apprentice, who stood at the gangway and passed his "things" aboard. One quick glance I have in his face as he passed me, and the world of sorrow that lurked in those sombre eyes touched me with a feeling of intense pity; though I knew little, save that he had lost his wife after a brief space of married life. Afterwards I learnt something of their story. How he had fought and saved to make sufficient to marry the woman he loved. How for her sake he had lived straightly and honourably, working at his profession until at last he had obtained a Master's certificate. Then they had married, and for six brief weeks' joy had been theirs; and now—this!

During our outward voyage the Captain was grimly silent. He acted like one who had lost all interest in life. As a result, the two Mates after a few attempts to draw him into conversation left him pretty much to himself, which indeed was what he apparently desired.

We reached Melbourne after an uneventful voyage, and having discharged and re-loaded, commenced the homeward passage: the strangest and weirdest, surely, that ever man took. Even now, I scarce know what was real, and what not. Sometimes I'm almost persuaded that the whole dread incident was a fearsome dream, were it not that the things which happened (things I cannot explain away) have left all too real and lasting traces.

We had a tedious passage, with continual headwinds, heavy gales and long calms, and it was during one of these that the strange thing I have to tell of befell.

We had been out a hundred and forty-three days. The heat had been stifling and thankful I was when night came, bringing its shade from the oppression.

It was my "timekeeping," and I walked the lee side of the poop sleepily.

Suddenly the Second Mate called me up to wind'ard. "Just have a squint over there, Hodgson, I seemed to see something just now," and he pointed out into the gloom, about four points on the port bow.

I looked steadily for some minutes, but could see nothing. Then there grew out of the darkness a faint nebulous light of a distinctly violet hue. "There's something over there, Sir," I said. "It looks like one of those corpse-candles."

The Second had another long look, and then went for his night-glasses. For some time after, he watched the thing at intervals, taking short hurried strides up and down the poop between whiles. Evidently he was puzzled; so was I for that matter. The light was not that of another vessel; it appeared to be, as I have just said, more of the nature of a corposant, or "corpse-candle."

Presently the hail of the "look-out" came hollowly aft. "Light on the port bow, Sir."

"Thanks for nothing," I heard the Second Mate mutter: then louder, "i, i."

There was not a breath of wind. The "courses" had been hauled up to prevent chafing, and we were lying silently in the night.

A little later, after a prolonged gaze, the Second again called me to him, and asked if I thought the light any plainer. "Yes, Sir," I replied. "It's much plainer, and larger, too, Sir."

For a while he was silent.

"Queer thing, Sir," I ventured after a bit.

"Damned queer!" he replied. "I shall call the 'old man' soon, if it comes any closer."

"Perhaps it's not moving," I suggested. The Second Mate looked at me a moment moodily, then stood upright with a sudden movement.

"I never thought of that," he cried. "You think we may be in a current taking us towards it?" I nodded silently.

He went to the side and looked over, then returned irritably. "I wish to heaven it was daylight!" he snapped. In a while he looked again; then an exclamation of surprise came from him quickly, and turning, he handed the glasses to me.

"See if you can see anything queer about it," he said.

I had a long look, then passed them back to him.

"Well?" he questioned impatiently.

"I don't know, Sir," I answered. "It beats all I've seen while I've been fishing: it seems tons larger too."

"Yes, yes!" he growled, "but don't you notice anything about the shape?"

"Jove, yes, Sir, I do now you mention it. You mean it looks like a great wedge? And the colour, Sir, it's wonderful. You might almost fancy..." I hesitated somewhat shyly.

"Go on," he grunted.

"Well, Sir, you could almost fancy it was a tremendous valley of light in the night."

He nodded appreciatively, but said nothing.

An hour passed, and the thing grew visibly. From the maindeck came a subdued hum, the voices of the watch discussing the strange phenomenon in awestruck tones.

It could be seen plainly now with the naked eye, a great chasm of violet light like the opening of a huge valley into dreamland.

The Second Mate beckoned to me, and I went quickly.

"Take the poop," he said, "and keep your eyes lifting while I go and call the old man."

"Very good, Sir," and he went below. Presently he came up again.

"Can't make him hear at all," he said uneasily. "Better run down and call the Mate."

I did, and in a few minutes he joined the Second on the poop.

At first the Mate did little but stare astonished at that uncanny sight, while the Second Mate told him what little we knew. Then we went to the chart room, and presently returned. I saw him shake his head in answer to a question from the Second, and after that they watched that growing mystery in silence. Once the Mate said something, and I thought I caught the words "luminous clouds," but was not certain.

On we moved. The sight grew vaster.

A little later the Second Mate had another try to wake the Captain, but returned unsuccessful.

Down on the maindeck had gathered the whole crew. Once a man's voice rose blasphemously. There was a growing mutter of anger, and the blasphemer was silent. Time passed slowly.

The gulf of light rose right up into the midnight sky spreading fan-wise, and vanishing into further space.

We were apparently some two miles from it when I heard the First Mate whisper something and go back to our binnacle. When he came back I heard him mutter hoarsely that we were drifting directly into the thing. The words were caught by some of the crew, and passed round quickly in accents of fear.

Strange to say, no light came to us from the rift and this, I think, made it the more spectral and unearthly.

The two miles had dwindled down to half, and I saw the Second Mate raise his glasses and look towards where the gulf had joined the sea. In fearful curiosity my gaze followed his, and there came to me a fresh feeling of dread as I saw that the point of the shimmering wedge seemed to drive far below the surface of the silent deep.

Still nearer, now but a hundred yards from that luminous gulf. I stared, but could see nothing.

Nearer, and I looked up one slope of the riven night showing like the side of an eternal mountain.

The ship's bows drifted into the light. A moment, and I saw the foremast with its maze of ropes loom ghostly against that weird effulgence.

The Mate spoke jerkily.

"Damn!" he said, and was silent.

I looked forrard again, and stared, terrified.

The fore-part of the ship had vanished. In place rolled a sea of violet clouds, out of which rose grotesquely the frightened face of the look-out man. Further aft came the impalpable billows of mist. Forward of the foremast, nothing showed save that frightened face.

The ship drove forward and the mainmast faded into nothingness. I saw the crew in the waist stare fearfully out of those trembling waves of mystery. A moment later it was upon me, and I found myself submerged in an ocean of violet shades that gleamed wondrously.

The two Mates still stood together, and I saw them look bewilderedly at one another, though neither spoke.

I looked astern and saw a mighty shape of blackness, with a glimmer of dark waters. It was the night we had left.

Slowly, as my faculties began to work, I saw things more plainly. Afar on my left, rose a vast range of shadowy peaks, showing ghostly.

Between them and where I stood, rolled an immensity of luminous misty waves that fluctuated eternally.

To the right, the eye swept away into unutterable distances, and over all reigned an intolerable silence. A coldness like that of a tomb crept over me. I shivered. Once the brooding silence was broken by a moaning, as of a distant wind.

Presently I put out my hand through the winding mist and felt something hard; it was the rail running across the break of the poop. I looked down, but could see nothing. I took a step forward and stumbled against a hard object; it was a hencoop, and gropingly I sat down on it. I felt strangely tired and bewildered. How long I sat there it would be difficult to say. Time seemed to have no part in that dread place. The cold grew more intense, and I have an indistinct memory of shivering through an indeterminable space of time.

Suddenly there came again that windy moan, and then a cry of indescribable fear from many voices, followed by a sound as of whispering in the sky. I leapt to my feet and looked to where I had last seen the crew. There they were, all huddled together like frightened children, their eyes staring fearfully upwards into the void. Instinctively my gaze followed theirs. At first I could not make out what it was they watched so steadfastly; but slowly there grew out of the mists shapes, shapes clothed mistily, that watched us with great sombre eyes. Nearer they came, and looking towards the distant mountains I saw dusky masses of clouds sweeping steadily from their towering heights in our direction. On they came, and as they drew nearer I saw that they were not clouds, but legions upon legions of those spirit forms. Still they came, floating like great clouds of intelligence above us. The weird sight impressed me terribly. I felt that the end of all things was approaching. Then as I watched, a strange thing happened. From those unnameable beings above, there drove a single dim enshrouded figure. It came headlong like a storm-driven cloud, and stopped before the crowd of cowering sailors. Then, as the wrappings of a shroud, rotten with extreme age, might fall away showing the corpse within; so did the dusky mist slip away and reveal to my astonished gaze—not a corpse, but the face and figure of a lovely young girl. I gave a gasp of astonishment, and leaned forward to get a better look; even as I did a tall form sprang from amongst the crowding sailors and shouted hoarsely.

"Mary! Mary!" it said, and ended in a harsh scream. It was Langstone, one of the A.B.'s. The girl put one ghostly hand to her heart, and I saw the handle of a sailor's sheath-knife showing starkly. What she meant, I could not at first make out. Then Langstone's voice rose shrilly, "Mary! Mary! forgive..." He stopped abruptly. The girl-spirit after that one accusing gesture had turned away coldly and unforgivingly. I saw Langstone give a despairing glance at the shrinking men, then with a cry of "God help me" he leapt away out into the purple billows, and faintly to my ears as though from miles beneath my feet came the sound of a far distant splash, and then a long dread silence.

In a while I looked again towards those gloomy heights, but now I could no longer see the spectral hosts; instead it had grown wonderfully clear, and far into the void I saw a speck of snow-white fleece which grew rapidly larger as I watched, until presently it floated just overhead, and I made out a tender womanly face smiling down upon me. It was the face of my mother who a short year previously had passed into the arms of the Great One. I took a step forward and held my arms out supplicatingly—I felt as though the tumultuous beating of my heart would suffocate me. I called "Mother," first softly, then loudly, and saw the dear lips move tremulously. Then even as I watched, it faded and like a dream was gone. For some moments I stood looking tearfully and unbelievingly upwards, until sorrowfully it was borne upon me that she had indeed gone.

A moment it seemed, and a voice spoke. The words came to me muffled, as though through mists of eternity—unmeaning they seemed and unreal. A dreamy feeling stole over me. I felt disinclined to listen. Again the voice came and I roused myself to catch the words. Two words only, but they woke me thoroughly. The sound echoed from the far heights with a tender insistence: "My Love! My Love! My Love!" And presently a step sounded muffled and soft. I turned, and lo! the Captain's face showed palely. He was looking up into the wide with a rapt expression. I looked also, but though I searched earnestly, could see nothing. Suddenly I heard again the vague murmur of a deep splash, and glancing down quickly, could nowhere see the Captain. I stood confounded. The cry above had ceased. Then it seemed I saw a shadowy form with a face like that of the Captain's, float upwards into the violet twilight.

And thus, stupefied, I stood waiting; waiting for I knew not what.

Presently I roused myself and made my way gropingly towards where I judged the side of the vessel to be. In a while my hand rested on something that I knew to be the rail running along the port side of the poop, and thus I leant upon it and peered over and down into the strangeness of that unearthly sight. Sometimes I looked and saw nothing, save the illimitable deeps of that billowy, misty ocean. It seemed to me as though ages passed over my head and still I watched dreamily. At times I dimly saw weird things that peered up at me and vanished. Thus I stood, and the monotony of time passed over my head in silent aeons. Then, it might have been half-way through eternity, something drove up out of the boundlessness, a dull green glow that shone lividly through the purple gloom of that infinite mystery. Steadily it grew, a cold malicious gleam that frightened me, and in a while, looking far to my left I saw another ghostly glimmer strike through that dark-hued sea.

Brighter grew the brilliance of those lights until their vivid greenness smote intolerably up into the violet impalpableness like two transparent pillars through which played a shiver of lambent flame, and suddenly the murky vastnesses beneath were heaved upwards into a mighty wave that drove towards us threateningly. Yet ere it reached us, my eyes had seen something, something terrible—eyes that blazed out of mystery, and beneath, lips—white, vast and slobbering had opened, disclosing the blackness of an everlasting night. Then, like an awesome wall that reached up into the nothingness above and blotted out everything, the wave was upon us, and instantly we were wrapped in a surging blackness that seemed to weigh down upon us and suffocate. My head began to sing queerly and I felt my knees give weakly. Then the blankness of unconsciousness swept over me, and I passed into dreams.

I opened my eyes and looked around bewilderedly. For a moment I saw things through a violet haze. It passed and I saw that the sun was shining brightly. I glanced aloft, noting that a fresh breeze of wind filled the sails; then down on deck to where the two Mates still stood, just as I had seen them last. Even as I gazed, the Second Mate stood upright and yawned, then looked round him in a puzzled manner. As he did so, his eyes fell upon the Mate still sleeping. The Second stared stupidly a moment, then put out his hand and shook his superior roughly.

"What the devil's up, Mr. Gray?"

The Mate jumped, and swore quickly.

"What the hell's the matter with you?" Then seeming to realise that he was not in his bunk, he rubbed the sleep out of his eyes and looked around—dazed.

The Second Mate spoke again, "Blarst!" and stared over the break of the poop. The Mate turned slowly and looked also. I heard him give a little gasp. Wondering what it was they eyed so earnestly, I ran to the break, and glanced down on to the maindeck. Great God! what a sight. There, lying on the deck, and huddled on the top of one another, lay the crew. The watch on deck, and the watch below, mixed up in an inextricable senseless heap. As we watched them, one of the men stood up shakily. His lips moved, but no words came. I saw the two Mates look at one another, and their eyes were full of doubt. Then the First Mate turned and tottered to his room. The Second Mate said nothing, but continued to watch the men, as at intervals they rose and with suspicious, bewildered looks stumbled forrard. Some cursing there was, yet most preserved a glum and vacant silence. True, a little Frenchman—excitable like all his nation—started to question volubly, but ceased in surprise at the blank looks that were cast upon him.

During the day, and indeed the rest of the voyage, the subject was strictly tabooed. It was as though each one of us felt afraid to admit that which according to our knowledge could not be.

Strangely enough, seen in this light, no surprise was expressed when the Captain's and Langstone's disappearance was formally announced. Instead, each one received the news tacitly. All, that is, except the little Frenchman, who swore softly in several languages at the—to him—incomprehensible behaviour of his comrades.

Once, a few days later, I had some work to do for the First Mate in the cabin. On the table was the Log book, and with a mingled dread I turned up the date of that fearsome night. There I found the following entry—

> *Lat.—S. Long.—W. Heavy gales. About 2 A.M. shipped a tremendous sea which washed Captain Ronaldson and Langstone, one of the A.B.'s, overboard.*

At the bottom were the signatures of the two Mates.

BRITISH LIBRARY TALES OF THE WEIRD

Haunted Houses:
Two Novels by Charlotte Riddell
Edited by Andrew Smith

The Platform Edge:
Uncanny Tales of the Railways
Edited by Mike Ashley

The Face in the Glass: The Gothic
Tales of Mary Elizabeth Braddon
Edited by Greg Buzwell

Doorway to Dilemma:
Bewildering Tales of Dark Fantasy
Edited by Mike Ashley

British Library Tales of the Weird collects a thrilling array of uncanny storytelling, from the realms of gothic, supernatural and horror fiction. With stories ranging from the 19th century to the present day, this series revives long-lost material from the Library's vaults to thrill again alongside beloved classics of the weird fiction genre.